# THE GREATER GLORY

†

Andrew Fogarty

2QT (Publishing) Ltd

For Paul and Mark

# CHAPTER ONE

THOMAS RUFFORD WIPED his perspiring face with his hands and adjusted the collar of his doublet. Beside himself with pent-up fury, his eyes rolling ferociously, he plunged forward into another vehement attack.

'Why must we always run? We must stand firm and resist!' he shouted defiantly, his voice trembling with raw emotion, his hand clutching impetuously at the hilt of his sword.

'Yes! We must resist the temptation of those heretics that would have us destroy ourselves,' replied John, glancing across at his brother with an air of exasperation.

'So while you wander freely through the seminaries of Europe,' persisted Thomas, throwing his arms about wildly, 'we who are left abandoned must continue to suffer this unrelenting persecution.'

'You know why I must leave,' said John, pursuing his brother across the cobbled yard at Mythe Hall, their father's ancestral home. 'My plan was always to return to the Continent, to continue with my studies, travel to Rome and, by God's grace, enter the Society. Our dear friend Anthony Babington sacrificed much to secure my release from the Marshalsea and now, at last, the chance I have been waiting for is here. You must try to understand.'

John's quiet, firm voice was full of conviction and there seemed to be a permanent smile beneath his full beard which, though he was three years younger than his brother, made him look older.

Thomas frowned and turned away from his brother's outstretched hand. He loved John more than anybody else for his intellect and his strong will, but right now he felt only angry resentment towards him.

The Ruffords were of the Old Religion. They had watched helplessly as England, the country of their birth, had turned into a ruthless and divided land. And like for so many Catholics, it had become a dangerous struggle to uphold their faith. Many had drifted into conformity or gone abroad.

Several moments passed in awkward silence. Thomas leaned against one of the stone entrance pillars, listening to the distant rushing of the river, his eyes far away. He was a slight man and possessed a reticent charm though he found it difficult to make friends; although good looking, he often passed unnoticed. He had dreaded the inevitability of this moment.

He spun round.

'Then take me with you!' he begged, abruptly changing his plea. 'Since we were small boys we have always been inseparable. You were no more than five years old when they took Father away and we were sent to live with the Ashtons ... do you remember?'

Thomas spoke rapidly and his eyes filled with tears. 'For three long years while Father was imprisoned, we had to look out for each other,' he went on. 'We shared our food and our clothes; we played games, we laughed ... and we shed a few tears too. And do you recall those long winter nights when we used to sit by the fire and I would read to you?"

John smiled and nodded silently.

'And later, when we were at Oxford,' Thomas continued, 'when you stubbornly refused to attend church at Easter and receive the Protestant sacrament, I stood by you and defended you even though I knew we would both be expelled from college! I tell you John, there is nothing left in this miserable, bloody country for the likes of us.'

Thomas paused, silent and morose.

'Thomas, I know in your heart you love England as much as I,' said John, taking his brother by the arm and leading him back towards the house. 'Believe me! I will forsake neither my home nor my friends. My absence from these shores will only be a temporary one. But you, on the other hand,' he continued resolutely, 'you must remain here, at Mythe Hall. It is your duty. Father and Mother are both getting older. And Jane ... well, you know how she dotes on her elder brother's every word. Thomas, you are meant to stay. And besides, the Faith is still strong in these parts and has many influential friends who are sympathetic. You have no need to worry. You will be left undisturbed if you are discreet.'

Thomas sighed deeply and a feeling of resignation crept over him.

'Thomas ... Thomas,' John's voice was even more soothing and reassuring at the sight of his brother's pained expression. 'It is good for us to have trials and troubles at times,' he said, smiling and throwing an arm around his brother's shoulder, 'for they remind us of our greatest need … to place all our trust in God.'

†

February, 1586. Thomas Rufford was standing in the same walled courtyard at Mythe Hall. This time he was alone. It was two years to the day since his brother had fled England for the safety of the Continent. He tried to fight against the flood of memory that surged over him: the despair, the anger, the unanswered questions that burned like fire within him. He shut his eyes but it was to no avail; the image of his brother was still there and their parting words, painfully vivid as if they had been uttered only yesterday, still echoed.

'To place all our trust in God,' Thomas repeated silently, bitterly. The words had seldom left his thoughts from that day to this. His heart ached. Too simple, too easy, he thought, shaking his head.

Thomas shifted his weight from one leg to the other, shivering miserably as an icy mist crawled around the courtyard and wrapped itself around him. The crumbling stone entrance pillars, not more than ten paces in front of where he stood, had become strangely distorted in the gloom while the raucous cries of a nearby crow were the only sounds to violate the ghostly silence.

The memories, the seeds of discontent he felt, were smothered in a numbing coldness and his mind wandered back to the present. In truth, he was angry with himself and annoyed at his own weakness. He liked to imagine he had remained in England out of a sense of loyalty and out of the deep love he had for

## CHAPTER ONE

his family but the real reason owed more to his lack of courage, his anxiety and his fear.

Mythe Hall lay secluded in the flattened bottom of a deep broad valley at the confluence of two great rivers, two miles north of the small town of Whalley, deep in the Lancashire hills. The house faced south, looking out over a wide expanse of flat marshland, overgrown with alder and birch, while to the north and west ran the wide deep waters of the river with steep undulating hills rising dramatically beyond.

But with the increasingly severe recusant fines taking their toll, the family was now on the verge of ruin. The Hall, its former splendour now decaying and rotting, looked sad and gloomy and unkempt; its appearance epitomised the change in fortunes that had befallen them. The old perimeter wall, once a fortification against the encroachment of the outside world, now lay broken and breached. Thomas had overheard his parents talking in hushed voices about selling the Mythe Hall estate, although a final decision had not yet been made.

Thomas's only escape was hawking. How he cherished those precious few hours when he managed to steal away into the surrounding fells. The sensation of freedom and exhilaration, of seeing his hawk soar effortlessly high above him and then in the next instant, swoop down low at lightning speed, was pure delight. But now, by some cruel twist of fate, even this pleasure had been denied to him when his young male hawk had sustained a deep gash to its flank and badly broken one of its wings.

Thomas gently caressed the pair of hawking gloves

which he held in his hands. He had given his heart and soul to nurturing and training the bird but now all that was gone forever. He tucked the gloves inside his doublet. He had no use for them now.

As he waited in the stillness of the courtyard, Mythe Hall seemed more desolate and lonely than it had ever been. Pondering on all his frustrations, Thomas was completely unaware of how the direction of his life was about to change.

†

As Thomas turned wearily back towards the house, he heard the dampened sound of hoofs in the lane, still some way off but coming slowly and inexorably towards him. His head jerked stiffly towards the narrow meandering track which led up to Mythe Hall but the mist was like a thick shroud, hiding everything from his searching gaze. He heard the murmur of low voices drawing nearer and nearer. His eyes and ears strained frantically. Eventually, after several minutes, he saw the shadowy outline of two men on horseback. The man on the right was unknown to him but Thomas recognised the extravagant clothes and flamboyant good looks of the other rider. It was Anthony Babington, the Ruffords' trusted friend and benefactor.

Pulling up his horse only a few feet from where Thomas stood, Babington immediately jumped down. He was a tall, thin man with striking, clear-cut features. His black breeches and boots were splattered with mud from the journey and his chestnut mare was muddy up to the saddle girth.

## CHAPTER ONE

'Thomas!' Babington's wet, dirt-stained face beamed with tired yet genuine excitement. 'It has been too long!' He held out his arms to embrace his friend.

For a moment, Thomas stood silent and motionless. Then a smile crept over his face and he reached forward, threw his arms around Anthony and hugged him as if he were his younger brother who had just returned from St Omer or Reims.

'What's the matter Thomas … lost your tongue?' Anthony mocked, holding him at arm's length.

'Thank the Lord you have come,' gasped Thomas at last. 'We thought you were lost! Besides,' he added, a sparkle in his eyes, 'you are so much delayed, the mutton is all but ruined!'

Babington let out a great bellow of laughter and embraced his friend again.

Anthony Babington and Thomas Rufford shared many things in common. Both had been born in October 1561 into wealthy Catholic families, Anthony in Derbyshire and Thomas in Lancashire; areas which still clung to the old faith. Later in the same year that Pope Pius V had issued his bull 'Regnans in Excelsis' pronouncing a sentence of excommunication against Queen Elizabeth, a youthful Anthony had been inconsolable at his father's death from influenza. Thomas, meanwhile, had watched in horror as his father was imprisoned on a charge of complicity in a plot to rescue Mary Queen of Scots. And more recently, Anthony had paid sureties for Thomas's younger brother John and made safe his release from the Marshalsea prison.

These were two restless, angry young men who had grown up in turbulent times and who had lurking within them a boiling, seething bitterness towards the Queen for the split in their beloved country and for her government's unjust penalties on fellow Catholics. Feelings of rebellion stirred in their hearts.

Standing and hugging each other like beleaguered comrades, their bond of friendship appeared closer than ever.

After a few minutes, Thomas glanced over Anthony's shoulder at his friend's companion. With the hood still concealing his face, the stranger had remained in his saddle, calmly observing their cheerful reunion.

'Ah, forgive me Thomas,' said Anthony. 'Allow me to introduce my good friend, Captain Foscue, recently returned from Flanders.'

Thomas turned to face the stranger as he dismounted.

'I am pleased to have the opportunity of making your acquaintance, Master Rufford,' Foscue said, stepping forward with a self-assured yet courteous bearing. He threw back his hood to reveal the narrow face of a man in his middle thirties, with a hooked nose, neat close-cropped black hair and beard and friendly eager eyes. 'Anthony has told me much about you and your good family.'

'Captain Foscue, you are most welcome,' Thomas replied. 'Any friend of Anthony Babington is a friend of the Ruffords.'

'It is a relief to know I am among true friends,' said Captain Foscue, his eyes shifting from Anthony to Thomas. 'I understand your brother is abroad, Master Rufford, going about his sacred duties? I pray it won't be too long before he rejoins us in restoring England back to the Faith.'

# CHAPTER ONE

'Sweet Jesu, it's cold!' exclaimed Babington, stamping his feet. 'Thomas, are you going to keep us out in this freezing cold much longer? What about that mutton, eh?' he said, clapping his hands on his friend's shoulders.

'What?' snapped Thomas scowling, distracted by Babington's clumsy interruption. He shrugged off his friend's arm and moved away hesitantly; all the while his curious, uneasy gaze remaining fixed on Captain Foscue's smiling face. What did he mean '… before he rejoins us in restoring England back to the Faith.'

'But where are all your servants?' asked Anthony, stretching his aching limbs. Without waiting for a reply, he strode past Thomas towards the dark shape of a half-timbered building at the far end of the courtyard. 'Are we to take care of the horses ourselves?' he cried, with a hollow laugh.

'Leave the horses!' shouted Thomas, clearly irritated. 'Philip will tend to them directly.'

Babington returned across the courtyard and the three of them entered Mythe Hall through the solid, carved oak entrance door.

'Now I see!' Anthony went on, crooking a finger. 'You have been forced to release all your other servants, haven't you?'

Thomas made no reply though he could feel his temper rising. Instead, he led them swiftly through the vestibule, at the end of which a heavy curtain was draped across an opening.

'Ah, I knew it!' exclaimed Anthony slightly breathless. 'It is intolerable that we should all face destitution and imprisonment for remaining loyal to the true religion.

Even death!' he added and he glanced back towards his companion, who was loitering a few feet behind.

Thomas lifted the curtain and entered the gloomy stillness of the Great Hall, closely pursued by Babington. Lastly, Captain Foscue crossed the threshold and paused. In the dim light, he could see that it was a vast hall, with wainscot panelled walls and a nobly proportioned oak hammerbeam roof, enriched with carved angels on the column capitals. To his right, there was a decoratively carved screen with an arched opening at its centre partly concealing a short flight of stairs leading to a gallery above; at the other end of the Great Hall there was a long table perched upon a dais, with a tall bay window to its side adorned with the fading Rufford family coat of arms in painted glass. In the middle of the wall opposite, a wretched looking fire burned low in a large stone fireplace.

The sound of their heavy footsteps on the flagged floor echoed noisily through the Hall as they crossed to the screen. Babington and Foscue lingered for a moment by the gallery stairs, sniffing the aroma of roasted mutton and freshly baked bread that escaped from behind a closed door on the left. Thomas, already opening the door to the right of the kitchen, beckoned them to follow.

'And I tell you, Thomas,' said Anthony, hastening into the chamber after him, 'the Holy Father was right when he excommunicated the bastard tyrant. It will not be too soon when we have the Queen of Scots on the throne and the true Faith restored to the nation.'

'Guard your tongue!' a brusque voice rang out.

Thomas, Babington and Foscue stopped abruptly,

taken aback by the harsh tone.

It was almost dark in the room. Two candles burned on a modest dining table, casting flickering, sinister shadows across the floor. An imposing sideboard covered with pots, jugs and pewter plates filled the length of one wall while chairs, small tables and cabinets were scattered at random about the room. The silhouette of a tall, silver-haired man was standing before the window. He had his back towards them.

'Father!' Thomas burst out. 'You of all people should understand.'

The silver-haired man turned round sharply. With his tall stature and broad shoulders, his presence was formidable. 'We must guard against uttering such treasonous words,' said Sir William Rufford, with rising fury, 'for they may rebound against us all.'

Thomas drew breath and persevered. 'How long must we bite our tongues?' he asked belligerently.

'Enough!' snapped Sir William. 'I will not have such talk in my house!'

He broke off suddenly, embarrassed at his own vehemence and turned to Babington. 'It is good to see you again, my friend,' he said softly, with a warm smile that showed his sound but yellowing teeth. 'Tell me how you are.' He shuffled forward to greet him.

Thomas regarded his father with impotent fury; he looked as if he were about to continue the quarrel but evidently thought better of it. Sir William Rufford no longer had the influence on high officials in the county that he'd had when he was High Sheriff of Lancashire, but to those around him, from his family to his servants, he still inspired respect and deference. Any further discussion on the subject was prohibited ... at least for the time being.

# CHAPTER 2

SUPPER WAS SERVED in the informality of the modest dining chamber rather than the fine surroundings of the Great Hall, which was now rarely used to entertain.

Lady Katherine Rufford, a portly, imposing woman who had once been handsome but whose appearance had faded, sat at the opposite end of the table to her husband, while Thomas and his flaxen-haired sister Jane sat facing Anthony Babington and Captain Foscue. Philip, the squat, snub-nosed peasant who had faithfully served the Rufford family for nearly twenty years and who, owing to his worsening sight, was constantly squinting, shuffled back and forth, bringing food from the adjoining kitchen.

The fare was plain and simple: roasted mutton with parsnips, freshly baked manchet and a quince pie to follow. But the wine was passed around liberally and the conversation was amicable, and any further mention of the Queen was temporarily set aside.

As the evening wore on, they talked and laughed and joked. Anthony Babington was in good humour and with his characteristic urbane charm, he made flattering remarks about how attractive Jane had become since he had last seen her. Jane, although secretly delighted at such compliments, blushed crimson. Everyone laughed and Anthony added, with a playful smile on his lips, that he was mystified why she was not yet married.

'Because she is a stubborn, headstrong young girl,' Lady Rufford said, 'who does not know what is good for her.'

'Oh, Mother!' Jane cried indignantly, averting her eyes to avoid her mother's searching look.

'Jane, you know it is both your father's will and mine that you should marry Richard Shirebourn. He comes of noble Catholic stock and an alliance between our two families would bring many advantages. He is a good man and you know he has been very fond of you since you were a little girl.' As a loving and doting mother, Lady Katherine wished only happiness for all her children but she also knew that if Jane married their wealthy neighbour's youngest son, the Rufford fortunes would soon be restored.

'Richard Shirebourn!' Jane's shrill voice echoed. 'He is a conceited, immature, foolish young man,' she said, breathing faster. 'How can you contemplate such a marriage for your only daughter?' The mere thought filled her with revulsion.

'Oh, don't be so unkind,' cried Lady Katherine, wagging a threatening finger. 'He is a worthy, excellent young man and…'

'But I do not love him,' Jane interrupted. 'Do you expect me to sacrifice my feelings for the sake of his money?' Agitated and flushed, she rose from her seat and paced about the room.

'But you will grow to love him in time.'

'Never!' Jane's voice broke and tears came to her eyes.

'I would rather marry a Protestant heretic whom I love, than a Catholic man I do not!'

There was a lull as Jane wiped away her tears and an astounded Lady Rufford contemplated her daughter's violent outburst. Thomas felt a lump in his throat. He loved his sister dearly, admired her feisty spirit and her beauty, but he felt sorry for her too.

'Do not upset yourself, Jane,' said Sir William, pushing back his chair and crossing to the fireplace to console his daughter who was staring absently into the flames. 'We will not talk about it any more, my dear.' He took her by the arm, led her back to the table and then sat down himself.

Babington poured himself some more wine. Feeling responsible for the sensitive emotions he had unwittingly aroused and anxious to make amends, he remarked, 'It was a most excellent and delicious supper, Lady Katherine. It amazes me how you…' His words petered out as he was momentarily distracted by Philip who had entered the dining chamber, wheezing and red-faced, carrying a precarious bundle of kindling.

'God's blood!' Thomas snarled. His fist thundered on the table making everyone start a little and turn towards him. His face pale and distorted with fury, he pushed himself to his feet, sending his chair crashing to the floor. 'It amazes me how we … how any of us survive,' he raged. 'I tell you, our Sovereign Lady will not be content until every Catholic has been bled dry and every recusant household has fallen.'

Babington nodded approvingly. 'Quite so,' he said, casting a wary glance towards William.

But William, seemingly not heeding his son's

outburst, was scrutinising the firewood being stacked on the hearth. 'Is that kindling dry, Philip?' he asked, leaning forward across the table.

Thomas glared at his father and mumbled incoherently, his eyes blazing.

'Er, No, Sir William, I'm afraid it's still a little damp. But…'

'Then leave it to dry where it is. It is warm enough in here as it is!'

'Very well, Sir William' Philip replied dutifully, wiping his enormous hands on his breeches. He laboured to his feet. 'If I may be excused, I'll attend to the horses now.'

'Certainly Philip … and thank you.' William looked at Philip's rather tired countenance and dishevelled livery. It would have been far more practical to have retained one of the younger, stronger servants as his wife had wanted but William would not hear of it. 'We are fortunate to have retained one so … faithful!' he added, grinning widely.

Philip smiled awkwardly, evidently flustered at receiving such a compliment. He bowed and hurriedly left the room.

Everyone fell silent. Lady Rufford looked at their visitors with an affected smile, barely able to conceal her shame at her family's predicament and hoping the guests would get up and leave. Jane smoothed her dress and looked mournfully at her mother, while the two guests fixed their eyes eagerly on William as if anticipating his response to his son's remarks. William merely leaned back in his chair and stretched his legs before him, quite content to savour the last drops of his wine.

Impatience crept into Thomas's voice: 'Well, Father?' he said at last.

Sir William rose and ambled over to the fireplace. He leaned forward, staring into the dying embers and rubbed his hands together as if he were attempting to conjure up more heat. Then he turned round and faced his expectant audience.

'We survive,' he began calmly, 'by our wits. We have loyal friends and trusted neighbours. We have our good health and we work hard to retain mastery of our own destiny. We have this land,' he went on, gesturing towards the window. 'We are not starving.' He advanced towards the table, leaned forward, picked up the jug of wine and peered inside. 'And we still have good wine to drink!' he said, beaming. 'We should count our blessings.'

'Such opulence!' retorted Lady Katherine ironically, raising her eyes.

'But it's not enough, Father,' Jane said gloomily.

'Not enough! Is the wine not to your liking, Daughter?' William returned facetiously. 'What more could you possibly need?'

'Masters of our own destiny! How can you say that!' cried Thomas angrily, flushing an apoplectic red.

Captain Foscue, who had listened attentively, shifted uncomfortably in his seat. Now keen to participate in the debate, he cleared his throat.

'We cannot simply shut our eyes to what is disagreeable; we have to face up to it. We all live in constant fear of losing our property today, our liberty tomorrow, our lives the day after. None of us escapes the shadow of these times.'

Babington smiled to himself, pleased to see that for the first time since their arrival Foscue was roused and looked eager to express his opinion on the matter.

'Sir William,' Foscue went on, 'how can you view so frivolously the persecution suffered by honest Catholics such as your good selves?'

'I assure you, Captain Foscue, I am most earnest,' William replied.

'Masters of our own destiny!' Thomas interjected, trying to restrain his wrath. 'John is forced into exile and I am prohibited from practising my chosen profession – simply because we are Catholics.' He crossed the room to where his mother and Jane were sitting and gently laid a hand on each of their shoulders. 'And have you forgotten how our family was torn apart,' his voice wavered, 'by your imprisonment on some concocted charges against this heretical Queen.'

'All the more reason for not speaking treason now,' retorted William. 'Or for encouraging sedition among friends that would see us all on the scaffold!' he added gravely, glaring first at Captain Foscue and then at Babington.

Lady Rufford looked aghast at her husband's last remark.

'But he only speaks his mind, Father,' said Thomas.

'Then he speaks irresponsibly and with the rashness and foolish courage of youth.' William frowned with more than a hint of irritation.

There was another pause as everyone seemed to gather their breath.

'It seems to me,' lamented Lady Rufford, 'that we would all be better off if we simply attended church and had done with it. Yes, why can't we do that?' There was a glimmer of excitement in her voice. 'Why can't we attend the Protestant service and rid ourselves of this poverty, while we carry on with our faith in private. Outwardly we would be seen as good honest folk, loyal to the Queen and her laws, but inwardly our hearts and minds would remain true.'

Thomas exchanged incredulous glances with Anthony and Captain Foscue. In spite of the enforced hardships, the question of acquiescing or remaining true to the old faith had never been discussed … not until now.

Lady Rufford gazed at her husband with imploring eyes.

'Others have done it,' she went on. 'I've heard that Sir Robin Catterall has declared that he will go to church at Easter and that his family and tenants must do likewise. Poor Robin, he has a wife and five children to support. Surely God cannot persecute a man for preferring to be a good husband and father than a…'

'I don't believe my ears!' Thomas yelled. 'How can we crawl out during the hours of darkness like ghosts to practice the faith and then, as soon as the cock crows, cower away and conform. Hypocrites, I say!'

'Not necessarily,' said William, considering for a moment and folding his arms across his chest. 'Survivors!'

Thomas smiled wryly in acknowledgement at his father's response.

'How dare you call us hypocrites!' Lady Rufford cried indignantly.

'But what you suggest; is this not to surrender all we hold dear?' said Thomas, lowering his voice to almost a whisper.

'No!' Lady Rufford said defiantly. 'We may act out whatever play they have us perform, but if in our hearts and minds we think otherwise … then, no! We may keep our consciences to ourselves and you would be free at last to study and practice at the great Inns in London!'

Thomas's head ached and his senses reeled. Perhaps he had taken too much wine or perhaps his mother understood him only too well.

'Well, it is certainly practical,' William said pensively.

'And you, Sir Anthony,' said Jane, gazing across the table. 'Can you not understand the need for practicality? After all, you have a wife and child to support, do you not?'

'Indeed, I do,' Babington replied, slowly and deliberately. A charismatic smile crept over his handsome features, yet Jane remained unmoved. Somehow, his charm failed to work its usual magic on her.

'Recently, I have often considered my duty towards Margaret and dear little Meg,' he continued wistfully. 'Of taking us all to the safety of the continent, to France or Spain, where we may travel and study to our hearts' content, and where we may practise our faith openly without fear of persecution. But on the other hand…'

'But you need a licence to travel abroad,' challenged Jane. 'Obtaining a licence is virtually impossible for a Catholic. How do you think you are going to get one?'

'But on the other hand…' Thomas said, turning back to Anthony, urging him on.

'On the other hand,' Anthony resumed, 'I confess

that I am ill at ease at the thought of abandoning our country to its fate.' He paused for a moment and poured himself some more wine. 'But there is hope,' he went on, casting a furtive glance at Thomas. 'There is a choice. I saw the Queen of Scots while I was a page in Lord Shrewsbury's household at Sheffield. I used to glimpse her as she rode out to take the air. Her beauty is indeed far greater than Elizabeth's. And when I had reason to deliver her some trivial letter or message, she bestowed such a heavenly smile on me as I knelt before her. There and then, I made up my mind.'

As Babington spoke, Thomas imagined the scene and was captivated by it.

'She is our beloved country's rightful sovereign. My companions and I are convinced that with true and ardent support … it is possible,' Babington's words drifted away as he gazed absently at the last flickering embers in the fire. It was as if he were suddenly transcended to another world.

'That what is possible?' said Thomas, puzzled.

Babington instantly awakened from his dream. 'Why, that she can be rescued and restored to her throne, of course, and the true Faith restored to the country,' he exclaimed. His face showed both enthusiasm and fear. Then, staring directly at Thomas as if issuing a rallying call: 'We have just cause, my friends. Let us take up arms and defend ourselves! As the phoenix, we shall rise out of the ashes. Now is the time to act, now is the time to fight, now is the proper time to…'

'Enough! Enough!' cried William. 'Think of what you are saying. Such actions would court disaster. This is not the means to advance our religion but to see its destruction.'

There was silence again while they reeled at the gravity of what they had just heard. Even Thomas was alarmed at the implications of Anthony's seditious words and he remained motionless, staring wide-eyed at his friend.

After several moments, William's low, ominous voice broke the stillness. 'You have become a dangerous friend!' he pronounced grimly. 'Take care, Anthony; take great care.'

Lady Katherine winced and shifted her position. Her face was contorted but whether it was simply from spending too long sitting in a cold damp room or the danger that Anthony Babington had placed them in by confiding such treasonable ideas was impossible to distinguish.

'Come now, the hour is late,' William said, observing his wife's discomfort. 'Time for bed, Kate, you too, Jane. That's enough excitement for one evening!' He wandered over to the table and, stooping low, kissed them both gently on their foreheads.

Lady Rufford and Jane rose from their seats and moved towards the door together, supporting each other. Jane stopped and glanced back over her shoulder. 'It is a foolhardy thing you suggest, Sir Anthony!' she declared furiously.

Babington coloured slightly but made no reply.

Thomas felt a cold draught on his neck as his mother and sister opened the door and disappeared hurriedly along the corridor.

'It is time we retired to bed, too," said Babington, turning to his host. 'We need to rise early tomorrow and be on the road back to Derbyshire.'

'Already?' said Thomas.

'From Dethick, we go on to London,' Babington continued.

'To London?' echoed William.

'To London,' replied Babington, throwing his gold-laced cape onto his shoulders. 'There we will meet with some friends. Something is rotten in England, Sir William; we cannot rest and sit idly by.' His voice was hushed but deliberate.

†

Thomas set down the candle on the small table next to his wooden-framed bed and sank wearily onto the striped wool and linen coverlet. The bedchamber was tucked away at the rear of the house and faced north so it always felt cold and damp. The candle gave off just enough of a glow to show that besides the bed and the table next to it, the only other furniture in the room was a solitary elbow chair in one corner and a heavy oak chest beneath a latticed window.

He unbuttoned his doublet and the gloves which he had stuffed there earlier fell onto the rush-strewn floor. He cursed under his breath. He had intended giving the gloves to Anthony as a gift but had completely forgotten about them during the course of the evening. He bent down to pick them up, brushed them against his breeches and laid them neatly on top of the table. He resolved to present them to his friend in the morning.

He pulled off his boots and fell back onto the bed exhausted, a little drunk with the wine and the excitement of Anthony's talk. The candlelight cast strange, ominous shadows on the wall as it flickered in the draught. Thomas lay there, gazing at the plaster flaking from the ceiling. In spite of his tiredness, he was restless and agitated. He went over and over the evening's discussion, turning and twisting first one way then another, hoping yet dreading. He was astonished, even flattered, at Anthony's thinly-disguised proposal that he join with him in his audacious plan; but while greatly admiring his friend's courage, Thomas could only foresee danger and inevitable tragedy along that particular path.

He drew a long, shaky breath as a grotesque vision of severed heads and butchered limbs flashed through his mind. He knew that he did not possess sufficient courage or hold such high moral principles. The idea of turning schismatic, although initially abhorrent, now intrigued him. Away from influence or persuasion, it provoked his own suppressed desire to free himself from the shackles of recusancy and truly become 'master of his own destiny'.

Thomas stretched and slid down under the coverlet. His eyelids grew heavy and he began to dream that one day he might be able to leave the confines of Mythe Hall and forge out a career of his own. A position of wealth and status and the respect of his contemporaries – it was what he had always yearned for.

✝

'Thomas! Thomas!' cried Jane, bursting noisily into her brother's bedchamber the next morning. 'Look what

I've found!' She held up her clenched fist. 'They must have left it in their room by mistake.'

Thomas prised open his eyelids. A grey light drizzled in through the window. He took a deep breath and forced himself groggily up onto one elbow.

'What?' his parched voice croaked. He began massaging his forehead as his sister thrust a small object into his clammy hand.

'I think it must belong to Captain Foscue,' she said excitedly. 'If indeed that was his real name. Do you think he's a priest?'

'A priest?' Thomas repeated, still half asleep. Gradually, his eyes began to focus on the small object he was holding in his hand. Recognition struck and at once, he was alert, sitting stiffly upright.

'An Agnus Dei!' he whispered softly, solemnly holding up a silver chain at the end of which hung a little wax oval, impressed with an image of the Paschal Lamb. These discs were made from the remains of Easter candles and blessed in Rome by the Pope.

Thomas swallowed. Such 'popish trumperies' had been outlawed by Parliament and the penalty for possessing one was death.

'We must get rid of it straight away!' he said frantically and made to move but Jane swiftly snatched the consecrated object from his hand.

'No, Thomas!' she shouted. Her large eyes shone with defiance.

'But to keep it would place us all in great danger.'

'I'm not afraid – and besides, it is a beautiful and blessed thing. I think I'll keep it.' She crossed herself and kissed the wax disc before tucking it into her skirt pocket.

Thomas shook his head and smiled. It was strange to think that this independent, handsome young woman was the same Jane, the freckled, shy little girl who used to follow him obediently everywhere.

As she turned to leave, the expression on Thomas's face became quizzical. 'Did you say that Anthony has already left?' he asked.

Jane looked back over her shoulder and smiled. 'Yes, they left over two hours ago, Sleepy. It's already past ten o'clock.' And with that she was gone, her footsteps retreating back along the corridor.

Thomas glanced over at the gloves still lying neatly on the oak table where he had placed them the night before. He gave a heavy sigh and fell back onto his bed.

# CHAPTER 3

EASTER HAD COME and gone at Mythe Hall. An unusually wet and warm spring had given way to an unbearably hot and dry summer, and life had once more resumed its monotonous round of daily chores.

In the herb garden on the other side of the walled courtyard, Lady Rufford and Jane were busy at work. The garden had become overgrown with weeds and the plants which had once thrived there now looked ragged and chaotic. While Philip clipped the box hedging, Lady Rufford and Jane were cutting the herbs back into some semblance of order.

'I cannot understand why William did not relent and attend church at Easter. Then we could have hired a gardener to do this,' grumbled Lady Rufford as she rose stiffly to her feet and stretched her aching back. Her face was red from the sun and beads of perspiration glistened on her forehead. Her wrinkled hands were dirty and sore.

'But you know why,' said Jane, setting down the basket of lavender and red mint trimmings, which would be sprinkled among the floor rushes, helping to mask the smells of the house. 'Come, you should rest for a while, Mother. This June sun is the hottest I can remember.'

Wearily, they sat down on a wooden bench beneath

the shade of a rose arbour; a welcome respite from the stifling summer heat. They watched in silence as a bee hummed and probed the flowers for nectar.

'Then your father is a stubborn old fool who puts his conscience before the welfare of his wife and family. I hope he remembers that when he is faced with an empty plate for supper!' Lady Rufford raged. 'And where is Thomas,' she added, looking round and frowning. 'He has become extremely slovenly and neglectful of his duties of late. Ever since Anthony Babington came to visit, Thomas's head hasn't stopped spinning; he doesn't seem to know what he wants these days. Well, it won't do, I tell you. It won't do.'

Jane's lucid blue eyes were tinged with sadness. 'I think he and Father quarrelled again this morning,' she said softly. 'He was in a dreadful temper when he left for Whalley.'

Lady Rufford sighed despairingly. 'Thomas seems to find fault with every little thing and then vent his frustrations on the rest of us. What was it about this time?' she added, raising her eyebrows.

'Over some dealings with a brogger, I think,' replied Jane. 'But don't be too harsh on him,' she continued, taking her mother's hands in hers. 'He feels confused. He is torn by the promise he made to John to remain at Mythe Hall, and by his desire to break away and make a success of his life; something he knows will only be achieved if he yields to the Protestant laws. He feels trapped.' She paused, raised her mother's hands to her lips and kissed them.

'It is hard for him to know what to do,' she continued. 'His mind wanders and his head is easily turned. Much of what the charming Anthony Babington said would have tempted him.' As she spoke, she stiffened and her voice became stern. 'But Babington is nothing but a romantic fool!'

'Well, let's hope he prevails over his dilemma soon before he drives us all to distraction,' said Lady Rufford, forcing a feeble laugh.

Jane gave a good-natured smile and was still defending her brother's sullen moods when they were distracted by a confusion of sounds from the courtyard: raised, threatening voices; heavy footsteps running across the cobbles; the snorting of horses, and the ominous rattle of steel.

'Philip, will you go and see what all the fuss is about?' asked Lady Rufford, agitation showing in her face. 'We'll follow you in a moment.'

Philip straightened up from his crouched position.

'I'll go with him,' said Jane, jumping up and running after him towards the house.

Oblivious to the rising commotion outside, Sir William was sitting in an elbow chair in the study, hunched over the table before him, writing a letter. Even the thundering of impatient fists against the main door did not prevent him from continuing his work. Only when he was satisfied that he had completely finished did he raise his head. He peered through the open casement. Returning the quill to its stand, he sealed the neatly folded parchment with melted wax and slowly heaved himself out of his chair. He placed the letter on the table, adjusting its creases with lingering fingers. His hands were trembling a little.

As Philip rushed headlong into the Great Hall, he

almost collided with William emerging from the study.

'It's alright Philip,' William said stiffly. 'I'll deal with it.'

There was a rustle of a woman's dress as Jane ran into the Hall. The door shuddered under more furious hammering. She stopped abruptly and looked about her with wide, scared eyes. 'Who is it, Father? What do they want?' she asked.

William did not answer but moved through the porch towards the heavy oak door. The two iron bolts screeched as he pulled them back. The wooden crossbar was lifted from its sockets and set to one side and the door was opened.

'Sir William Rufford?' enquired a stern voice. It belonged to a sergeant-at-arms, a tall man past middle-age, with grizzled eyebrows and whiskers and powerful broad shoulders. He was sweating profusely beneath a high collared black and white cloak. Behind him were several stout young men, all of whom were wearing buff leather jerkins which had badges sewn onto the left front breasts. One of them stayed by the stone gateway and held the horses while the others, brandishing pikes, swaggered arrogantly about the courtyard.

William nodded in acknowledgement but didn't speak. His expression was grave but without fear. It almost seemed as if he had been expecting them.

'Sir William Rufford, I have here a warrant for your arrest,' continued the sergeant-at-arms, thrusting an official-looking piece of parchment at him.

Jane felt a sharp stab of terror in the pit of her stomach. Her face turned ashen and her mouth gaped in disbelief.

'A warrant for my arrest,' repeated William slowly.

'On what charge?'

'The charge is high treason,' the officer replied, 'for conspiring with Anthony Babington and others to plot the death of her most glorious majesty, Queen Elizabeth and to place Mary of the Scots on the throne.'

At that moment, Lady Rufford hurried into the courtyard via a side gate. 'I have never heard such nonsense in all my life,' she bellowed, pushing her way through the soldiers towards her husband.

'I have my orders, Sir William, and I will use force if necessary,' the officer asserted coldly. Two of his men stirred and moved threateningly towards William as if to reinforce their intentions.

Lady Rufford clung fiercely to her husband's arm. 'But he has done nothing wrong,' she cried. 'You cannot take him, I beg of you!'

'This is intolerable!' said Jane indignantly, stepping out from behind her father. 'The accusation is false. Anthony Babington has neither the wit nor the cunning to imagine such a plan ... and as for my father being complicit in such an obvious invention...'

'Sir William, if you please...' said the officer with growing impatience and unmoved by the women's appeals. 'I will carry out my duty without hesitation. Should there be any resistance I will have no qualms about taking you all!'

'Why, you thick-skinned brute!' screamed Lady Rufford, and she made a desperate lunge towards the officer.

William, gripping her by the arm, managed to hold on to her. For a moment, she struggled feebly against her husband's strength and then she relented.

Taking both her hands in his and pressing them against his chest, William looked directly into her eyes. 'Kate, I beseech you, there must be no confrontation,' he said. 'Any show of defiance would only play into their hands. It may be misconstrued as an indication of guilt.' Lady Rufford made to speak, to remonstrate, but he continued swiftly to prevent her. 'I was innocent all those years ago and I am innocent of this charge now. Their deceit will be exposed and my innocence revealed. In the meantime, we must play along with this little game if it amuses them.'

'But Father, this is no game they play,' said Jane, her eyes moist with tears.

William put his arms round both his wife and daughter. 'Come now,' he said with a good-humoured smile. 'It won't be for long.'

'We must set off at once, Sir William!' insisted the officer, frowning angrily. 'I am charged to bring you to London without delay. To the Tower.' Jerking his head, he ordered his men to take William away.

'To the Tower!' exclaimed Lady Rufford. Her body began to heave with convulsive, choking sobs. Jane, fighting to restrain her own tears, drew her mother closer, hugging her tenderly.

'Now, that is most inconvenient,' William said and for the first time, his voice betrayed a hint of irritation. He put his hand under Katherine's face and turned it towards him. 'Do not lose heart, my dear,' he said softly, wiping away her tears. 'They have no case against me.' He kissed her lovingly on both cheeks. He gently stroked Jane's long, golden hair and was about to speak when his daughter's eyes widened in astonishment.

'Father, look! ... it's Thomas!' she cried out.

Everyone turned to look.

'Yes, it is. It's Thomas!'

Instantly, the soldiers were alert. Hoof beats drummed on the parched ground. The sergeant-at-arms squinted as he scrutinised the distant figure galloping along the rutted bridle path which curved towards Mythe Hall.

Thomas kicked his horse into a longer stride. He could see soldiers in the courtyard.

Earlier in the day, Thomas had overheard a small group of farmers and local tradesmen gossiping excitedly outside the De Lacy Arms. They had been talking about the recent discovery of yet another treacherous popish plot to murder Elizabeth. He had heard them say that one of the conspirators was believed to live nearby and that the whole area was swarming with soldiers and constables with a warrant for his arrest. Wallowing in their beer, they had gloated that there was little chance of escape and the traitor would get what was coming to him.

'As far as I'm concerned, you can't trust any of them,' one of them had said. 'Everyone knows that all Catholics are dirty scheming troublemakers and deserve to be hanged.'

'No mercy for the traitor!' agreed another, with a stupid grin on his face. Thomas thought he had heard the name of Babington being bandied about but he couldn't be certain. Though he still had unfinished business in town, he decided to return home at once.

Still some distance from the old perimeter wall, Thomas leapt from his horse and sprinted across the open ground. His heart hammered against his chest so forcefully that his vision blurred. He rubbed his eyes with his gloved hand to clear them. He was close enough now to recognise them: the tilt of a fair head ... the round tear-stained face ... the erect, dignified figure of a man.

Holy Mother Mary, keep them safe, he prayed.

He entered a little way into the courtyard with his sword drawn, drenched in sweat and gulping for breath, struggling against the rising fear within him. He was still haunted by the memory of that sickening day in his childhood when the soldiers had seized his father. It had left deep painful scars. Now the soldiers were here again. The wound was re-opened.

Thomas's eyes flashed around the courtyard and locked with those of the sergeant-at-arms. For some moments, they gazed silently, impassively, at one another, each one looking the other up and down, deliberating. Everything seemed unreal ... still ... peaceful. The only sound he could hear was that of his own heavy breathing.

'Spoiling for a fight, eh? One blow from this and your head will be split right down the middle.'

The brutal voice fell on Thomas's ears with a crash and he was overwhelmed with an intense, seething rage. Now is the time to act, now is the time to fight ... this was his chance for glorious fulfilment. He swung round and raised his sword to strike.

'Thomas! Not that way!' yelled William.

Thomas glanced back at his father, infuriated, incensed, hesitant. He heard the shuffle of feet behind him but before he could react, a heavy blow struck the side of his head. He sank down onto his haunches, clutching his left temple, his sword clattering on the cobbled ground before him.

'Thomas!' The cries of Lady Rufford and Jane rang out in unison. 'Stop it! For God's sake, stop it!'

The sergeant-at-arms stepped forward, shaking his head at the crumpled figure lying prostrate before him. His eyes were cold. 'Now, that was a foolish thing to do,' he said mockingly.

The young soldier who had delivered the blow looked keen to continue his assault but the officer gestured for him to remain where he was.

Jane rushed forward. 'Thomas ... Thomas! Are you alright?' she asked.

Thomas pushed away her offer of assistance and, picking up his sword, rose groggily to his feet. Blood was already trickling down from his temple into his face.

'They've come to arrest Father!' Jane said, her voice quivering with despair and frustration. 'For being involved in some half-baked plot of Anthony Babington's! They're going to take him to the Tower!'

Still hazy, Thomas tried to adjust his focus.

'Do not make it any worse for him,' said the sergeant-at-arms quickly and beckoned two of the soldiers take William.

'But you are mistaken!' Thomas clutched his temple and moved to block their way.

One of the soldiers growled at him impatiently, demanding that he stand aside.

'If there is any conspiracy, then it lies with those who would fabricate such deception,' continued Thomas, standing his ground and glaring at the burly figure opposite. 'Our father is completely innocent of this preposterous charge. Listen to me!' But his protestations fell on deaf ears. The soldiers moved quickly and efficiently, as though they had encountered such situations a hundred times before.

Jane gripped her brother's sword arm tightly, pulling him away. 'It's no use,' she whispered. 'It's no use.'

Thomas's fragile nerves were in tatters, his belligerent confidence disappearing fast at being confronted with that which seemed inevitable. He was a weak and helpless child again.

William glanced back over his shoulder as he was escorted away. There was calm resignation about his expression. Thomas felt a lump in his throat and angry tears filled his eyes. Before long, his father had disappeared from sight and Thomas became conscious of feeble sobbing next to him.

# CHAPTER 4

'I SHALL GO to London immediately,' Thomas said, pacing restlessly up and down the Great Hall. His face was stained with dried blood and his head pounded. Every now and then he paused, raised his hand to his mouth, shook his head with disbelief and then continued to pace the floor. 'Father will be depending on me and I know exactly what I must do. I vow before Almighty God they shall not get away with this outrage.'

He stared at his mother and sister who were clinging to one another for support.

'Anthony is no conspirator,' Thomas went on. 'And Father was fervently opposed to any talk or suggestion of treason. I blame myself; I should not have allowed them to take him. In God's name they cannot be allowed to do this.'

Just then, the study door opened and Philip came hesitantly into the Hall, clutching something in his stubby fingers.

'Forgive me … My Lady,' he stammered, 'but Sir William left this on the table. Would you have me see that it is delivered?' He tentatively presented the neatly folded and sealed letter to Lady Rufford.

She stared at him as though she did not understand what he had said.

'Let me have a look,' Jane murmured, taking the

letter from Philip's grasp and glancing at the elegant handwriting. A pensive smile crept slowly over her lips.

'Ah, that's it!' she exclaimed. 'That's what we'll do.'

'What is it? What do you mean?' said Lady Katherine, bewildered.

'Why, Lord and Lady Molynieux, of course!' said Jane, pointing to the names written on the parchment and wondering why it had not occurred to her before. 'Father always said that if there was any trouble, we should go to them at Broad Oaks.'

Lady Rufford nodded. 'But of course,' she said hoarsely. 'If anyone can help they can.' She forced a feeble smile and there was a glimmer of hope in her eyes.

'I know they will discover the truth of the matter and then we will be able to prove Father's innocence,' Jane went on eagerly. She glanced across at her brother.

Thomas's gaze was lowered. Guilt and frustration weighed heavily upon him. He was desperate to prove himself; it was his duty and his alone to save both his father and Anthony Babington. But, raising his eyes and looking at his sister and mother, he knew it would be irresponsible to refuse help from such influential friends as Lord and Lady Molynieux.

'Very well,' he said tersely. 'But I shall go to Broad Oaks alone.'

'What? And leave us here?' said Jane indignantly. 'I shall most certainly come with you!'

Thomas made to object but was interrupted.

'Yes, we shall all go,' said Lady Rufford, with renewed firmness in her voice. 'Philip, have three horses saddled and ready for the morning,' she added, turning to their faithful servant.

Thomas mumbled his disapproval and hastened from the room.

Early the following morning, all three departed for Broad Oaks.

† 

Broad Oaks, situated midway between Thaxted and Saffron Walden in Essex, was Lord and Lady Molynieux's family home. The mansion house was a fine one. Its setting was dramatic, edged by a forest and surrounded on all sides by gently undulating hills. A great herd of red deer roamed its parkland.

Lord and Lady Molynieux had first encountered the Rufford family at Oxford, where their eldest son, Ambrose, had attended Magdalen College at the same time that Thomas and John were at Exeter College. The families had been introduced by a mutual acquaintance, a tutor, and a Catholic. They had remained good friends ever since.

Lord Molynieux was a respected and trusted government official. While outwardly conforming, he continued to give covert support and allegiance to the old religion by maintaining a large Catholic household and encouraging the activities of his devoted but recusant wife. Indeed, Lady Margaret was a quite remarkable woman. At the beginning of Elizabeth's reign, she had bravely spoken out against the Oath of Supremacy. More recently, she had taken to publicly flaunting her Catholicism by wearing the forbidden rosary and crucifix in full view; and though readily admitting she was no saint, she was often seen assisting and feeding the poor.

When they arrived at Broad Oaks, Thomas and his mother and sister were welcomed by the whole family. Lord Molynieux, whom Thomas had once condemned as hypocritical for clinging to his wealth and status while sacrificing his faith, now seemed a most honest, sincere and kindly man.

When Thomas promised they would not be a burden and that their stay would be brief, Lord Molynieux stepped forward and insisted that they could remain at Broad Oaks for as long as was necessary to resolve this terrible business. Beneath a shining bald head, a lace cartwheel ruff framed Lord Molynieux's round face; when he spoke, his deep voice had the distinguished tone of a man who had spent his life in society and at court.

Lady Margaret would also hear nothing of their leaving and showed great sympathy for their plight. Her tall, majestic figure swept across the Great Hall and she warmly embraced both Lady Rufford and her daughter. 'Come, you must be exhausted. You must have something to eat before you collapse,' she said softly, leading them into a richly-decorated dining chamber.

Later, after a hearty supper, Lady Katherine and Jane retired to their upstairs bed chambers. Lady Margaret announced that she was also going to her room and dismissed the servants. She instructed her husband not to detain Thomas for long and on no account was he to get the young man drunk, and then she withdrew.

Thomas reached for the flagon of wine and replenished

his pewter goblet. He took a large swig and leaned back in his chair, closing his eyes for a moment. Perhaps, he thought, when he opened them again he would be back in the Great Hall at Mythe Hall and it would be his father sitting opposite him. Perhaps this was all a bad dream and when he awoke the nightmare would be over.

'Thomas ... you are tired,' said Lord Molynieux quietly. 'Perhaps it is time we all rested and prepared ourselves for the difficult task which lies ahead.' He leaned forward slightly. 'And we dare not disobey Lady Molynieux!' he added, and his round face lit up with a cheeky irreverent smile.

Thomas opened his eyes.

'How can you smile?' he snapped, sitting bolt upright and fully alert again. 'How can we rest while my father and Anthony and who knows how many other innocent men are unjustly imprisoned. The charges are fabricated, I tell you. It is yet another attempt by our Queen and her ministers to pour scandal and ill repute on us all. But none of us traitors!' He sighed and slumped back in his chair again. 'Why can't they leave us alone?'

'Understand this, my friend,' said Lord Molynieux solemnly. 'These are turbulent times. Our enemy will try to destroy us using all means within his power. Turn where you will, above, below, left or right, he will be there and he will never leave us alone. Faith...' he smiled encouragingly, 'we must all have faith.'

'Faith! Believe me, sometimes I wonder what good it does me. What good it does any of us. Tell me, how are we to live and prosper? What is there to aspire to when all is forbidden to us? Are we merely to exist? We would be better off without it.'

'If you do not have faith, you are like a rudderless ship blown hither and yon...' began Lord Molynieux but Thomas cut him short.

'Fine elegant words indeed, My Lord, but it seems to me that faith has imprisoned my father and Anthony Babington!'

'It is not faith that has imprisoned them,' said Lord Molynieux, shaking his head, 'but fear; fear and suspicion. Elizabeth demands loyalty from all her subjects and she is surrounded by those who have secured high office by swearing such allegiance. They have forged a new order throughout this land and one which they will defend with all their cunning. But her position on the throne has always been vulnerable to forces within and without this realm. Her advisors, Burghley and Walsingham, sow the seeds of mistrust in her and through their propaganda they have fastened the hatred of the nation on us. Indeed, they see conspiracy and plot in every Catholic. They will contrive to preserve this new order from any storm which threatens to sink it.'

Thomas continued to listen out of politeness and respect for he did not see how such talk would help either his father or Anthony Babington.

'But there are some at Court,' Lord Molynieux went on, 'good people, influential people, who say that Her Majesty doesn't have the stomach for religious persecution and is slow to condemn any man without good proof.'

'Then that is it!' Thomas blurted out, his eyes bright

with hope once again. 'They have no proof!' His mind raced. 'If you will speak with them, my father and Babington will be free within the week!' There was renewed optimism in his voice and he hauled himself out of his chair, strode to the window and threw open a casement. He breathed in the cool night air.

'Thomas, believe me.' said Lord Molynieux, rising from his seat and following him to the window. 'I truly accept that your father is innocent in this matter and I give you my word that I will speak with my friends but you must understand…'

'When?' interrupted Thomas impatiently, banging the casement shut and turning round.

'The matter is delicate, Thomas, and we must all have patience if we are to prevail.' He sighed. 'However, I am afraid Anthony's is already a lost cause.' His eyes fell to the floor, avoiding Thomas's confused bewildered stare. 'I am informed that certain letters exist.'

'Letters? What letters?'

'Correspondence between Anthony Babington and the Queen of Scots.'

Thomas frowned. 'Correspondence?'

'Aye, it is spread like the plague through the corridors of Richmond and Whitehall. It is reported that Walsingham seemed to be congratulating himself, such was the detail – the damning detail – contained within them.'

'And what did they say, these letters?' Thomas asked.

'It would appear that Sir Anthony has exchanged several letters with the Queen of Scots in which he describes a plan whereby he and several of his noble friends would carry out the execution of Queen

Elizabeth, rescue Mary from her confinement at Chartley and set her on the throne. It is said that in the last of these letters,' Lord Molynieux went on, 'the Queen of Scots signed her own death warrant by agreeing to such a folly.'

There was stunned silence as Thomas struggled to grasp what he had just heard. His face began twitching with anger.

'I don't believe any of it!' he said at last, pacing the floor. 'Anthony may have spoken of such things in the past but they were fanciful boasts. It was just his way of showing off. He would never have gone through with such plans. I tell you, Walsingham has wanted rid of the Queen of Scots for years and has spun a great web of lies to ensnare her. Anthony has been trapped. The letters are faked.'

'You may be right,' said Lord Molynieux, 'but faked or not, it makes little difference. It is the evidence they have sought, the proof the Queen demands. I fear Anthony's fate is a foregone conclusion.'

'But we owe him so much. There must be something we can do,' Thomas shouted despairingly.

For a few moments, they stood in silence. Lord Molynieux's keen eyes looked out from beneath his thick brows, an intense look which seemed to see right through to a man's soul. He made no reply for there was nothing he could say.

Thomas sank onto a chair and buried his head in his hands. Lord Molynieux laid his hand on the young man's shoulder and squeezed gently. 'Come, Thomas. You need to get some rest.'

Thomas tried to force a smile. He felt sick at heart. If

what Lord Molynieux said was true, then the cruellest of deaths awaited his friend. And what of his father?

'We'll talk some more tomorrow ... and of course, we must also write to your brother and inform him of what has happened,' said Lord Molynieux. With a sympathetic smile, he left Thomas alone with his thoughts.

Some time later, he returned. The candles on the table had dwindled almost to nothing and cast flickering shadows across the figure of Thomas, lying fast asleep against the table, with his head cradled on his arm.

# CHAPTER 5

THOMAS, HIS HAT pulled low, stood amid the great seething mass of people at St Giles Fields near Holborn. It was early morning on the 20th of September 1586 and it seemed as though the entire population of London had gathered to witness the execution of the Papist traitors. It was rumoured there was even one of those despicable Jesuits amongst the condemned. Many had lined the route from the Tower to glimpse the deathly procession meandering its way through the narrow cobbled streets, to give vent to their hatred and to throw their filth at the helpless victims. The vast majority, however, had congregated at St Giles Fields around the specially erected scaffold. Whole families had gathered for this entertainment. The smallest children were being lifted up to get a better view. Vendors selling gingerbread and hot cockles mingled with the crowd; some people sang newly composed ballads while others distributed printed sheets of the 'Last Dying Speeches and Confessions'. Everywhere, excited voices chattered in relish and anticipation.

Thomas had learnt about the executions through a letter sent by Lord Molynieux from his apartment in Whitehall which had arrived at Broad Oaks only two days previously. The letter contained implicit instructions that on no account was Thomas to come to London; 'Walsingham's spies and informants will be everywhere; eager to note down the names of anyone suspected of Catholic sympathies'. But Thomas felt he had no choice. There was a force deep within him compelling him and he had departed for the City later the same day.

Suddenly there was a disturbance in the crowd and Thomas craned his head. At first he saw only the halberdiers forcing their way through the crowds, resplendent in their scarlet and black uniforms, their pikes stretching upwards. What he saw next made him shudder. Horses, their hooves quietened by the damp turf, pulled wicker hurdles; strapped upon these wooden sledges, with their feet uppermost and their heads level with the soil, were pitiful unrecognisable figures spattered with mud. Thomas felt as if his very soul had been wrenched from his body. He could not think; he could only look and listen.

'There's Ballard! There's the Jesuit traitor!' someone shouted as the leading horse reached the scaffold.

A broken, crippled figure was helped up from his hurdle. It was Captain Foscue! Or at least that had been Ballard's alias. Thomas's eyes shifted to the scaffold where the hangman, dressed in a woollen apron, calmly adjusted the seven nooses. There was a table nearby with butcher's knives laid out upon it and next to that, over a fire, a cauldron which spewed out thick acrid smoke. Surrounded by constables, the sheriff and the distinguished gentlemen of the Privy Council had assembled, talking gravely to one another from their bejewelled saddles.

'That's Babington!' yelled an excited eager voice as another horse was brought to a standstill not more than twenty paces away. Thomas reeled as he caught sight of his friend. A constable bent forward to cut the bonds that bound the victim to his hurdle and Babington staggered to his feet. The vibrant, handsome and confident man that Thomas remembered had disappeared; in his place, there was this frail, pathetic creature. Thomas trembled with rage and revulsion; he was desperate to strike out at those nearest to him, to retaliate for the pain they were inflicting but all he could do was stare helplessly at his friend.

'See how he prays!' jeered the man standing next to Thomas, and some others around him laughed and mocked. All their faces and voices seemed to merge together.

Thomas stared at his friend with glazed eyes. It was true; Babington's lips did seem to be moving in silent prayer. Waves of compassion swept over Thomas, threatening to overwhelm him. Dear God, let it be over quickly, have mercy on him.

The boisterous clamouring of the crowd gradually faded to an expectant hush as the first victim, Ballard, offered his head to the noose. He showed no fear; on the contrary, he seemed calm and impassive. There was a surge as those around Thomas shifted forward for a better position. Moments later, after just one swing of the rope, Ballard was cut down and the butchery started on the still conscious priest. The men in the crowd cheered with approval but some of the women, their faces deadly pale, turned away in horror and shame. Some members of the Privy Council shuffled and murmured uneasily at the brutal speed of the executioner.

'Their fate has been ordered by Her Majesty and we are all bound by our loyalty to her. We must carry out our duty!' the sheriff said coldly and he continued to direct the bloody savagery upon the next victim.

Thomas tried to shut out the voices, the sounds, the smell, the ugly world around him. 'This dreadful world is gone mad,' he thought. 'How can God allow such a thing to happen?'

'Now for Babington!' someone shouted.

Thomas wanted to turn away but again something inside compelled him. He gazed in horror as his friend's head was roughly bundled into the noose. He stood on tiptoe, trying to catch a final glimpse, to show Anthony that he was not alone, that he had not been abandoned. But his friend did not look up. The crowd quietened and they noticed Babington's lips moving as he murmured to himself during his last few moments. Some said he was repeating the name 'Mary' over and over, but Thomas knew it was not 'Mary' but 'Miserere'.

Thomas closed his eyes; he could bear it no longer.

'Behold, the head of a traitor!' came the triumphant cry at last. The crowd roared its approval, cheering and applauding. Dark shadowy figures jostled and pressed on all sides. Thomas staggered. His head pounded. Then he felt a hand grab him by the arm.

'It's me, Thomas,' whispered a familiar voice. 'Let's get you away from here.'

Thomas stared vacantly into the face of Lord Molynieux who tugged his arm insistently.

'Come, we must leave immediately,' he urged. With

nervous haste, he fought his way back through the crowd and led Thomas away. Neither of them looked back.

They walked and ran for what seemed like an eternity until they approached the large houses along the Strand. Thomas had no idea which route they had used, or how long their journey had taken. He had heard and seen nothing along the way but had merely stumbled blindly on behind Lord Molynieux.

Thomas rested his head against a wall and closed his eyes but immediately saw the dreadful face and broken body of his friend Anthony Babington. He opened them again and stared absently about him at the blurred faces and figures in the street.

'Why did you go?' demanded Lord Molynieux, holding Thomas close. 'Why did you not heed my advice? Your presence at the executions is sure to have been noticed. It will confirm how inextricably linked your family is with Anthony Babington. And that is dangerous for your father.' He glanced around to ensure he could not be overheard. 'We must be mindful of our actions at all times, you must understand that,' he added.

Thomas shook his head. He was still numb with the horror of what he had witnessed, but there was anger as well. 'I had to be there,' he said. 'Anthony was a good friend. But today I feel ashamed … I could only stand by and watch him being butchered. I couldn't even cry out to him. Can't you understand?'

'Yes, I do understand, my friend,' replied Lord Molynieux, his voice softening. 'How can a man not feel ashamed? How can any of us not feel sick at heart at what we witnessed today? I know it is hard not to lose our belief and our trust in God at such moments but we must remain strong and true. The pain you feel now is like an open wound, raw and tender to the touch, but in time it will close over and heal. Remember, after winter comes the summer, after night the day.' After a short pause, he straightened up. 'Come. Let us return to the safety of Broad Oaks. Let us concentrate all our efforts on freeing your father.'

These last words were spoken with such tenderness that Thomas felt his lips tremble and the tears rise in his eyes. The despair in his soul gave way to new hope.

† 

Several weeks passed and the mood inside Broad Oaks reflected the sombre colour of the leaden sky outside. In the small winter parlour, situated off the Great Hall, Lady Rufford and Jane were sitting on a high backed settle in the centre of the room looking mournfully at Thomas. Lady Molynieux, rising slowly from her seat, drew her chair a little closer to them while her husband, on the other side of the room, standing next to an elaborately carved oak cabinet, leaned forward with his arms resting against the back of a wainscot armchair.

Thomas was standing with his back to them. Facing the great stone fireplace with its heavy overmantel, his eyes heavy and dull, he continued to gaze at the flames dancing before him. However desperately he tried, he could not shut out the hideous images of the recent executions. The pitiful sight of his friend on the scaffold had burned itself deep into his memory. Neither would he forget those who had tormented Babington. What level of ignorance must a man have that he becomes consumed with such hatred? But Thomas also remembered that some, hidden amongst the crowd, had been mortified at the cruelty of the executioners; they, at least, had shown some pity. There was good amongst the bad, Thomas thought. And then there was the priest, Ballard. Something about his calm serenity, right up to the last dreadful moment, stirred Thomas's soul. He was so strong and unwavering in his faith, he was willing to embrace such a horrible death. Such courage made Thomas feel ashamed, for he doubted that he would ever possess such courage or belief.

'It is Babington's wife and child who I feel sorry for,' said Jane, breaking the silence and looking up from the unopened book on her lap.

'Yes, poor little Meg,' agreed Lady Molynieux, keen to engage in conversation. 'I do so pity them from the bottom of my heart. We must offer whatever consolation we can,' she added, turning to her husband.

'Yes, we must write to them. Invite them to stay,' agreed Lord Moynieux.

'Neither must we forget our father,' snapped Thomas, frowning and casting a sideways glance at his host. 'We must act now before he suffers the same fate as Babington and Ballard.'

'Oh, Thomas, what are you saying?' exclaimed Lady Rufford, aghast at the suggestion that her husband could face the same cruel death.

'No … what I mean is … it has been over three months since his imprisonment and we have heard nothing,' Thomas said quickly.

'Pay no attention, Mother,' said Jane, scowling at her brother's tactless outburst. 'I'm certain Father's alright.'

'It's true,' began Lord Molynieux. 'I have made discreet enquiries and Sir William is indeed well. Do not despair Lady Katherine,' he continued soothingly, looking her steadily in the eyes. 'We will make every effort; we will not rest until this ordeal is over.'

'There, you see,' said Jane. 'We will soon secure Father's release and everything will be fine once again.' She smiled and, using her own handkerchief, wiped away her mother's tears.

Lady Molynieux leaned forward and put a hand on Lady Rufford's sleeve.

'We will all pray to God that he is delivered to us free from harm and without further delay.' Then she rose and started towards the door. As she passed Thomas, she stopped and looked at him. 'If we have faith and turn to God, then our prayers will be answered.'

Thomas sighed and turned his head away. 'I'm afraid that it may take more than prayers,' he muttered softly to himself.

# CHAPTER 6

## July, 1588

THE OPPRESSIVE HEAT and stench of London during high summer was overpowering, permeating every narrow alleyway and entering buildings through carelessly opened windows. July storm clouds jostled and rolled as they threatened from south of the river, and there seemed to be a nervous anticipation that weighed heavily on people as they laboured over their everyday business. Ominous rumours swept through the city: 'the Spaniards are coming, with orders to slaughter all English men and women over the age of seven.'

Walsingham's propaganda was devoured eagerly. Strained emotion lurked everywhere, just below the surface; in the taverns, the timbered tenements, Whitehall and Westminster, the need to point the finger of blame for all England's troubles and a person's own misfortunes upon a perceived enemy was swept along by a tide of ignorance and hysteria. London was no place for a Catholic to loiter at such a time.

The large sign over the door showed a boar's head with peeling gold letters beneath. Thomas hesitated, staring up at the inn with its three storeys and many windows, and felt his heart sink. It was shortly after midday and he was in a foul temper. He beat his hands together in frustration and wiped away the sweat that trickled down from beneath his hat. Noisy, raucous laughter drifted into the street. Sighing wearily, Thomas reluctantly followed his companion through the arched doorway and entered the murky shadowy interior.

'A flagon of your best Canarian, landlord!' roared Lord Molynieux in the careless manner of a gentleman of wealth and high social status.

'Be with you in a moment, sir!' shouted the landlord over his shoulder, before he was swallowed up by the smoke and noise of the revellers crowding around him.

Lord Molynieux nodded in acknowledgement at the other drinkers in the inn as he and Thomas made their way to a quiet secluded recess at the rear and sat down at a round table, a safe distance away from prying ears; a place where they would recede into the shadows.

Thomas peered around the dingy, low-beamed room. The room was full of all manner of people: gentlemen, merchants, labourers, and soldiers recently returned from the Low Countries, all in various stages of drunkenness. Games of dice and cards were being contested; the powerful odour of stale sweat, beer and smoke was everywhere. Along the far wall, a fire burned in the grate of a brick fireplace, in front of which three men in their mid twenties, wearing patched wool and leather jerkins, slouched at a table. An older man, who sat alongside them, was coughing repeatedly into his lace handkerchief. His dress was old-fashioned: he wore a linen frill on the collar of his high-necked doublet and, despite the warmth of the day, a black velvet coif with ear flaps and a furred mantle reaching to his knees.

Thomas continued to gaze absently as the man unscrewed the silver knob on the top of his walking stick and sniffed at the aromatic herbs it contained. There was a mournful look about the man's face; Thomas didn't know why, but he seemed vaguely familiar.

'There you are gentlemen!' bellowed the deep voice of the landlord as he arrived at the table, clumsily setting down the wine and two cups. 'Now, will you be wanting something to eat? A plate of my fine stew, perhaps?'

'We'll call for it when we're ready, landlord,' replied Lord Molynieux, pouring the pale wine into the cups.

'As you wish,' said the landlord and quickly disappeared again.

Thomas took a large gulp of wine from his cup. His face immediately distorted into a grimace. 'Sour as vinegar!' he grunted and set the cup down with a thud. 'That rogue of a landlord…' He wiped his mouth with his sleeve and turned to Lord Molynieux. 'My father has been imprisoned without trial, for two years now. Surely after all this time they must know he is innocent. We do not seek charity from them, only true justice. If they possess any conscience, they must free him.'

Leaning his elbows on the table, Thomas pushed the half-full cup of wine aside. 'We have now spent three months in London and yet Walsingham still refuses to listen to our petition or grant us an audience,' he went on. 'We have visited Whitehall and Cheapside more times than I care to remember. We are kept waiting for hours, pacing up and down corridors or in some tiny ante-chamber, where we observe all manner of comings and goings, only to be informed that Sir Francis is not to be disturbed, that he is occupied with far more important matters of state. Why? What reason does he have?'

Lord Molynieux inclined his head towards Thomas. 'And amongst those comings and goings, did you not observe Francis Drake and the Admiral of the Fleet? Or the Spanish Ambassador being sent away from court?' he asked.

His eyes downcast, Thomas did not answer.

'Ministers are restless,' continued Lord Molynieux. 'There is a great deal of political manoeuvring ... on all sides. The Queen's realm is under threat and while Lord Burghley continues to exercise cautious restraint and advocates diplomatic solutions, Walsingham's counsel to Her Majesty is to secure the country against a Spanish invasion.'

Thomas looked up. 'A Spanish invasion!' he repeated, in a voice that seemed deliberately raised. 'But is that not a cause for celebration for us? Are not the Spanish our allies?'

Lord Molynieux scowled at him and leaned across the table. 'Lower your voice, I beg you,' he whispered under his breath.

Thomas scanned the crowded inn in response to his friend's alarm. The low room throbbed with conversation and laughter. He shook his head and sighed. It was impossible for him to have been overheard in such a din, although in his present mood, he half wished he had been.

'There are many who believe that the real purpose of

such an invasion is to restore the true religion to this country,' Lord Molynieux went on, his voice barely audible, 'and that it has been endorsed by the Pope. And there is a strong conviction amongst the Queen's advisors that many English Catholics would take up arms to assist the Spanish in their enterprise...'

'Well, I for one am prepared to pledge my sword,' Thomas interjected.

'...which gives Walsingham perfect cause to keep English Catholics like your father locked away,' Lord Molynieux added bluntly.

Thomas felt an unpleasant lurch in his gut. He knew Lord Molynieux had spoken a painful but evident truth. Averting his eyes from his friend's piercing gaze, he glanced across at the men by the fireplace who were enjoying some jovial banter with the older man who had now joined their group. Distracted for a moment, he rested his chin on his elbow and looked again at the face of this man sitting only a few feet away. Recognition stirred and then faded.

He had been watching for several minutes when the older man, suddenly conscious of being scrutinised, turned quickly and fastened a severe look of admonition directly on Thomas.

Thomas did not have enough time to look away and felt a warm red flush sweep across his face. He fumbled with his cup and spilled some wine onto the table.

One of the others at the table, a broad-shouldered man of about Thomas's age, who was partly obscured by a stout timber post which supported the ceiling, also swung round and glared menacingly at him. The older man muttered something to his companions and immediately all their faces beamed with contemptuous grins. Another gestured as if holding a knife, ripped upwards from his belly in a slashing motion. Laughter, cruel and harsh, bellowed from their midst.

'That's it!' cried Thomas, remembering. 'They were at St Giles' Fields, at the executions. They were no more than a few feet from me. The older one…'

'…is Robert Poley,' said Lord Molynieux, grabbing Thomas's arm to prevent him from turning around again.

Thomas paused, bewildered. The name did not mean anything to him.

'Robert Poley is known to have befriended Anthony Babington. But beware; he is not what he seems.' Lord Molynieux's expression was grave and his grip on Thomas's arm tightened. 'Robert Poley is a renegade Catholic and a spy for Walsingham.'

Thomas's jaw dropped. 'Anthony was betrayed?' he asked weakly, hardly able to get the words out. But there was no need for a reply; Thomas could see the answer in Lord Molynieux's eyes.

'Our hasty departure from the field that day would not have gone unnoticed, Thomas. No doubt Walsingham was duly informed. We should exercise caution,' continued Lord Molynieux. 'Do you hear what I say?'

Thomas's eyes burned, his lips tightly compressed. He could feel anger swelling up inside. 'Let me be … I'll kill him … what do I care?' he growled, wrenching himself free from his friend's grasp.

'Don't be a fool, Thomas!' said Lord Molynieux. 'Listen to me … think of your father!'

In the split second that Thomas hesitated, Lord

Molynieux pulled him back down on to the bench.

'What!'

'Anthony, God rest his soul, is dead, the Queen of Scots is dead. Thomas ... it is done and cannot be undone,' Lord Molynieux said, his voice shaking with emotion. 'But think now of your father. He is all that matters.'

Thomas simmered with hate but he had enough sense to heed Lord Molynieux's advice. He choked as he thought of his father locked away in the Tower. He remembered Babington's death and, in particular, those vile creatures now seated only a few feet away. At the executions, he had paid no great attention to them for they had been inconspicuous among the rest of the howling mob and Thomas was concentrating on his friend and the priest.

Thomas gazed wearily into the middle distance. The noise and chaos of the inn intruded again, confusing his thoughts. Though he felt contempt towards Poley and desired vengeance for his friend's cruel death, he knew in his heart that Lord Molynieux was right.

A few moments passed. Lord Molynieux took another sip of wine and glanced at Thomas. 'I understand your anger and your sorrow, my friend,' he said softly, 'but whatever troubles we face, we must not lose sight of that which is most important.'

Thomas forced a smile. He was aware of something comforting and soothing in his friend's voice, in his gentle kindness and simple truth. But the smile faded almost immediately, for these qualities in Lord Molynieux reminded him of his own father.

'I fear for him ... my father,' Thomas said, without

raising his eyes. 'He is kept closely confined in the Tower, with no visitors to bring him food and clean clothes … even some little hope.' He drew a long, deep breath and shut his eyes. Lord Molynieux watched attentively but without stirring. 'He is no longer a young man and I tremble when I hear such disturbing tales about the Tower,' Thomas went on, his moist eyes flickering open again. 'Few men ever go free; there is no escape except by the block or hangman's noose. And then there is torture and the rack! I ask you, how long can a man exist in such a terrible place?'

'You underestimate your father's strength and courage,' replied Lord Molynieux with a wry smile. 'And you Thomas, my friend, you too must be steadfast and resolute in order to see this business through to the end.'

Thomas's face was haggard. In spite of their combined efforts, it seemed as though they had come up against an impenetrable stone wall. The anger, the frustration, the despair, all weighed heavily upon him; he sensed he was beginning to lose faith, to doubt that they would ever succeed. But as he looked at Lord Molynieux's kindly face, his words of consolation and encouragement rekindled new belief in his heart.

'Such trusted and loyal friends are rare these days,' Thomas murmured. 'And you may rest assured that I have no intention of giving up on my father.'

Lord Molynieux drank the last of his wine and got to his feet. 'Come, let us return to Broad Oaks,' he said, squeezing between the end of the table and the wall. 'A few days' rest will do us both good while we wait for news of the warrant we seek. Besides, we must not forget we have a duty to your mother and sister.' As he turned to leave, he added: 'Remember Thomas, there is value in adversity however painful it may appear at the time.'

Thomas dragged himself out of his seat, forced his way through a bunch of drunken soldiers re-telling yarns about their heroic deeds in Flanders and followed Lord Molynieux towards the doorway.

'You keep good wine landlord!' Lord Molynieux's voice boomed over the chatter and clinking of mugs. 'I hope we shall have the good fortune to take some with you again soon.'

The portly, middle-aged landlord forced a smile, nodded out of courtesy and returned to impatiently shouting orders at a young serving girl.

Thomas glanced back towards the fireplace where the harassed serving girl, a pretty little thing who was no more than twelve or thirteen years old, was making a clumsy attempt at clearing the tables. Getting more agitated and flustered by the minute, she spilled a half full mug of beer down the trunk hose and silk stockings worn by a distinguished looking young gentleman. As the landlord's fury boiled over in a tirade of abuse she screamed back at him and, with tears streaming down her face, fled from the room.

'You fool!' the landlord hollered, his face purple with rage. Head hanging low and his eyes flashing wildly, he shoved aside those nearest to him. 'I'll show that stupid bitch…' he muttered.

'Leave her be!' cried Thomas, rushing forward to obstruct the landlord's way. 'She's only a young thing, for pity's sake.' He bent down, picked up the mug and thrust it into the landlord's hand.

He turned to the gentleman, a handsome young novice of the Inns of Court who seemed to be finding the whole episode rather amusing. His doxie, a diminutive, red-haired woman in a loose beige gown and a low-fronted bodice, leaned against him, idly caressing his smooth hands with her large stubby fingers.

'Good kind sir!' Thomas began politely. 'The girl meant no harm, I'm sure. Allow me to buy you another drink...' He broke off suddenly. The benches nearest the fireplace were empty; Poley and his companions had gone.

Thomas spun around, his eyes frantically searching the inn. Lord Molynieux had also disappeared. Panic threatened. An image of Lord Molynieux's lifeless body lying face down in a pool of blood, his throat slit, flashed before his eyes. Poley was standing over him, clutching a dagger with his bloodied hands. Thomas felt a chill run down his back. And now Poley lay in ambush for him...

Thomas plunged into the street outside. His eyes blinked rapidly as they grew accustomed to the sudden change from the gloom and smoke of the inn to the blinding glare of a mid-summer's afternoon. He glanced down the narrow alleyway, first one way then the other, then let out a long sigh and breathed again. His mouth curled into a grateful smile; Lord Molynieux was striding confidently down the street, his legs kicking out at a curious angle as they propelled his bulky figure along. Poley and his companions were nowhere in sight.

'Did you see where Poley disappeared to? What

happened to those other rogues?' Thomas asked, coming alongside him. He glanced nervously over his shoulder; perhaps their assailants were simply biding their time, waiting to carry out their ambush surreptitiously, away from unwanted witnesses.

Lord Molynieux turned his head as if to ignore Thomas and continued his brisk pace. The noise of the inn gradually receded and the only sound was that of their breathing and their echoing footsteps on the cobbles.

'We must be on our guard, for if they did recognise us…'

'Oh, I'm certain they recognised us,' Lord Molynieux remarked. 'But I think their sort of courage comes and goes with the mob. We needn't worry too much.'

'I don't understand,' said Thomas, sounding surprised. 'In there you advised caution…'

'And indeed we must be cautious but you must not let your imagination blind your senses. Their bravery does not extend beyond a cruel taunt or jest and that will never harm us.' Lord Molynieux smiled at Thomas. 'But if it dispels your fears, we will be careful and avoid the side streets.'

Thomas returned a feeble smile. 'But what about Poley?' he persisted.

Lord Molynieux stopped abruptly and turned to face him. 'Yes, Poley is cunning and devious but he is also a weak man. Like many, his crime is one of avarice. He does what he does out of greed, not out of some high ideal or deep hatred. He has not the stomach to become embroiled in such unruly thuggery; rather, he relies on a plausible manner which makes it easy for him to take advantage of honest people…'

'Like Anthony!'

'Yes! Like poor Anthony,' Lord Molynieux agreed. 'And yet, in our hearts we should pity him, he is as much a victim…'

But these last words, softly spoken, crashed upon Thomas's ears.

'Pity! Victim!' he exclaimed, incensed. 'How can you speak so? I saw the look in his face that day. I tell you, I shall never feel pity for the likes of him!'

'At the end of the day you must make up your own mind, Thomas,' Lord Molynieux said. 'But I hope you do not become another victim. Now, come along, my good friend. We must collect our horses. We must not dawdle if we are to be back at Broad Oaks before nightfall!' And he set out once more with that peculiar gait of his.

# CHAPTER 7

'It is small consolation I know, but we should content ourselves we have at last been permitted access to Father,' said Jane, smiling brightly, brandishing aloft the precious warrant that was necessary to visit confined prisoners and which had been delivered to Broad Oaks by messenger that morning. With a slight rustle of her fitted blue velvet gown, which she wore over a cream high-necked bodice and matching skirt, she crossed the room to where her mother was sitting.

'But of course. This should give us all cause to hope,' Lord Molynieux asserted, glancing round the room.

Thomas looked at his sister's cheerful face and nodded dumbly. He was impatient for his father's release and had hoped for more. 'Very well, very well,' he said, grudgingly reconciled to accepting what he saw as nothing more than a token gesture on Walsingham's part. 'But I will go alone. You and Mother should not come; the Tower is no place for either of you.'

'Nonsense!' retorted Lady Rufford indignantly. 'The Tower does not intimidate me! And nothing will keep me from attending my husband.'

Thomas glanced anxiously at his mother. In the two years following her husband's imprisonment she had aged visibly; her plump face had become gaunt and pallid and though she spoke bravely and tried to conceal her pain, her sunken eyes were filled with melancholy and fear. She was far weaker than she would ever admit.

'And you needn't think you will prevent me from seeing Father either,' said Jane defiantly. 'We must make the necessary arrangements immediately – food and such like. Some freshly-baked bread and wine.'

'Yes, we'll bake some cheese cakes and a syllabub and his favourite apple tarts,' said Lady Rufford eagerly. She rose from her chair and accompanied her daughter from the room.

Thomas gazed after them,shaking his head, the corners of his mouth slightly upturned.

†

Two days later, the Ruffords entered London via the Bishops Gate and, after stabling their horses, began to make their way on foot towards the Tower. Both women carried covered baskets laden with supplies for William. The weather was still and sultry, the calm before the storm.

Along every street, carts and coaches thundered past; at every corner, men, women and children met in shoals. The City was so overwhelming that the two women huddled close to Thomas. Curiously, in spite of his earlier misgivings, their presence seemed to strengthen Thomas's resolve.

They went along Tower Street, with its mix of wealthy merchants' houses, shops and inns, past All Hallow's parish church until eventually they reached Tower Hill, the site of so many public executions. Street vendors, oblivious to the grisly sight of the gallows only a short distance away, were busy plying their wares. There the Ruffords came to an abrupt halt. Across a broad deep moat, the imposing stone edifice of the Tower of London reared menacingly before them. For some minutes, they stared in awe at the medieval fortification. Thomas shuddered. Jane nudged his arm and, with some trepidation, they advanced towards the drawbridge gate.

A stout, broad-shouldered man dressed in the scarlet uniform of a Yeoman Warder, and wielding an intimidating halberd, barred the entrance.

Thomas, his heart pounding and sweating profusely under his heavy leather jerkin, drew closer, stopping only two or three feet away. 'We are here to visit my father, Sir William Rufford,' he announced, his voice sounding surprisingly bold.

The warder's contemptuous eyes stared back from beneath his black woollen cap. 'Rufford? Why, he's one of those Catholic conspirators, one of Babington's lot!' he said in a husky voice. 'No, you can't come in here. You need a warrant to visit a close confined prisoner.'

'Yes, we have such a warrant here,' said Thomas. He fumbled in his pocket and produced the crumpled piece of parchment. Lady Rufford and Jane stepped a little closer.

The warder seized the document and studied it intently as if hoping to discover some mistake or omission which would give him a reason to refuse these people entry to his prison. 'Sir Francis himself eh?' he muttered, observing the signature and seal. He cocked an eye at the covered baskets and brushed Thomas to one side with his muscular forearm. 'And what have we got here?' he grunted.

'We have brought my father some food,' replied Jane, drawing back the cloth cover on the basket to reveal bread, cheese and apple tarts. 'And I dare say he'll be in need of it with the rubbish you serve him!'

The warder was oblivious to Jane's remark and lifted the cover on Lady Rufford's basket.

'Some medicines, that is all.' Lady Rufford swayed a little and her voice trembled. 'Might I be permitted to bring my husband these?'

The warder snorted. Over the years, he had grown hardened to insults and pleas alike. He turned away, still clutching the warrant in his hand.

'Sir?' Jane enquired, tugging at the guard's sleeve.

The warder shrugged his arm free and swung round. He stared intently at Jane. A smile crept over his thick lips.

'Look here, I don't like your attitude nor the way you look us up and down,' interrupted Thomas with growing impatience. 'That warrant is signed by Sir Francis Walsingham himself. We have rightful authority to enter the Tower.'

'Sir Francis Walsingham or not, I still have my job to do,' said the warder. 'I swear, you can't be too careful, especially at a time like this.' He had his routine to follow, his duty to carry out, and he would not be cajoled into hurrying for anyone. He found it irksome to allow visits to any prisoner; the thought of granting such a favour to the kinsfolk of one accused of plotting to kill his Queen did not sit comfortably with him at all.

'Ten minutes is all we ask, please,' whispered Lady

Rufford. 'If you have any mercy at all, you will allow me to see my husband.'

Thomas frowned. He reached for his purse, grabbed hold of the warder's gloved hand and thrust several groats into his outstretched palm.

The warder looked greedily at the coins and grunted again. 'Wait there!' he snapped. He turned and walked across to another warder slumped against the wall at the far end of the gate lodge. After a few minutes' conversation, he returned. 'Very well, my colleague over there has agreed to escort you. Ten minutes only, not a minute longer!'

The other turnkey was a squat older man in his late fifties and he walked with a slight stoop. His face was weather beaten but his eyes seemed kinder and his manner more sympathetic. He ushered them through the gate and into the prison, leading them towards a tower situated at the corner of a small garden. As they walked, the warder's bunch of keys, hanging from the leather belt around his waist, jangled noisily, a stark reminder that freedom was out of reach.

'That three-storey tower yonder is the Salt Tower, that one the Lanthorne Tower, this, the Queen's Privy Garden,' the turnkey informed them as if he were a guide showing them the sights. 'And this one 'ere is known as the Cradle Tower. This be where we look after your father.'

They ascended a small flight of stone steps to the first floor. Their new guide unlocked one of the doors and peered inside. 'Wake up Sir William! You have some visitors!' he said almost gently.

Thomas, Jane and Lady Rufford paused on the

threshold. The room was dark, lit by a single narrow slit window nine feet up in the wall opposite the door. At first Thomas could not see anything and he was overwhelmed by panic; perhaps his father was dead. He was aware of a furious thumping in his chest and a cold sweat broke out on his forehead.

Gradually, as his eyes grew accustomed to the gloom, he made out his surroundings. The cell was small, about nine feet long by seven or eight feet wide and it had a low, vaulted ceiling which made it feel claustrophobic. There was a small table directly beneath the window, a stool with a broken leg, a pitcher of water in one corner and a chamber pot in another. A thin bed of rotting straw covered the floor. The dank, fetid air, heavy with the stench of urine and filth, enveloped him. For an instant, he felt he was going to retch.

'Ten minutes now!' came the harsh reminder from the turnkey and the door was slammed shut and locked behind them.

There was a faint scuffling from the straw. At last, Thomas saw his father and his eyes widened in horror. He barely recognised him. William's hair, usually neat and well groomed, was unkempt and completely grey. His pale face was covered with grey stubble and his sad eyes were sunken.

'Thomas! It's good to see you!' His father's voice was hoarse and the words barely audible. He raised himself to his feet, grimacing with the effort; his shirt and breeches fell loosely from his emaciated body.

Words failed Thomas. He reached out and hugged the wasted figure that was his father. 'This is an awful place!' he said angrily and pulled away from the embrace. 'They have no right to treat you like this!'

'But what's this?' His father's voice, though still weak now contained that note of authority Thomas knew so well. 'Jane … and Kate too! Thomas, you should not have brought them here.' But his tone softened quickly as a weak smile creased his face. 'Jane, my sweet Jane, it is good to see you. And Kate, how are you, my dear?' The three wrapped themselves around one another, hugging and kissing.

'It is so dark and gloomy,' said Jane, looking up at the weak trickle of light that came through the window.

'Yes, I'm afraid you have come at the wrong time of day, my dears – the window faces east,' William said, gently stroking her face. 'But every morning when the sun rises it fills the room, visiting me like an old friend – and without the permission of the governor or my warder. When its warmth disappears, as indeed it must, I have enjoyed its presence for four or five hours. That is more than enough.'

Thomas choked back his tears. He had indeed underestimated his father's strength.

'We miss you so…' Jane began, but then stopped, and gave her father another hug. 'Look Father, we've brought you some things,' she went on, uncovering her basket. 'Some bread and cheese…'

William held the bread up to his nostrils, closed his eyes and inhaled deeply. 'It smells absolutely delicious,' he said. 'God bless you!'

'And an apple tart. We know how you adore mother's apple tarts,' Jane added, crossing to the table.

'I have also brought some medicines and restoratives, my husband,' added Lady Katherine.

'Better than any apothecary in London!' William said, peering into the basket. 'Thank you … thank you … thank you,' William expressed his deep gratitude to each in turn. 'I am indeed a favoured mortal.'

He took a mouthful of the bread and closed his eyes. It tasted good, not dry and stale like that served up by his warder, but soft and fresh.

'The finest manchet. Yes, I am privileged – but happier still to see you, my dears.' He grinned at their loving but melancholy faces; they were unconvinced by his exaggerated cheerfulness.

'We should be grateful,' William continued quickly. 'There are some in a far worse position than I am. Why, there is a condemned man in the room above this, another from the Babington affair. My warder informs me that his name is John Arden, from one of the old Catholic families of Northamptonshire. He was arrested in January last year and moved here from Windsor. Sometimes, on calm evenings, I can hear him through the window reciting his prayers when he's out on exercise. And in all this time, his poor wife has never been allowed to visit him. Not once. So, you see my dears…'

'Are we to thank them for their kindness and generosity then, Father?' retorted Jane.

'Now then, Jane, don't be silly…' But he broke off, distracted by his son flicking aside some of the putrid straw with his boot. 'Thomas?'

'May God help me!' screamed Thomas, shaking with rage, no longer able to restrain himself. Lady Rufford recoiled at the suddenness of his outburst. 'I swear we will get you out of here, Father. You are no more guilty of treason than any of us. This whole affair reeks of trickery and deception and has no doubt been perpetrated with the full knowledge and complicity of…'

'Thomas!' William implored, his voice breaking.

'Oh, Father!' Thomas exclaimed. 'We all know that Walsingham and the others were desperate to be rid of the Queen of Scots. But to do so without good reason would be too uncomfortable for they knew that such an unprovoked act would harm Elizabeth's reputation, both here in England and abroad. Such an act would be a sign of weakness and she must remain omnipotent, Gloriana to her subjects!' Thomas flung out his arms in a wild gesture.

'For God's sake Thomas … and mine, remember where you are!' William rebuked him.

But Thomas ignored his father's desperate reproach. 'So a scheme was hatched, a devious, cunning scheme. But in order for it to succeed, they needed scapegoats – and what better than a Catholic, a gullible Catholic, or better still a Jesuit. They invented new accusations to ensnare their victims but I tell you, they went too far with you.' Thomas's eyes smarted as he gazed at the wretched figure before him. His temper subsided and compassion welled up in its place. 'You are an honest man who has done no wrong. You do not deserve such injustice.' He suddenly spun round and beat his fists on the door. 'I should never have let them take you! I should have cut them down when I had the chance and we would all have been spared this humiliation.'

'You sound more and more like Babington!' remarked Jane ironically, crooking a finger at him.

'I stand by what I say!'

'God preserve you, Thomas!' said William, dismayed. 'Such words will achieve nothing save put all our lives at a greater risk. Pray, have you not considered your responsibilities to your mother and your sister?'

'I have considered the degradation of simply submitting without a fight!'

'Then you care more for appearance's sake than simple truth,' William snapped. He fell silent for a moment, exhausted. Teetering a little, he wrapped his threadbare coat around himself a little more snugly.

'Come now, let us quarrel no longer,' he whispered and glanced over at Lady Katherine, who had remained silent the whole time. 'My dear, you mustn't fret so … they have no case against me,' he said, observing her distress.

'We're sorry mother!' Jane said. 'We didn't mean to upset you; it is so inconsiderate of us.' She shot an angry glance in Thomas's direction.

'They have no case against me,' repeated William, stepping closer to Lady Katherine and tenderly taking her hand. 'They scratch around in the dirt like rats trying to rake up some evidence – but it is to no avail for there is none to be found. They are so desperate they have even suggested the money Anthony paid as surety for John was some kind of bribe to recruit me to their ranks!'

'Unbelievable!' Thomas muttered. 'How low will they stoop?'

'All that may be so,' said Lady Katherine, drawing away from her husband's embrace. 'They know you to be a recusant; they know about your previous imprisonment and they know Anthony Babington was a close acquaintance.'

'That is neither here nor there, my dear,' replied William. 'I have spoken no treason, nor have I at any time encouraged or had any part in treason. They have bartered words with me on many occasions in an attempt to gain a confession but it is in vain. I sense they are becoming increasingly impatient with their lack of progress. Indeed, I would go so far as to say that in recent months they have even lost interest in me!' He gave a low, forced laugh.

'Then in God's name why do they keep you here?' demanded Lady Katherine bitterly.

'My dear, it is only a matter of time. We must remain patient just a little while longer. Indeed, if it were not for all this gossip about some great enterprise then I am confident Walsingham would have already seen fit to return me to you.'

'You have heard the rumours of a Spanish Armarda in here?' asked Jane, surprised.

'It is the warders' sole conversation!' William smiled.

'How can you be so certain?' Thomas asked. 'About Walsingham, I mean.'

'Sir Francis is a meticulous man and a committed Protestant, none more so, but he has already accomplished what he set out to, as you have so vehemently pointed out – that is why I am certain.' William shrugged. 'His attentions are now shifted elsewhere.'

'If that is so, then you should be released without further delay,' Thomas said.

'Thomas,' began William in mild reproach, 'you have

a tendency to impetuosity; remember these are still dangerous times. We must have our wits about us and we must all steer a prudent course in the coming storm if we are to find safe harbour.'

Then he looked at Jane and smiled. 'Now, if you would be so kind as to pass me one of your mother's apple tarts,' he said brightly.

As she did so, the key rattled noisily in the lock and the door scraped open. 'Time's up Sir William!' shouted the turnkey.

'What! Already?' cried Jane. 'A few more minutes – give us a few more minutes!' She clutched at her father's arm.

But the warder was unyielding. 'You must come away now ladies, you'll only stir up trouble.' He seized the two women by their arms.

'Let us at least take our leave in a proper manner,' begged Lady Katherine. She pulled away from the warder's loose grip and fell into her husband's arms.

Thomas grabbed the warder's shoulder to restrain him. 'For pity's sake! Have you no heart?'

'You must leave right away. All of you!' the warder said, with growing impatience. His mood appeared to have changed: now he seemed tense and uneasy at carrying out a necessary but unpleasant duty.

William released his wife and daughter from his embrace, kissing them tenderly as he did so. 'Goodbye, my dears. Take heart, I'll be home soon.' His voice faltered as he spoke. Lady Katherine and Jane began sobbing uncontrollably. 'Remember Thomas,' he added, clearing his throat to regain his composure, 'think on what I've said.'

'Thank you, Sir William,' the turnkey said gratefully, as the visitors fell grudgingly into line. 'Let's go then, shall we!'

As the cell door was locked behind them, they could clearly hear the sounds of William blowing his nose with sharp angry blasts.

# CHAPTER 8

### October, 1588

THE SUMMER GALES, which had dashed the hopes of the Spanish Armada and of those English Catholics who had prayed that its success might once more return a Catholic sovereign to rule their country, had now abated. The people, though, were unable to breathe a sigh of relief. Fear and suspicion was still widespread and watchers remained vigilant, guarding the coastal towns and villages with orders to apprehend anyone suspected of stirring up further trouble or rebellion. Englishmen everywhere waited for the Queen's victory celebrations to give tangible proof of the Armada's final and comprehensive defeat. A mood of tense and eager anticipation descended over the nation.

Though news from London would often take a day or two to reach Broad Oaks, Lady Molynieux was kept abreast of events by her husband's letters which he sent every day from court.

On a day towards the end of the month, Lady Molynieux was busy with the arrangements for a great feast, scurrying between the kitchen and the Great Hall, giving instructions to the steward, the chief usher and the head cook. The tables must be covered with the finest white cloths, the sideboards dressed with wines, flagons and drinking cups; the numerous fish and meat dishes which must be cooked in the kitchen. Her servants listened carefully to her considerable demands, aware that few knew how to organise a dinner as capably as Lady Molynieux.

Having given her orders, Lady Molynieux was about to go to her private chambers to rest when she remembered something else of importance. She turned back, summoned the steward, the chief usher and the head cook again and began giving yet more orders.

She heard light footsteps and the gentle rustling of a dress as Jane entered the Hall, radiant in her blue velvet gown.

'Ah, there you are, my dear!' said Lady Molynieux. She hurried over and took her by the arm. 'I think everything is in hand. There is so much to think about on such occasions and I cannot help worrying that I've overlooked something.'

'Lady Molynieux, I do believe even the Queen's celebrations will not be as well prepared nor will they have a greater assortment of food or drink!' said Jane, smiling.

Lady Molynieux laughed nervously. At that moment Thomas stepped noisily into the room. His boots were muddied and his face was flushed and perspiring. He had risen early and spent the day roaming despondently through the deer park which surrounded Broad Oaks.

'Thomas!' said Jane, approaching her brother. 'Where have you been? Never mind, it is going to be a marvellous feast. I don't know how Lady Molynieux does it…' She stopped short, seeing the anguished look in her brother's eyes.

'I don't understand,' Thomas said, struggling to stifle his emotions. 'How can we celebrate when Father remains imprisoned? I tell you, a Spanish invasion may have brought him and the rest of us our freedom.'

Lady Molynieux looked at Thomas and was moved by pity and compassion.

'Thomas! Thomas!' she cried, walking swiftly towards him with outstretched arms. 'Believe me, my dear, we all pray for your father's release every day but such an invasion would have brought nothing but chaos and destruction. It is not God's will to save souls through hatred and violence; your father understands that.' She kissed him on his forehead then addressed both Thomas and Jane: 'You have been allowed to visit your father on several occasions, taken him food and clean clothes, even paid for a bed for him. Is he not better for these visits?'

Jane nodded. 'Yes. Father was much improved when we saw him last,' she said.

'There, you see, Thomas! You must not fret so,' Lady Molynieux continued. 'We must keep up our courage and remain patient. I'm sure it won't be long before your father is granted his freedom. Lord Molynieux is working tirelessly to this end … but in the meantime, he was most insistent about the celebratory feast. Indeed, he said what better way to demonstrate our true allegiance to the Queen than to sing the praise of Francis Drake and the rest of our glorious navy for scattering the Spanish threat to the four winds.'

Thomas shook his head. 'Well, I still don't agree

with it! There are many of us who pay dearly for our nonconformity and who consequently cannot afford such a feast!' he added spitefully, glancing at a servant placing more flagons of wine on the sideboard.

'Don't be so ungracious, Thomas!' Jane scolded. 'Please forgive my brother's impudence,' she said, turning to Lady Molynieux. 'He has no right to speak to you like that. We have become a burden to you... You have lavished nothing but kindness and generosity on us and we repay you with our selfishness. We owe you and your husband so much. We should be ashamed of ourselves.'

'Nonsense, my dear child.' Lady Molynieux smiled at her. 'Come, Thomas,' she said, leading him by the arm towards the door. 'I know how you must be feeling. You are angry and frightened and yes, perhaps even a little resentful towards us. You see how well we live, how rich we are – but without our faith it counts as nothing. My husband is an honourable man. He struggles constantly to reconcile the dictates of his conscience with those duties he is required to do under his oath of allegiance. But in his heart he has never broken faith with God. He is resolved to use this position of wealth and power,' these last words were spoken with a slight lilt, 'to plead the cause of Catholics, including that of your father, in the halls of great houses and before the Queen and her court. And in doing so he puts himself at great risk, acquiring many enemies. But he does it anyway. So, let us have the feast, for his sake.'

Thomas smiled ruefully but he still felt troubled and uneasy. At that moment her words meant little to him.

'I have spoken out of turn ... it was most uncharitable

CHAPTER 8

of me,' he said hesitantly. 'Please forgive me.'

'There is nothing to forgive,' replied Lady Molynieux. 'Now, if you will excuse me, my dears, I am tired and in need of a little rest.' She turned and went out of the room.

Jane came alongside her brother. 'Well, I hope you are ashamed of yourself,' she snarled. 'I don't know what you were thinking of!'

But Thomas did not hear his sister's reproach. 'When is your husband expected to return?' he called after Lady Molynieux.

'His last letter indicated he would be back at Broad Oaks by this evening ... perhaps he will bring further news of your father,' Lady Molynieux replied as she started to climb the stairs.

†

It was around four o'clock in the afternoon when Lord Molynieux finally returned to Broad Oaks. Passing swiftly through the vestibule, he entered the Great Hall and paused. He smiled. It seemed that the entire household had mustered there in readiness for the feast; the steward was in his gown, surrounded by servants and guests alike; Lady Molynieux's attractive younger sister, Mary and her husband Sir Henry Leigh were there; Master Christopher Sutton, a much respected neighbour and friend, together with his charming young wife and son; Lady Rufford, Jane and Thomas drifted from one group to another, looking a little sad and bewildered; and Lady Molynieux of course, wandering back and forth, still fussing over last minute details and directing the servants.

'Ah! There you are, my dear!' exclaimed Lady Molynieux, observing her husband. She smiled the special smile which she always reserved for him. The buzz of conversation quickly faded away and all eyes turned in his direction.

Lord Molynieux stepped forward and heaved a weary sigh. 'Forgive my untidy appearance.' He glanced down at his mud-stained breeches and boots and ran his grimy hand across his sweating forehead. 'It has been an arduous journey! I would have been here earlier but it was the devil to get away.'

'And we will no doubt hear of your adventures in due course, my dear, but you must first refresh yourself and change your clothes before dinner!' said Lady Molynieux, fussing over his bedraggled appearance.

'All in good time!' replied Lord Molynieux, shrugging off her attempt to usher him away. 'I have brought someone with me from London. Can we arrange for another seat?'

'Well, of course. But why didn't you send word?'

'There was no time. Indeed, I wasn't sure until the last moment if he would be able to come.' He gave an imperceptible nod to the steward.

The steward cleared his throat and announced pompously: 'May I present … Sir William Rufford!'

Suddenly, William appeared in the doorway, his fragile figure dwarfed by the door frame. He looked exhausted and on the verge of collapse. Rubbing his eyes and blinking hard as he gazed into the brightly lit room, the merest suspicion of a smile came to the corners of his mouth.

CHAPTER 8

Thomas, Jane and Lady Rufford stood as if paralysed, staring silently in disbelief; Lady Molynieux also seemed to be in a state of shock and was, for once, lost for words.

'Are you not pleased to see him, then?' ribbed Lord Molynieux.

Jane and Lady Rufford's expressions transformed into delighted astonishment. With tears of joy streaming down their faces, they rushed forward, smothering William with hugs and kisses. A hundred questions spewed out simultaneously and then a sound, which had become almost extinct in recent months, was heard again ... the sound of laughter.

For Lady Rufford it was almost too much to bear and she began to sob, burying her face in her husband's chest. Thomas, however, remained hesitant. He seemed unable to share the excitement around him. He glanced at Lord Molynieux who, blushing with embarrassment, had surrendered to Jane's heartfelt embraces.

Thomas had wanted more than anything to be the one who freed his father but he had been so helpless, so powerless. He felt this weakness was not due to lack of physical strength but something that was missing within him, some inner force, some faith that their good friend, Lord Molynieux, possessed in abundance. Thomas lowered his eyes as if to hide his shame.

William seemed to sense his son's turmoil and crossed the room towards him. 'Thomas,' he said, 'I never once doubted your resolve. The certainty that this reunion would come gave me such cause to hope.' A tender smile came to his lips as he spoke.

The familiar sound of his father's voice, the warm

smile and gentle compassion in his eyes which made William's thin, sickly face beautiful, soothed Thomas. Tears welled up in his eyes and he brushed them away. His anxieties, though never quite disappearing, melted into the background.

'As God is my witness,' Thomas said, his voice quivering, 'you are the most remarkable man I know … or am likely to know!' The two men fell into a long, affectionate embrace. Thomas closed his eyes, savouring the moment he had yearned for for so long. The dignified manner in which his father conducted his life, the way he remained true and honest even in the most dire times, filled him with pride and admiration.

'That is the most sensible thing he has spoken these past few months!' Jane grinned as she joined in their embrace.

At length, Thomas pulled away and went to his mother. He kissed her on the forehead and gave her a warm, affectionate embrace. 'All is well, is it not Mother?' he said happily.

'We should thank God that this terrible ordeal is over,' Lady Rufford said, crossing herself reverently. 'But I think only when we are all returned safely to Mythe Hall will my mind rest easily again.'

'But first, we celebrate!' exclaimed Lord Molynieux and he gestured to the steward to begin the proceedings.

Thomas went to Lord Molynieux and seized him firmly with both hands. For a few seconds, they faced one another silently. Thomas seemed to grow taller and his chest swelled. 'You are a good man and we are forever in your debt,' he said hoarsely. 'In our hearts, we will never forget what you have done for us.'

## CHAPTER 8

†

The celebration feast was a splendid affair, magnificent in every way. Oysters, carp, assorted baked meats, mortreux – a sort of stew or broth, goose stuffed with parsley, a haunch of venison which had been spit-roasted all day, and wafers, cheese and gingerbread. The diversity and quantity of food and wine on offer astounded the Ruffords, for they had not enjoyed such luxury for many years.

As the early evening light gradually faded and the combination of first-rate food and strong wine conjured up their magic, the assembled company grew more relaxed and content. Thomas looked around the room; he saw the same happiness that he felt on the faces of everyone there. For once they were able to disregard plots and conspiracies and the threat posed by Walsingham and his agents; to ignore the consequences of a failed Armada and the bitter struggle by the state to retain supremacy over the soul of Rome; to forget the conflict between Protestant and Catholic. The Ruffords could be forgiven for imagining that their lives would resume a semblance of normality again. 'We have prevailed and the crisis is over!' slurred a bleary-eyed yet euphoric Thomas.

He was unaware that on that very same October night, two young Englishmen had been put ashore on a shingle beach a mile north of Dunwich in Suffolk. Landing in secret, the two men were on a divine mission: to succeed where the Armada had failed and to return England to the Catholic Church. Both were Jesuit priests – and one of them was Thomas's younger brother, John.

# CHAPTER 9

STILL PHYSICALLY WEAK from his imprisonment, William Rufford was in no fit state to make the demanding journey to Mythe Hall so the family decided to remain at Broad Oaks until he was sufficiently recovered.

There was little sign of improvement over the following weeks but, as the prayers and fasting of advent began, William announced that it was high time he and his family departed. In spite of Lady Molynieux's remonstrations, his mind was made up.

At dawn on the second Sunday of Advent, half a dozen servants rushed to and fro preparing for the journey. Lady Rufford made vain attempts to supervise but was constantly distracted. 'Do you think your father is strong enough to make such a long journey?' she asked Jane. 'Lady Molynieux is right, perhaps we should stay a while longer. We have been away from Mythe Hall so long, I dread what state we shall find it in.'

Her daughter, keen to reassure her, responded, 'Father is fine. Nothing will keep him away from Mythe Hall a day longer. I think we have enjoyed Lady Molynieux's generous hospitality for long enough. And you mustn't worry, Philip will have watched over the house in our absence.'

Saying he felt hot and queasy Thomas escaped into the courtyard. Outside, it was cold and still. The early-morning light gave the courtyard a peaceful, tranquil appearance. Thomas breathed in heavily and pulled the collar of his cloak around his ears. As he looked up at the gloomy sky, he heard footsteps on the gravel approaching from behind.

'May I join you?' Lord Molynieux's voice rang out. 'It's absolute bedlam in there!'

Thomas glanced round at him but did not answer.

Standing next to him, Lord Molynieux fixed his gaze on Thomas's face. 'What is it, Thomas? You look unhappy. Are you not eager to return home?' he asked.

Thomas's features hardened. 'To return to the same life as before, to endure the same hardships as before, the same pretence.' There was desperation in his voice.

'You asked for my advice before so now I will give it,' said Lord Molynieux. 'But it is up to you whether you accept it or not. We each have a choice to make and we must have conviction in our decision. If you wish, you can live in the religion which the Queen and the whole kingdom profess. You will have a good life; you will have none of the vexations which Catholics have to suffer.'

'I am a simple soul,' said Thomas, regarding his shabby cloak and faded leather jerkin. 'Surely a man's first duty is to himself.'

Lord Molynieux smiled. 'It is natural that every man wishes to gain knowledge and make progress amongst his fellows, to be highly thought of. But what good is that knowledge, that progress, if we lose our soul? Look into your heart and there you will find the truth. You alone can keep your conscience, for there is no-one in this land that will keep it for you.'

Thomas looked away. 'You are a fine, noble man and I have nothing but admiration for you. I hope that one day I will be able to see things as clearly as you.'

Lord Molynieux sighed and touched him on the shoulder, then turned and went back into the house.

Thomas glanced up at the heavy sky and shook his head; the weather was closing in from the north east and the first snow of winter would fall before the day was out. Of that much he was certain.

His gaze returned to the near distance and, as he looked, he glimpsed a stranger, mounted on a pony, advancing slowly along the main approach to Broad Oaks. The rider's hat was pulled low and a fur collar was wrapped around his lower face. The steward appeared, brushed past Thomas and hurried forwards.

When he reached the gatehouse, the stranger dismounted, handed the reins to the steward and turned around, removing his hat as he did so.

A look of astonishment came over Thomas's face. 'John ... is that you? God be praised! It is you!' he said joyfully, recognising his brother.

'It is good to see you again, Thomas,' John replied simply.

Clumsy and awkward, for a moment the two brothers could only grin sheepishly at one another. Gradually, as they overcame the initial shock, they started to laugh and finally, they embraced warmly.

'But why did you not come sooner?' Thomas frowned. 'Did you not receive any of our letters?'

'It is not so easy,' John began, shaking his head,

his countenance a little more weather beaten than Thomas remembered. 'My presence then might have condemned Father. It puts you all in danger now. We are hunted men.'

'But you are here...'

'Yes.' John smiled. 'Father is released and the time now is right. There is much work to do.'

'Well, I'm glad you've come at last!' Thomas said. 'But look at you!' He looked his brother up and down. 'You're a man of nobility now!'

John was stylishly dressed in a satin doublet with a buff leather jerkin, canions and pansid slops, velvet hose and leather boots. A black velvet cloak with an ornate gold and red trim was fashionably draped over one shoulder.

'Come, everyone will be delighted to see you!' said Thomas, taking his brother's arm.

'Tell me, is Father in good health?'

'Yes, yes. Though still a little weak. When he was released...'

'Was he released because he gave up his faith?' John interrupted, drawing away his arm and looking sternly at his brother.

Thomas halted. 'What? No, and he never will!' replied Thomas indignantly. 'But on our return to Lancashire he is bound to report to the sheriff at the end of every three months.'

They walked on a few paces.

'I fear that Anthony Babington forfeited more than his freedom,' Thomas added mournfully. He glanced anxiously across at John to catch his reaction for he was unsure if his brother knew of Babington's fate.

John remained pensive and silent.

'London has witnessed many executions these last three months,' continued Thomas. 'Mostly priests but also Catholic laymen; even a woman, I hear.'

At the porch, Thomas bounded up the stone steps and entered the house through the great oak door. 'Anyway, it is you we must hear about,' he said eagerly. 'You must tell us every detail of your adventures!'

In the Great Hall, Lady Molynieux was speaking with Jane while Lady Katherine, weariness etched on her face, had sat down on the settle and was being attended to by one of the servants. Sir William, his eyes closed and apparently resting, was sitting beside her. As the two brothers entered, everyone looked up. Almost immediately tired expressions were transformed into joyful amazement.

'Is it possible? Yes, yes, it is! God be praised!' William cried and he rushed forward and threw his arms around John's neck. Moments later, Jane was smothering John with hugs and kisses before she gave way to Lady Katherine, who fell sobbing into his arms. On all sides eyes glistened with tears of joy and faces beamed with rapturous excitement.

† 

As a consequence of John's arrival, the Ruffords return north was postponed. That evening, as a blanket of snow covered the ground, they all settled around the huge stone fireplace in the Great Hall to learn about John's time abroad.

'Tell us, is Rome as magnificent as we are led to

believe?' Jane asked eagerly.

John smiled and gave an exaggerated sigh. 'Give me time to collect my wits,' he said. 'Why, I haven't had time to settle down yet!'

He seemed to take an inordinate time collecting himself, infuriating the women with his teasing but eventually, after much cajoling, he gave a brief account of his life at the English College in Rome: his studies of theology and controversy, his ordination and his eventual admission to the Society of Jesuits.

'Are all priests emerging from Rome dressed in such an extravagant manner?' interrupted Lady Molynieux's younger sister with a hint of sarcasm.

John glanced at Mary and then at the rest of his gathered audience. 'Please understand the hazards and perils we face,' he said gravely. 'We are hunted men, regarded as traitors by this heretical queen and her government. We must take whatever precautions are necessary if we are not to be apprehended. We travel under assumed names and we disguise ourselves in this way so as not to attract unwelcome attention.'

'But how did you come by these clothes?' asked Lady Katherine.

'My superior, Father Garnet, provided them for he was anxious that I should be able to move about freely and with authority.'

'Forgive my outburst, my impertinence is well rebuked,' Mary said contritely.

'Understand this, also,' continued John, fixing his gaze on Lord and Lady Molynieux. 'By harbouring me, even for a single night, you place yourself and your family at considerable risk. Now that the Armada is defeated, our Majesty and her cohorts will turn their hatred from the Spaniards to their own subjects. All their fury will be directed on English Catholics.'

'My wife and I are glad to welcome you to our house,' said Lord Molynieux.

'It's true, Father John,' agreed Lady Molynieux, reaching out and taking her husband's hand. 'And it is quite safe. Perhaps, if you have the time, you will say Mass while you are here?'

There was a slight pause as the steward, who had remained in attendance the whole time near the door, waved to a servant who rushed into the room, placed another jug of wine on a small side table and then left quickly.

John shot an anxious glance at Lady Molynieux. 'You have no need to concern yourself, Father,' she assured. 'They are all to be trusted.'

John smiled at Lady Molynieux and promptly agreed to her request.

Thomas rose from his seat, quickly replenished the wine cups and urged his brother to continue his tale. John was happy to oblige. He described his journey from Rome: how he and his companion travelled through Switzerland, Lorraine and Reims, through Paris and finally reached Eu on the French coast, from where they set sail for England.

'We sailed across the channel and up the English coast. After three days we saw a good place to put ashore. The ship cast anchor off the point until nightfall and on the first watch of the night, we were taken ashore in the ship's boat.

'We wanted to put as much distance between us and

the coast before dawn but in the dark and pouring rain it was impossible to find the right path that would lead us to the open fields. First, we almost stumbled into an old leper hospital and then, shortly after, we passed close to the ruins of an old church where we could hear voices and dogs barking. We quickly retraced our steps and took what little shelter we could find in a nearby wood and we rested there till morning, entrusting our keeping to God.'

'It is by God's grace you didn't catch your death!' exclaimed Lady Katherine.

'It is true; God's mercy and goodness is infinite,' said John. 'Anyway, we decided it would be safer if we parted company and travelled separately to London. So at first light we drew lots as to who should leave the wood first – it fell on my companion.'

Thomas was about to ask the name of his brother's companion but thought better of it and remained silent.

'As soon as he was out of sight, I left the wood by a different path, taking great care to avoid villages and public roads where I knew watchers would be on the lookout for strangers. By the end of the day I was soaked with rain, tired and hungry, so I was obliged to take refuge in an inn on the outskirts of Yoxford.'

'Did the people there not suspect anything?' Thomas asked.

'No. Indeed, they were quite sympathetic when they saw my weary condition. They gave me food and drink without question. We sat down by the fire to warm ourselves and God's providence came to my assistance again. It happened that one of them was a local Catholic and later, when he was alone I confided in him that I too was a Catholic and on my way to London. He offered to help and invited me back to his house where he lived with his family and brother. I stayed a few days, purchased a pony from his stables and left for London. I arrived there safely and met up with my superior.'

'Father Garnet?' said Jane.

'Yes,' said John. 'While in London, we discussed what I should do and he gave me splendid advice; I tell you, he is a good and wise man. He is kind and compassionate also, with a great love for music. He is most skilled with the lute and has a delightful voice. He is an inspiration to us all.'

As he listened to his brother's narrative, Thomas was captivated. The tone of authority, the sincerity in his voice, the assuredness of purpose which radiated from John's whole being impressed Thomas. It contrasted strongly with his own unhappiness and lack of purpose.

'Father Garnet agreed that my first call should be here, to Broad Oaks, to see my family and friends,' John continued after taking a sip of wine. 'Later I plan to visit the home of the Catholic gentleman I mentioned earlier.'

'We are overwhelmed,' said William, rubbing his eyes 'and rejoice that our dear son is returned.'

'May we expect you at Mythe Hall anytime soon?' Lady Katherine asked her son.

'There are many people who are depending on me...' John began hesitantly.

'Oh, please!' begged Jane, tugging at his sleeve.

John relented. 'Be assured, I will return to Mythe Hall before the last snow of winter has melted.'

'Is that a promise?' Jane asked, grinning widely.

'And you and I will go hawking on the moors again, just as we used to!' cried Thomas excitedly. 'What do you say to that brother?'

John turned and looked at him intently. 'Thomas ... what would you say if I asked you to accompany me on my mission?'

Instantly, everyone in the room fell silent and all eyes fell on Thomas.

'Believe me, Thomas, it is God's work we do and nothing is more important.'

Thomas stared at his brother but remained silent, unable to say anything.

'Besides, it would be most agreeable to have you as a companion on my travels,' John added with a smile. He grasped his brother's hand and looked him straight in the face. 'But be aware that we are as lambs among wolves and there will be many tests along the way. It will be your greatest challenge ... if you have the courage to accept it.'

Thomas's heart skipped a beat; it was not so much a request as an ultimatum.

# CHAPTER 10

Lady Rufford clasped her hands to her chest and turned angrily to her husband. 'I cannot comprehend what motivates both my sons to follow a path that at any time could lead them to a horrible and violent end.'

Sir William remained silent, lowering his gaze, evidently considering.

'Dear, sweet Mother,' John began affectionately, 'it is the only path that will lead us to our salvation. We must keep the faith and not be afraid of the battle.'

'John is right, Mother,' said Jane, taking her hand. 'I think it is a journey Thomas should make and it would be a poor excuse that forces him to stay. And besides, I don't think I could cope with him sulking around at Mythe Hall if he did not!'

But Lady Rufford was not convinced. 'And how are we to manage Mythe Hall in the meantime?' she demanded. 'What about duty?'

'Above all else, our duty is to God,' said John softly.

Lady Rufford gazed intently at her husband with a look that seemed to say 'why don't you say something, why don't you speak?' but he simply stared back at her, keeping whatever thoughts he had to himself.

'Don't worry. We'll get by,' Jane said, caressing her

mother's hand, although in truth she had no idea how they would cope with the demands of their old house.

'You are most welcome to take Master Richard,' interrupted Lady Molynieux, observing Lady Rufford's distress and glad of an excuse to offer some help. 'He is a reliable and trusted servant and will be more than capable of attending to your affairs at Mythe Hall.'

Sir William looked up, his wan face and sunken eyes revealing the torment of his experience in the Tower and the agitation he now felt over his weak and frail body. 'It is true, we will need help to get back on our feet when we return home.' His voice was barely audible. 'And it is a most kind and generous offer. But we cannot afford another wage at this stage ... not unless we renounce the faith!'

'Then we will continue to pay his wages and be content to do so,' said Lord Molynieux cheerfully.

'But we are already indebted to you. No, that is too much!'

'Nonsense! Nonsense! Good, that's settled,' said Lord Molyneiux. 'We'll hear no more about it.'

Sir William was silent, a sad smile on his face as he gazed at his devoted friend. He glanced at Lady Rufford who was expressing her gratitude to Lady Molynieux but he still saw a look of anxious foreboding in his wife's pale face.

John turned expectantly towards his brother. 'Thomas, do not put off the care of your soul till later. Life is a journey. Along the way we may find love and hatred, joy and sadness, hope and despair, but we must not allow ourselves to be distracted. We must not give up our search for God.'

## CHAPTER 10

Thomas stirred restlessly in his chair but remained silent, biting his lip. He drank some wine and, with an unsteady hand, refilled his cup again. What should he answer? He was inspired by his brother and moved by his wise words. The idea of travelling with John appealed to him greatly. On the one hand, John would show him the way to discover that sense of purpose which he so desperately sought; on the other hand, he saw that such a journey would present a great opportunity to avenge not only his family but also Anthony Babington and all the other Catholics who had suffered so much under Elizabeth's reign.

But he was also aware of the enormous risks involved in being caught aiding and abetting a Jesuit priest. He imagined rotting away in some squalid, fetid cell in the Tower or awaiting a hideous execution on the scaffold. He feared his own weakness.

And then there was his mother and father and sister. He loved them dearly; would they be able to manage Mythe Hall without him? There was the ever-reliable Philip of course, and now the additional help of one of Lord Molynieux's servants, surely that would be enough? After all, Thomas thought to himself, he would only be away for a few months.

He glanced around the room as if trying to seek counsel. All eyes were upon him. Jane smiled with encouragement. Swallowing hard and trembling with excitement, he rose shakily from his chair and went up to his father.

'With your permission, Father,' he said with slow deliberation, 'I would like to accompany John on his travels.'

Lady Rufford blanched. She knew what her husband's decision would be.

Sir William squeezed her hand gently and, raising it to his lips, kissed it tenderly. He got to his feet and faced Thomas, placing a hand on his shoulder and gazing at him with keen eyes. He cleared his throat. 'Of course you must go ... and with our blessing.' Grasping his son's hands with his long thin fingers, he added resolutely: 'Discover what God wants you to be, Thomas, and there is nothing you will not achieve. If you believe, everything is possible.'

After releasing himself from his son's embrace, Sir William announced it was high time he retired to bed. 'Now go, kiss your mother and tell her you love her,' he shouted back as he left the room.

Thomas stooped down to where his mother was sitting and kissed her gently on her brow. Jane hugged him, displaying the kind of deep affection that only exists between a devoted sister and her beloved brother.

Lord Molynieux stepped forward and ordered the steward bring more wine to mark the occasion. As the room filled once again with conversation and laughter, only Lady Rufford remained quiet, occasionally stealing sorrowful glances at both her sons.

† 

The following morning, the entire household arose shortly before six o'clock and was preparing for the brothers' departure. It was still dark outside and wintery squalls were blowing from the east but it had been agreed that, in the interest of everyone's safety,

Thomas and John should leave Broad Oaks without any further delay.

Lord Molynieux had insisted they take two of his finest mares and, as Thomas and John ate some bread and drank the last of their breakfast beer, two fine animals were being saddled up in the stables.

'I must confess,' said Thomas, 'it feels as if I'm about to embark on a journey into the unknown. I don't know what to expect.'

'Have no fear, brother. God is with us,' John said, smiling at the pensive expression on Thomas's face.

Outside the cold was intense and shards of ice slashed at their exposed faces. Thomas stamped his feet, readjusted the fur collar on his cloak and pulled his hat low but it did not help.

The main door to the house, caught by a sudden strong gust of wind, suddenly flung wide open and a shaft of light streamed out into the courtyard. The entire Molynieux household had crowded into the porch, waiting to say their farewells. Two servants rushed out carrying lanterns, closely followed by the hunched figures of Sir William Rufford, Lady Katherine and Jane.

Jane smiled tenderly at Thomas. 'I know it may be risky but will you wear this ... for me,' she said, taking something from her pocket.

Thomas looked down at the Agnus Dei she clasped in her freezing fingers.

'It is such a beautiful and sacred thing,' she continued. 'And it will serve to remind you of Him at all times.' She crossed herself, kissed the wax oval disc and handed it to Thomas. 'He will protect you.'

Thomas took the Agnus Dei, hung the chain around his neck and tucked the disc inside his doublet. 'Thank you,' he said. 'It will remind me also of those I cherish … and of their sufferings too.'

'Thomas, you must be careful!' Jane said. 'Take heed of our brother's advice and promise me you will not do anything foolish.'

'There is no need to worry about me…'

'Promise me!'

'Alright, I promise, I promise!' Thomas capitulated and kissed Jane on both cheeks. Both were silent for a moment.

'What about you?' Thomas asked.

'I am content to return to Mythe Hall; Mother and Father need me and there will be much that requires my attention. I will not have time to think.'

Thomas smiled at his sister's fortitude.

'And I shall read,' she added. 'I have not lost my love for the classics, for Ovid. And write. Yes, and I will correspond with Lady Molyneux's two daughters for I have discovered we share much in common.'

Thomas embraced his sister one last time before crossing to his father and mother. 'It won't be for long,' he said, trying to reassure them. 'Three months, I guess, four at the most! Then I will return to my duties at home.' His eyes shone brightly. He was not looking at them as he spoke but over their heads at a young stable boy who was bringing the two horses into the yard.

'Come Thomas, let us be off. We have a long journey before us,' urged John, taking the reins of the chestnut mare.

Thomas glanced round one last time. In the flickering

light from the lantern, he could see his mother was smiling and her lips moving in a silent blessing. His hand came up in a half-wave. 'God bless you and watch over you,' he whispered.

Moments later, he and John were beyond the fringe of oak trees that bordered the estate, two dark specks riding along the narrow lane that snaked in an easterly direction away from Broad Oaks.

# CHAPTER 11

THE HORSES WERE two of Lord Molynieux's strongest and healthiest animals and the brothers made steady progress. They did not stop to rest and Thomas, experiencing a sense of freedom he had hitherto not known, did not mind the harsh wintry conditions such was his contentment.

Before long, they were passing through the snow-sprinkled meadows and pastures surrounding the village of Long Melford. The easterly wind had dropped and in the gloom of a winter's morning everything assumed a hushed, almost eerie serenity. But as they crossed the narrow wooden bridge on the fringes of the village, the frozen stillness was abruptly shattered. They had failed to see the danger lurking in the nearby hedgerows and were caught completely off guard.

There were six watchmen in all, wearing varied liveries. One was dressed in a burgundy doublet, another in a black tunic and yet another in an old leather jerkin. All were armed with swords and rapiers.

Thomas and John were ordered to dismount. 'You are strangers to these parts?' enquired a large stout man, stepping forward, his heavy fur-lined cloak dragging along the frozen ground. His voice was suspicious and his eyes narrowed as he studied the two men facing him. 'Who are you and where have you come from?' he demanded.

Thomas was silent, incapable of uttering a word. Although he had supposed their might be trouble, he had not expected it so soon on their travels. As a consequence, he had not given any thought about a cover story. A sudden chill ran down his back.

'My name is Robert Staunton,' replied John calmly. 'I am in the service of Lord Draiton of Hanse Manor in the county of Norfolk; perhaps you have heard of him?'

There was a baffled expression on the stout man's face and a collective shaking of heads from the other watchers. Thomas glanced at his brother quizzically.

John had overheard this particular lord being discussed by some of the locals the night he had stopped at the inn in Yoxford. They had remarked that servants were coming and going all the time and John had decided that it would be good cover for him to assume the role of Lord Draiton's new steward. He reckoned that it would take a long time before the story could be disproved.

'And this is my cousin Richard Tanfield,' John continued, gesturing at his brother, 'whom I have been visiting in Bury St Edmunds.'

The stout man looked coldly at Thomas. 'Is that so? Then what business brings you here?'

'Well, before I return to Norfolk,' John persevered, 'my cousin wished to show me his new falcon. Unfortunately the bird has strayed and so we have extended our search into this area.'

The man's gaze remained fixed on Thomas. 'What's

the matter? Lost your tongue?' he said, and his lips curled into a sneer. His companions, who had until then appeared bored and disinterested, suddenly sprang to life and joined in with their captain's amusement.

'His tongue isn't the only thing he's lost!' they mocked.

'Who's lost his precious bird, then?' laughed another and, 'Be careful lad, or you won't be able to find your way back home!' taunted a third.

Thomas viewed them with contempt. Their gawping expressions and twisted smiles made them look stupid.

'Well?' the stout man barked. His renewed display of authority immediately silenced the heckling. 'Can't you speak at all?'

'My cousin speaks the truth, sir!' answered Thomas indignantly. 'As for my silence,' he continued, finding it impossible to restrain his anger any longer, 'I am not in the habit of replying to such meddling questions or responding to such bullying tactics! Do your orders permit such harassment of any fellow Englishman who happens to pass this way?'

'What!' screamed the man, his face flushing a blotchy, ugly red. 'You impudent little upstart! My orders come from Sir Francis Walsingham himself and give me the power to stop and apprehend anyone I choose. His intelligence reports that two Jesuit priests recently landed somewhere along the coast. It is my duty to hunt them down before they can spread their evil lies, and hand them over like the traitors they are!'

Thomas inhaled sharply. How could Walsingham possibly have found out so soon? He must have spies and informants in every village and town in the country.

## CHAPTER II

'Gentlemen ... gentlemen, calm yourselves,' pleaded John. 'My cousin means no offence. He is overly concerned with finding his falcon, that is all; it means the world to him. If you can tell us whether you have seen the bird or heard its bell or not, then by your leave we shall be on our way and you need trouble yourselves with us no longer.'

'No! We have neither seen nor heard your falcon, if it even exists!' the stout man exclaimed. 'I am not satisfied you are who you claim to be; nor am I persuaded by your story,' he continued firmly. 'You will accompany me to the village where the constable and the officer of the watch will determine what is to be done.'

Thomas was about to protest when John intervened once more. 'We shall do as you command, sir, but I assure you it will be a waste of the officer's time. We shall only be able to recount the same story as we have just told you.'

'Then we shall see what he makes of your fanciful tale!' the man scoffed. He barked an order, sending the obedient watchers into a frenzy of activity, shoving and jostling one another.

John cast an anxious glance at his brother, his eyes telling Thomas that any further resistance was useless and escape out of the question. He must submit.

Thomas felt some flakes of snow melt on his skin and trickle down the back of his neck as he struggled against his natural instinct to fight. He kept his sword hand free while he ran the fingers of his other hand inside the collar of his ruff. His mind raced. What might happen to them in Long Melford; would John's story stand up to further scrutiny? Would Thomas himself give the game away by some unwitting comment? He had set out not only to help his brother minister to beleaguered Catholic souls, but to use the mission as a way to strike back for all the persecutions his family had suffered. Now, as he stared at the stout man, he hated him for bringing all his hopes and plans to a shuddering halt.

Although Thomas was disappointed that his brother had not argued more vehemently and had given in far too readily, he was impressed at how unflustered and quick witted his brother had remained. In a way, John reminded him of their father when he was arrested at Mythe Hall. He flashed a reassuring smile at John and allowed himself to be led away.

They entered at the southern end of the village and proceeded up the long, wide high street. The village appeared empty and peaceful; most villagers were at church as it was Sunday morning. Thomas looked at the fine symmetry of the large timber buildings which flanked both sides of the street and pondered on the prosperity in these parts. They passed the Bull Inn, quiet and still, and the village stocks; then by way of a wooden bridge they crossed over a shallow brook. On their right, with its tall brick chimney stacks and fanciful octagonal turrets, was Melford Hall. Elizabeth and her court had been lavishly entertained here several years earlier. They continued up the gently sloping hill towards some almshouses on the edge of the green and, immediately behind these, they came to an imposing church. Here they halted in the graveyard.

'The constable and the officer of the watch are inside,' said the leader of the group, addressing John abruptly. 'Wait here!' He hurried through the porch and disappeared into the church.

John glanced admiringly at the cathedral-like proportions of the church. 'It is indeed a grand place to worship and glorify God,' he remarked.

'Aye, that it is, sir,' smiled an older watcher. 'Some folk say that you won't find a church anywhere in the county more superior than the Holy Trinity of Melford.'

'You must have a high regard for the people who built it ... and their faith,' John said.

The old watcher frowned. 'You misunderstand me, sir!' he said with obvious irritation. 'I am a poor man but an honest one, and I do not agree with the extravagances of past years. Those wealthy wool merchants indulged a corrupt church in the hope of buying their salvation. That was a false religion and I do not lament its passing. But all that is now changed, thank God and Queen Elizabeth, and that is why we must defend our English faith and our way of life.'

'You only have to ask the Spaniards about that!' another watcher said, sending the rest of his group into convulsions of laughter.

Thomas gritted his teeth behind a faked smile.

'And why we must take up arms against those papists who wish to return us to the old faith,' said the old watcher.

'Especially those scheming and lying Jesuit traitors!'

Thomas stared at the watcher who had uttered this last remark with loathing he could barely conceal but John appeared not in the least disconcerted.

'And how do you recognise these Jesuits?' he asked.

'They all have that same look about them – shifty and dishonest,' the man replied.

At that moment, the huge carved oak door to the church swung open and the officer of the watch appeared on the threshold. He paused and, without speaking a word, received the silence and respect from his subordinates that his rank warranted. He walked slowly around the two brothers, carefully observing every detail of their appearance. He stopped directly in front of Thomas and leaned forward so that his face was only inches away from Thomas's. His penetrating stare burned and Thomas was forced to avert his own eyes for fear they might betray their secrets.

'I am informed by my watchman that you are from Bury St Edmunds,' he said in a quiet, patronising tone.

Thomas shot an angry glance towards the stout watcher who had emerged from the church. Then he looked back at the officer and nodded in mute response.

'I am well acquainted with Bury. I lodged at The Angel back in '78 – during the Queen's progress. That was a summer to remember, eh?' The officer beamed and for a moment his eyes glazed as he recalled those heady days when Elizabeth had rested there for several days following the entertainments at Melford Hall.

Thomas relaxed a little.

'Perhaps you know the Landlord at The Angel?' the officer asked suddenly.

Thomas was caught off guard. 'The Angel?' he stuttered, struggling to control the rising panic. Although he had a vague recollection of Lord Molynieux and his father once discussing the plundering of its once great abbey, he was wholly ignorant of any other details about Bury St Edmunds. His heart pounded in his ears so loudly that he believed the sound must be audible to everyone around him.

'The Angel!' the officer repeated. 'You must know The Angel ... opposite the abbey ... it's the most popular tavern in town! No? Prithee, tell me where you do take your ale then?'

'Where we partake our ale is of no significance,' interrupted John, knowing he must create a diversion before their story fell apart. 'We have already given you our names and told you our reason for being here. You can see that we are not rogues or vagabonds. Surely, you must be satisfied and will send us on our way?'

'Yes! I am most anxious to resume our search without any further delay,' added Thomas quickly. 'Any longer and I fear my hawk may be lost to me for ever.'

'Ah, yes!' smiled the officer, pensively stroking his beard. 'I am intrigued by this hawk which is noticeable only by its absence. Tell me more.'

'The hawk is a gift from my cousin here,' began Thomas.

'You must be a favoured cousin to be presented with such a gift.'

'I have flown hawks since I was a child,' Thomas continued with genuine enthusiasm, 'and my cousin knows how much pleasure I derive from hunting.'

'It is a favourite pastime of both royals and nobles alike. I, too, used to have a hawk,' the officer said.

For the first time, Thomas thought he discerned a hint of understanding in the officer's tone and he pressed on, eager to exploit this shift in attitude.

'Today is the first opportunity we have had to see how well developed the bird is; how he handles and reacts to the game ... and as you may gather, he was too easily distracted. He is still young and inexperienced but with more training, more time, he will fulfil his potential and then he will be sure to reward his master with great pleasure.'

Recalling the first hawk he had possessed as a young child at Mythe Hall, Thomas went on to describe in detail this 'lost' hawk. 'He is a most handsome and elegant bird, sir, as I'm sure you would agree if only you could see him. He is grey on the back with white under parts, closely barred with brown. He has short rounded wings which are ideal for woodland hunting and can twist and turn through the trunks and branches at high speed. We had been out a goodly time and were about to return, when the hawk spotted a small bird and pursued it into some dense hedges. When he didn't return, we went in search of him. At first, we feared he may be lying injured but when we couldn't find him we presumed he had flown off. We gradually increased the area of our search but with no success and then your watchman there,' and he directed an accusing finger at the stout man standing by the church door, 'stopped us in our tracks.'

'He has his duty to perform,' replied the officer. 'He must apprehend anyone he thinks is acting suspiciously. You were found wandering along the lane and, although I grant that you appear most knowledgeable on the subject of hawking and have described what is undoubtedly a fine hawk, there is no tangible proof of your story ... or indeed, who you are.' Turning to face John, he added with creeping impatience: 'I have responsibilities too and without any such proof, I have no alternative but to bring you before the Justice of the

Peace.'

Thomas felt his hopes plummet. He must not panic. He glanced at John and then looked up at the side of the church as if searching for some form of inspiration. His eyes were drawn to the inscription carved into the stone under the eaves; although he couldn't make out all the words, he had no difficulty reading the first part: 'Pray for ye sowle of John Clopton.' The name meant nothing to Thomas but the prayer was very apt.

'If you consider it really necessary, then we are ready to go,' John said. 'But I am anxious to return to my master for I have been away long enough. As for my cousin, you can see how distraught he is. He will not rest until his hawk is recovered.'

The officer brushed away John's appeal and turned to go back into church, wrapping his cloak around him to keep out the wintry weather. The cold was intense and snow was beginning to fall more steadily: a freezing wet snow which numbed the senses and sapped the strength.

'In God's name, I beg you to let us pass,' John pleaded.

The officer halted at the porch, swung round and slowly began to retrace his steps. He stopped in front of John and gazed searchingly at him. For several seconds they looked at one another – and in that look Thomas and John were spared. In those few moments, the officer saw before him not two anonymous suspects but two fellow human beings shivering helplessly in the bitter cold. Minutes earlier he could easily have ordered the watchers to take them away, sealing their fate with a wave of his hand, without burdening his conscience; now, in his heart, he was dimly aware of something else. He recognised that these two men were like him and the watchers surrounding them, and the congregation inside the church, and the Queen and all her subjects: they were all part of God's infinite creation. His expression changed and he gave a long, deep sigh.

'You have the look of an honest fellow,' he said at last. 'Go in peace … in God's name. I won't detain you any longer.' Looking over John's shoulder at Thomas, he added: 'I would advise that in future, you have a greater care over those things you cherish most.'

John bowed his head in gratitude and thanked him politely. Taking the reins to his horse from a rather bemused watchman and summoning his brother, he left the scene, keen to be on his way before the officer changed his mind.

Thomas followed close behind, still trying to grasp what had transpired. He was amazed at their good fortune when only a few moments earlier all had seemed lost. He felt tremendous relief and had to use all his resolve to stop himself from shouting in triumph. Riding swiftly away from the church, neither brother turned to look back at the aggrieved face of the stout watchman staring after them.

They left Long Melford and galloped northwards along the Bury road. They had gone some distance before John eventually decided it was safe enough to stop and rest. He dismounted, sat on a log at the side of the road, carefully observed their surroundings and then whispered a silent prayer of thanks.

In contrast, Thomas leapt from his horse full of exhilaration. It had been a near escape and he understood only too well how close they had been to arrest.

'I thought that officer was never going to relent!' he announced, uttering the words so hurriedly he had to gulp for air. 'And when he said he was to take us before the Justice of the Peace, I thought we were done for!'

'It was God's providence that we should prevail,' said John.

'Maybe so,' Thomas replied, sounding unimpressed. 'I have to admire your composure. I don't know how you managed to remain so calm.'

'With God's help anything is possible ... that and a plausible story!' John added with a smile. 'It was your accurate and detailed account of the hawk that gave credence to our story and finally convinced him, of that I'm certain.'

'What about you!' Thomas laughed. 'How did you dream up our names?'

'Robert Staunton is an amalgam of the names of two fellow Jesuits I met in Rome.'

Thomas smiled and shook his head. 'And my nom de plume?'

'The same. But now we have used them,' continued John, looking solemnly at his brother, 'we must assume different ones.'

# CHAPTER 12

Two days later, and without further incident, the brothers arrived at the small hamlet of Brettenham, four or five miles to the north east of Thetford. They quickly sought out the family home of Edward Hopton, the gentleman with whom John had first stayed after landing back in Suffolk several months before.

Hopton Manor was situated in the midst of a large park, well stocked with deer. There were many fish ponds, and a great store of wood and timber. The whole estate extended to some two thousand acres.

Edward Hopton was a handsome youth of medium height with clear-cut features, not much older than Thomas. He was a widower and had inherited the property after his father's death. As was the fashion, he kept open house not just with his own family, but also his younger brother, a sister who had also been widowed and who acted as his housekeeper, and a brother-in-law. He kept all manner of sport hounds that ran buck, fox, hare, otter and badger, and long- and short-winged hawks. In many ways, he was the epitome of what Thomas had always dreamed of being: a country gentleman.

Edward was delighted to see John again and greeted

him with much enthusiasm. 'You must tell me how you are and about the latest news from London.'

'Firstly, may I introduce my cousin, Richard Tanfield,' John interrupted.

'Of course, where are my manners?' said Edward flushing red. 'You must forgive me, Master Tanfield; you are most welcome. You will both stay for Christmas, I hope?'

'If it is not too much of an inconvenience,' John said, removing his dripping cap and shaking his wet cloak.

'Not at all. In fact, I insist!'

'Then we will gratefully accept your hospitality.'

'Excellent! Come, let me show you inside,' said Edward, rubbing his hands together. His face assumed an expression of contentment, tinged with melancholy. 'In my father's day,' he went on as they hurried along a dimly-lit stone passage, 'this house held many feasts and celebrations. Now it usually stands empty and quiet, but tonight it will echo to the sound of cheerful voices and laughter once again.'

Thomas returned Edward's smile. Exhausted after their long journey, and after constantly being vigilant and alert for fear they might run into further trouble, he could finally relax. Their host seemed an amiable fellow and his grand house offered secure refuge and much-needed respite. Yes, they would be safe while they rested there, Thomas thought ... and yet one thing still puzzled him. Why had he been introduced as John's cousin? Surely there was no need to continue this pretence with friends; there could not be any danger lurking in such a magnificent place as this.

They went through a door at the end of the stone

passage and entered the Great Hall. Thomas stood for a moment, staring at the sight which greeted him. The Hall was a long room, furnished with all manner of tables, chairs, ornately carved court cupboards and oak chests. On a great hearth paved with bricks lay some terriers, hounds and spaniels dozing in the heat of the roaring fire; everywhere marrow bones were strewn across the flag stone floor. The length of one entire wall was hung with fox skins of this and last year's skinning, while two of the great chairs had litters of young cats in them. The large windows served as places for Edward to store his arrows, crossbows, stonebows, while the corners of the room were full of the finest hawking and hunting poles.

In the upper part of the room were two small tables and a desk, on one side of which was 'De Imitatione Christi' and on the other, Foxe's *Book of Martyrs*. On the tables were an assortment of hawks hoods and bells.

They crossed to the far side of the Hall and went through a set of double doors into a wide corridor, at the end of which was another door. Passing through this, they entered another room, far smaller in size and with only one tiny rectangular window. This was Edward's private dining parlour.

'Later, when you are refreshed, we shall have supper in here,' Edward said. Thanking his guests once more for agreeing to stay, he led them up a wide oak staircase and directed them to their rooms.

Thomas entered a large bedroom with oak panelled walls, a fine coffered ceiling and a timber floor covered with rushes liberally sprinkled with lavender and winter savory. In the centre there was an extravagant four-poster bed adorned with embroidered hangings; chairs were placed symmetrically on either side of it and there was an oak table with a stool in front of it along a side wall. A door led to a small private closet.

As he collapsed exhausted onto the bed's soft linen sheets, Thomas reflected on the changes he had observed in his brother since his return to England. He had always known that John had a vocation, a passion for the religious life but now there was something else; something that he had only detected in his brother's manner during the past few days. It was something he had seen before, though – in the eyes of the priest, Ballard, as he awaited his execution.

'What is it that motivates you, John?' he asked later as they were on their way down to supper. 'Oh, it's true enough we are both Catholics and we both believe in the teachings of the Church and the authority of the Pope. And I for one wish to stand up and be counted, to be seen as one belonging to the true faith. But for you I think there is something greater.'

'You must not concern yourself with how other people regard you,' John replied. 'That is nothing but vanity.'

'Easier said than done,' said Thomas slightly offended. 'When I am constantly reminded of what we have lost, what is denied us, I am tempted to hate and to seek revenge against those who profit by our sufferings.'

'Do not despair when you feel such thoughts, but instead submit yourself completely to the will of God, to the exclusion of everything else. His divine force is so powerful that it governs a man's whole being.'

Thomas laughed awkwardly. 'I'm afraid I could never manage to abide by such principles.'

†

That evening the two brothers dined with their host. After the initial excitement of their arrival had subsided, Thomas and John noticed a change in Edward's mood. The convivial smile disappeared, there was a preoccupied look in his eyes and his conversation became more awkward and stilted until finally he was silent. In an attempt to revive his host, Thomas recalled his delight at what he had observed in the Great Hall and remarked that he was keen on hunting and hawking, but it was to no avail; Edward simply shook his head and then buried his face in his hands.

'What is it that troubles you, Master Hopton?' asked John.

'I fear my sister is lost, Master Staunton, my brother too!' Edward said.

Thomas was puzzled. 'I don't understand. What do you mean, lost? Where are they?'

Edward's smile was ironic. 'What? No, they are staying in London with friends. Who knows when they'll return? What I mean is it is all the fault of my no good brother-in-law,' he continued, becoming agitated. 'He has corrupted them, turned them to heresy. Lucy is now a fanatical Calvinist. Just the other day, she proudly showed me the book he had given her as a gift, *The Institutes of the Christian Religion*. I couldn't even bear to hold it in my hands! She has changed so much since you were here last you would hardly recognise her. I simply don't understand her. What my late father would have made of it all, I don't know. He was such a staunch Catholic.' His eyes, which moments earlier had revealed only warmth and kindness, now flashed with irritation.

Thomas sighed. Although he did not know the sister, had never met her, he was immediately sympathetic to his host's predicament. He thought of Jane. 'I know how much I love my own sister,' he said, 'and how much it would hurt me, if she was corrupted or harmed in any way.'

'I am a Catholic like yourself, as you well know,' said John with a reassuring smile, 'as is my cousin also. We shall be pleased to offer you assistance in any way we can to persuade your sister and your brother to reject their heretical ways.'

'Yes, of course!' Thomas nodded enthusiastically.

'Thank you ... thank you both! It is providence that has sent you to me. I do not wish to impose my problems on you, but I fear that in our father's once great and noble house we are now a divided, unhappy family, tearing itself apart.'

'You must set your mind at rest, Master Hopton,' said John.

'We are glad to be here; we Catholics must rally together!' cried Thomas, roused by Edward's plight.

John gave his brother an irate glance. 'We must first put our faith in God and pray for His guidance,' he said quietly, in sharp contrast to Thomas's noisy outburst. 'Only when we have gained their trust and friendship will your brother and sister listen to our counsel. Only then will we be able to show them the error of their ways and return them to the true Faith. We must have patience and prudence if we are to succeed.' He directed this last remark at Thomas.

'You speak with such wisdom, my friend,' said Edward laying his hand on John's arm. 'I am in no doubt that as soon as they listen to you they will regret their mistake and return to their senses.'

John smiled. 'I do not deserve such compliments, Master Hopton, for I have yet to accomplish anything,' he said with genuine humility. 'I possess few talents or natural gifts and there are many men who are more learned than I, but it is a praiseworthy thing to make known the works of God. Whatever is done should be for the greater glory of God.'

'You undervalue yourself, Master Staunton. You are a good and honest man,' said Edward. He got up from the table and turned towards the door. 'Tomorrow, when you are recovered, we shall go hawking together,' and he flashed a wide smile in Thomas's direction.

# CHAPTER 13

THE NEXT MORNING was clear and bright. There had been a severe frost and the ground was stony hard. The parkland surrounding Hopton Manor was stained white and the bare, gnarled, misshapen branches on the lumbering oak trees were heavy with hoar-frost.

'It is a good day for hawking, eh?' Edward's voice boomed cheerfully, as he walked back towards the house. He was returning from the mews which were adjacent to the stables and he was proudly displaying a beautiful sparrowhawk which was tethered to his left gauntlet.

Wrapped up in a fur-lined cloak and with his velvet hat pulled low, Thomas made no reply but for several moments, stood there staring, poised as if ready to take to the air himself. The hawk was a female, larger than the male, with brown upper parts and dark barring underneath. The head was covered with a leather hood, and bells and jesses were attached to both its legs. Instantly, Thomas was carried away by that irresistible passion for hawking that makes a man forget everything else.

'She's been well trained and is ready to fly,' Edward said, observing the gleam in Thomas's eyes. Two small spaniels were following close on Edward's heels and, on catching sight of Thomas, they rushed headlong to the entrance porch where he was standing and began rubbing themselves against his legs.

At that same moment John appeared in the doorway behind Thomas. 'Surely you can't resist such an opportunity?' he said, addressing his brother with a mischievous smile. He looked up at the clear blue sky, tranquil without a breath of wind. 'It is indeed a perfect morning.'

'If it meets with your approval, I shall have the ostler saddle three horses,' Edward said as he reached the porch. 'But first my friends, we shall take some fresh manchet and wine together.' He ushered his guests back inside the house.

They did not linger over breakfast and within an hour were mounted on their horses and thudding over the frozen fields. When they had gone about half a mile and were approaching one of the fish ponds, two more horsemen, accompanied by a third horse with a lady riding side-saddle, appeared at the edge of a clearing in the trees and came galloping towards them.

'Good morning, brother!' shouted the young lady as she drew near.

Edward, his face like thunder, grunted incoherently.

Thomas glanced across at the girl. Edward's sister, he thought to himself. She was swathed in a full-length crimson velvet cloak with a capacious fur-lined hood which framed her oval face. Her shining eyes peered out and there was a charming smile upon her parted lips. She appeared so serene and dignified that he found it difficult to comprehend that this lovely creature could be the cause of distress to anyone.

'Well, brother! Are you not going to introduce your friends?' she asked.

Edward shifted uncomfortably in his saddle. 'Master Robert Staunton, you already know…'

'Ah, but of course! It is good to see you again, Master Staunton,' she interrupted, glancing at John and nodding her head.

'… and this is his cousin, Richard Tanfield,' continued Edward. He paused for a moment, exchanging uneasy glances with his sister. 'May I present my sister, Mistress Lucy Hopton,' he added, barely able to conceal his contempt.

Lucy looked straight at Thomas with clever, observant eyes. 'I am pleased to make your acquaintance, Master Tanfield,' she said. The disarming smile never left her pretty face.

'Your brother has told us much about you,' began Thomas, 'but he failed to mention your charm and beauty.' He dropped his eyes and then lifted them again. He was compelled; he felt weak.

'Your words flatter me,' said Lucy, lowering her hood to reveal long tresses of jet black glossy hair and a clear slender neck. But she did not mean it. She did not blush, as most women do when complimented on their beauty, but instead seemed to take it for granted, confident that all men would find her attractive.

'I trust my brother is being a good host, Master Tanfield. I hope you will be able to stay with us for a few days,' she said.

Thomas was so absorbed that he did not hear her.

'Your brother has kindly offered to shelter us over

Christmas,' interceded John. 'I pray that we will not inconvenience you too greatly.'

'To shelter you!' spluttered an astonished, harsh voice belonging to the burly young horseman reining in his horse alongside Lucy. 'A strange choice of words, Master Staunton. You make it sound as if you're on the run from something!'

'Oh, for pity's sake, Jack!' Edward retorted. 'It is a manner of speaking, that is all! Why is it you are always suspicious of any friends that I choose to invite to Hopton?'

Thomas glanced across at the robust young man. He was immediately struck by his likeness to Lucy and quickly deduced that he must be the younger brother. Yet in spite of this resemblance, there was an ugliness and coldness about him. Lucy's eyes flashed brilliantly with the vivacity of youth, full of life; by contrast this man's eyes appeared lacklustre and empty, and his bored expression was totally opposite to his sister's cheerful countenance.

'Because the friends you invite here are always *Catholic*!' Jack yelled. 'And they are likely to bring ruin on us all.' He shook his head contemptuously. 'I don't understand why you insist on clinging to the old faith when there has been more than enough evidence to convince me, and England, that it was a corrupt one. I tell you, the old ways are gone, the old faith is dead. You're living in the past and it is a past that will never return … however much you pray!'

The other horseman, who up until then had remained half hidden behind Jack and Lucy, brought his horse alongside. He was a thin man, about forty-five years old with a sallow complexion and a scornful expression. He doffed his cap and looked at Thomas and John disdainfully. This was Robert Beale, Edward's brother-in-law, and instinct cautioned Thomas to be wary of him.

'I do not wish to appear disrespectful but if I may speak freely,' began John in a conciliatory yet firm tone, 'I have found no sound reason or argument that causes me to doubt that the Catholic faith is the only true one. If it pleases you, we may debate the subject later, perhaps over a game of cards.'

Jack's face reddened but any response was interrupted by his sister. 'Come along, Jack, calm yourself,' she said gently. 'Master Staunton is right. The time for such rhetoric is later.'

Thomas glanced at Jack, whose angry face still seethed. Jack shrugged his shoulders and muttered dismissively under his breath.

'It is fortuitous that we should find you hawking because it is Jack's favourite pastime as well,' Lucy went on, turning to Thomas. 'I think there is much we may all share together. We should not quarrel. May we join with you?'

Edward frowned at his sister. 'Oh, very well, very well. Only don't get in the way.'

'I promise, I promise,' Lucy laughed. She moved her horse closer to Thomas. 'My brother takes this whole business very seriously,' she whispered. 'It is said that his hawks are unsurpassed in the whole county.'

They rode off at a gallop before slowing back to a more measured walk. Edward and John were out front, leading with the two spaniels; behind them came Thomas, with Lucy and Jack on either side, and following closely to the rear, the silent and menacing brother-in-law.

Every now and then, Thomas stole furtive glances at Lucy.

'My sister rides well, does she not?' ribbed Jack, with a hearty laugh. 'She carries herself with such grace and beauty. What do you think?'

Thomas smiled his agreement then lowered his eyes guiltily under Lucy's gaze. 'It is a noble sport, a royal pastime,' she said, as they followed a well-worn track round the edge of the fish pond. 'The Queen herself is very fond of hunting and hawking. Be it in the early hours or the foulest of weather, I am told that she is unrelenting in her pursuit of the prey.'

'She is our beloved and most glorious Majesty!' proclaimed the brother-in-law loudly. He raised himself up in his saddle as he spoke.

Thomas immediately stiffened, staring straight ahead, but keeping his thoughts to himself.

'Indeed!' shouted John, glancing casually over his shoulder. 'We are all the Queen's loyal subjects and we bow in obedience to those in authority.'

The brother-in-law settled back in his saddle, relaxing his grip on the reins slightly. They rode on in silence for a while. The sly, dubious expression on his face seemed to say that he did not believe what John had said.

'The three of us have just returned from London,' Lucy declared cheerfully, leaning across towards Thomas. 'Jack and Robert had some business at court. Have you ever been to London, Master Tanfield?'

Thomas nodded but did not elaborate.

'It is such a grand city, teeming with life, its people full of gossip,' Lucy continued with relish. 'The Strand, where many of the most wealthy and powerful noblemen reside, is so enticing and the gilded barges on the river look so resplendent, don't you think. Then there is the Royal Exchange where merchants have set up the finest shops and where almost anything can be bought or sold. Yes, it is a city very much to my liking.'

'And it is a city full of opportunities,' added Jack, with a cold smile.

Thomas turned his head to the brother, unable to conceal his interest. 'Mistress Lucy says you were at court?' he asked.

'I am indebted to Master Beale,' Jack said, indicating his brother-in-law, 'for it is he who introduced me at court. Nobility and knights everywhere! The Duke of Norfolk even spared me a "Good Morning" the other day! I tell you, Master Tanfield, if it is patronage or preferment you seek, then you will undoubtedly find it there!'

He paused and fixed Thomas with that same unpleasant smile. 'I was pleased to be granted an audience with Robert's brother-in-law, Sir Francis Walsingham, at his residence in Seething Lane not far from The Tower. I took the opportunity to present him with a gift, a pair of caged songbirds, which he admired greatly and was most delighted with. Subsequently, when I offered my services to him he seemed most keen to accept.'

'Sir Francis Walsingham is your brother-in-law?' Thomas asked, raising his brows in a gesture of surprise.

'And a fine, elegant gentleman he is,' replied Robert,

stirring in his saddle once again. 'It must have been predestined that Jack should meet with him, for he has little spare time. He is fully devoted to the queen's business.'

'Perhaps you will accompany us on our next visit to London, Master Tanfield?' asked Lucy. 'We could share its pleasures. And maybe Jack and Robert will introduce you to some of their friends at court. I'm certain it would be to your advantage.'

'Yes, of course!' said Robert eagerly. 'We could cross the river into Southwark and tempt you to take in some bear baiting. Of course, you would be welcome too, Master Staunton,' he added with a wry smile, revealing crooked, yellowing teeth.

'Master Tanfield, do say you'll come…' Lucy persisted.

'It is kind of you to suggest it Mistress Lucy and I would dearly love to…' Thomas stammered, marvelling at her pretty face and wondering how she both enticed and frightened him. He inhaled the fragrance of her scent and felt quite light-headed.

'Then I don't understand your hesitation,' Lucy replied. She shook her head in an exaggerated manner as if to say 'How can you refuse me?' In that moment, the sparkle drained from her smiling face.

'Our way leads us in the opposite direction,' interjected John, glancing back over his shoulder. 'Besides, we do not care for London's narrow cobbled streets and secret alleyways; one can easily become lost … and the stench!'

Thomas exhaled again.

'Oh, given enough time, one can become accustomed to the stench, Master Staunton.' Robert laughed sarcastically. 'It is a pity you will not be persuaded. But it is true, the city is compact. Why, it is such a short distance between the wealth of the Strand and the hanging tree in Holborn,' he added, giving John a significant look.

But John had already turned round and was facing to the front again. He did not react.

Thomas cast a glance at Lucy but she turned her head away. The party fell silent again, each occupied with their own thoughts. They rode on for a couple of hundred yards until they reached a glade at the fringes of a wood and here they stopped. The sun did not stretch to the clearing and it felt even colder though overhead it remained bright. The horses' flanks steamed in the raw morning air and the dogs lay panting with their wet tongues hanging out after their exertions. Behind them lay the woods, in front of them sloping open ground stretching back towards the pond, and to their right a dense, thorny hedgerow, thick with clusters of scarlet berries, winding its way along the estate's eastern boundary.

Edward looked about him and listened. He glanced at Thomas, smiled and then carefully, almost reverently, began to remove the leather hood from the sparrowhawk's head. It required great aptitude and considerable skill to be able to handle a hawk competently and Edward was no novice. Alerted, the dogs pricked up their ears, wagged their tails and began moving about impatiently, their eager eyes sparkling fiercely.

Edward raised his arm and cast the hawk loose. With a few beats of its broad, rounded wings the hawk soared upwards, landing on the tip of an outstretched branch of a birch tree some thirty or forty yards away. The two dogs were unleashed and leaped forward, racing away across the open ground towards the hedgerow.

'You know,' Robert began, leaning back in his saddle, addressing both Thomas and John, 'the vermin who think they are hidden from view in the hedgerows or in long grass at the edges of meadows always fall victim. Those powerful talons strike swiftly and deliver their fatal blow with unerring precision. In the end, they always get what they're after.'

Thomas shivered though whether it was with the cold, or with the excitement or with a sense of foreboding at Robert's sinister words, it was impossible to tell.

The dogs bounded towards the hedgerow. Nearer and nearer... A blackbird chattered deep in the undergrowth then, when they were within a few feet, four, five, six small birds, tits and finches, emerged into the open, startled and terrified.

Within seconds, the hawk was cutting across the sky like a shooting star. She tucked in her wings and began a breath-taking dive, bearing almost straight down on her prey, its streamlined silhouette growing larger until the small birds below spotted it and began to disperse frantically. But for one slow finch, slightly too young and inexperienced, it was too late. The hawk had already chosen her feathered target and moments later slammed her razor-sharp talons into its flesh, killing it instantly. The two birds fell to the ground as the hunters emitted a muffled cheer and immediately set out to retrieve both the prey and the hawk.

Half an hour later, they had all gathered together

again at the edge of the wood.

'Here, you take her,' said Edward casually, winking at Thomas and presenting the hawk to him.

Thomas's eyes lit up. He held out his arm. He was wearing the very same hawking gloves he had made two years earlier, which he had intended giving to Anthony Babington. With the other hand he reached into his pocket and took a small piece of bright red meat which he had secreted there earlier that morning and gently offered it to the hawk.

The hawk looked at him, her bright yellow-orange eyes wide and alert. Without any fear or hesitation, she suddenly hopped onto his glove and greedily took the meat. There seemed to be an instant and mutual bond between Thomas and the hawk, giving lie to the myth that a bird can only be handled by the master who trained it. For several seconds, Thomas looked at this sleek, beautiful creature of nature and marvelled.

Edward laughed with delight. 'You handle the bird with much skill, Master Tanfield,' he said.

'This is a fine hawk you have here, Master Hopton. You have trained her well,' replied Thomas, returning Edward's compliment. 'As for myself, I have nothing to boast about. I have flown hawks since I was child and enjoy nothing better.'

Once again, the dogs were set loose first, hurtling forward and reaching the hedgerow in no time. After a few moments, Thomas raised his arm and with strong, powerful beats, the hawk climbed rapidly skyward. Thomas's eyes followed her all the way but this time, instead of alighting on a nearby branch, she made her attack immediately, diving through the air at lightning speed.

At the moment of impact, Lucy gave an ecstatic shriek, so shrill that it set everyone's ears ringing. She leaned across from her horse and touched Thomas on the arm, her half closed eyes pleading with longing, his earlier rejection apparently forgiven.

Thomas also felt a longing. She is so beautiful, he thought. Life was good here.

The scene was repeated many times, over and over through the course of the morning and well into the afternoon, with Edward, Thomas and Jack taking it in turns to fly the hawk. The hunters shifted their location several times and more often than not, the hawk was successful, taking several tits and finches, a couple of thrushes and a rather plump wood-pigeon in one of her more ruthless attacks. The dogs were also allowed to display their terrific speed and agility, killing a full-grown hare they had chased into a ditch at the edge of a rye field.

Eventually, as the grey light of a mid-winter's day started to fade, Edward and the others assembled their spoils and with happy, exhausted faces, headed back across the fields towards the house.

# CHAPTER 14

Two servants, one tall and gangly, the other tiny and round, rushed out of the porch to meet their returning master and his guests. The appearance of Lucy, Jack and Robert caused the tall, gangly one to holler inside for additional assistance and moments later two young women servants popped their heads out from behind the door.

Edward dismounted at the porch and shouted at the women servants to take his guests inside and see to their comfort. He directed the small male servant to take care of the horses and dogs while he would personally return the hawk to its mews.

The house felt warm and inviting after the bitter cold outside and smelled strongly of wood smoke, grilled fish and baked bread. Thomas and John were taken to a small room off the main hall, where they removed their cloaks and sat down on a cushioned seat in front of a blazing fire. Their faces were flushed and burning; they were hungry and in good humour. One of the spaniels, still spattered with mud, came into the room and lay on the hearth, cleaning himself with his tongue.

After a while, Edward came in and crossed to the fire. He crouched down beside the spaniel. 'We will dine in the Great Hall this evening,' he announced, scratching the dog behind the ears. 'I am keen to preserve the traditions and habits that my late father so enjoyed.'

Shortly after Edward appeared, the door opened and a round-faced man of about forty with a double chin entered. It was the usher of the Great Hall and he had a stately, important manner about him. He glanced across at Thomas and John, and then gave Edward a respectful bow.

'Excellent! The table is prepared!' said Edward smiling, reading the look in the usher's eyes and rubbing his hands together in anticipation.

Edward led his guests through into the Great Hall. Lucy, Jack and Robert were already there, waiting to take their seats. Edward sat at the centre of the high table, with Lucy on his left and Jack on his right, while Thomas, John and Robert were at the single trestle table which adjoined it at right angles. Edward bowed his head and led Thomas and John in saying grace; the others remained silent.

Under the usher's critical eye, two servants in full blue and grey livery, came forward carrying towels and basins for the diners. After washing and drying his hands, Edward slung his napkin over his left shoulder, and leaned towards John. 'Well, this cousin of yours,' he said, addressing John but looking at Thomas, 'has shown us a thing or two about hawking, that's for certain. As a matter of fact, I think he displayed greater skill than either me or Jack!'

'Indeed, brother, I have never seen anyone like him!' agreed Lucy, coyly.

Jack merely muttered incoherently. He was renowned

among his associates for his enormous thirst and had already started drinking. He grasped his leather drinking cup, emptied it of ale in two or three gulps, beckoned a servant refill it and guzzled that as well.

The usher led half a dozen servants to the high table, each one carrying a dish. It was advent and the fast which prohibited meat, chicken, milk, cheese and butter was strictly observed by Edward. Nevertheless, they were still able to feast on many sumptuous dishes: grilled fish in a wine sauce, oysters in almond milk, crabs, mussels and assorted shellfish such as periwinkles. This was followed by a frangipane tart and spiced apples wrapped in pastry and baked.

Thomas was so ravenous that he sampled everything; it seemed to him that he had never tasted such mouth-watering oysters and delicious mussels; such scrumptious apple pie. Everyone talked at once, recounting their exploits earlier that day or about the Christmas feast still to come. As Thomas laughed and talked, he found himself gazing longingly at Lucy's face, transfixed by her beauty. She seemed to have a power over him that he could not resist.

At length Edward signalled that the tables be cleared and a commotion followed as the servants, directed by the usher, obediently bustled about carrying out their tasks.

Edward took advantage of this distraction to call for cards, which the yeoman officer provided. Along with Thomas and John, and Jack and Robert, he seated himself at a card table near the fireplace. All the players bestowed a small gratuity in the 'playing box' which would subsequently be distributed amongst the servants as was custom. Lucy sat on a cushioned settle behind Thomas but close enough for him to be conscious of the rustle of her gown and the slight creak of her bodice as she breathed.

Thomas spread his cards out like a fan while surveying the others. Edward, despite his best efforts, was struggling not to doze off while John wore an involuntary smile upon his lips as he perused his hand. Jack, his round face a little more flushed than earlier, shifted awkwardly in his seat muttering something about laying a wager and Robert, with his furtive eyes, looked preoccupied, absorbed in his own thoughts which Thomas suspected had nothing at all to do with the game.

They played a game of maw. Cards were dealt, bets wagered and play commenced. The reason for John's confident smile was immediately evident as he won the first three tricks, automatically taking the pot.

'Ah! Beginners luck!' exclaimed Jack, forcing a smile. 'Let's deal again.'

He gathered the cards together, shuffled them in his plump hands and dealt five cards to each player. He then placed the rest of the pack in the centre of the table and turned over the top card to reveal the queen of hearts. Bets were placed and a new game began.

'You should be careful, Master Staunton. It is a foolish man who trusts luck,' said Robert, with a sickly smile. 'One can never know what cards the other man holds.'

'That is true, Master Beale,' replied John cheerfully. 'But it is how you play the cards you have been dealt that is most important.'

Robert bowed his head in acknowledgement but

remained silent, carefully assessing his opponent. The game continued and once again, John was victorious.

'Aaah!" screamed Jack, lifting both hands to his head. 'I don't believe it.'

Lucy rose to her feet and moved alongside Thomas, her gown brushing against his legs. 'You do seem to play a charmed game, Master Staunton,' she said. She flashed a smile at Thomas as he glanced up at her.

John's 'luck' held for some time and he took the next five games before Edward, followed by Thomas and Robert, finally managed to recoup some of their money. Only Jack failed to win a single trick and, as time went on, his playing became more desperate and agitated. An hour and a half later, he threw his cards onto the table. 'That's it! I've had enough,' he said, slurring his words.

John glanced across at him. 'I agree. One gets tired of sitting still so long,' he said, stretching and getting up from the table. 'To play cards is no profession for a man.' He looked Jack straight in the eyes. 'Do not fret, Master Hopton. Charity begins at home and I never keep the money when I play with friends.' He pushed a large heap of coins back across the table.

Jack looked dimly at the money in front of him. For a moment, he seemed oblivious to everything else.

'I believe hunting is more Jack's pleasure,' announced Robert. 'In fact, why don't we arrange some as part of the Christmas festivities?'

'Splendid! ' cried Lucy. 'What do you say, Jack?'

But Jack did not stir or raise his lowered eyes.

'We enjoy the hunt the best of all,' Lucy added, her eyes resting on Thomas.

Thomas caught himself smiling. Though he knew it was not right, he did not have the strength of will to resist.

'And to make it more interesting,' Beale went on thoughtfully, 'let us invite some of Jack's hunting companions along. The more the merrier, as they say.'

'Yes, yes,' Jack murmured. 'I will send word immediately.' He glanced furtively at his brother.

Edward suddenly exploded from his apparent slumber, pushing his chair backwards and upsetting the drinks on the table. 'I will not tolerate your friends in this house and well you know it!' he shouted.

'Rowdy perhaps, a little boisterous maybe, but they mean no harm,' said Robert, quickly coming to Jack's defence.

'No harm!' Edward repeated. 'No harm! They disrupt the entire household by their very presence. By persistence and intimidation they attempt to influence me with their Protestant lies and falsehoods, though they well know my position. And to make matters worse, they are aided and abetted in their heresy by my own brother! My own brother!'

'It is not we who are heretics but you! You and your fellow Papists here,' said Jack rising from his chair. 'It is you who blindly swallow every utterance from that Antichrist in Rome. None of you are loyal subjects, true Englishmen. You are all traitors! And you will all get your just reward; Sir Francis will see to that!'

Thomas flushed and made to rise but immediately felt his brother's strong restraining grip on his arm.

'You will apologise to my guests for your outburst,' said Edward, tight-lipped.

'Oh, Jack!' said Lucy, aghast. 'I'm sure these are good men, whatever their beliefs. Why, you have already heard them express their allegiance to the Queen whilst we were out hawking; surely that is proof enough of their loyalty.'

'Why must it be me who always apologises? No, I will not apologise!' cried Jack defiantly. 'I am not deceived by their lies! They say one thing but mean another and I do not trust any of them.' He turned to John. 'You say that charity begins at home, Master Staunton. Well, it appears that neither I nor my friends are welcome in my father's house … that's charity for you! You will excuse me if I keep my own company.'

'I thought you were with us,' he added brusquely, sweeping past Lucy and out of the room.

After a moment's stunned silence, Beale rose slowly. There was a superior smile on his face which Thomas found repulsive. 'It appears that to consort with Catholics, however polite and well intentioned, brings with it nothing but disharmony and conflict. So, gentlemen, Mistress Lucy, I too must bid you good night.' With this, he also departed from the Hall.

'What is it!' exclaimed Lucy irritably. 'What is the matter with everyone this evening?'

'Your brother is a hot-headed idiot who doesn't know how to behave or hold his tongue!' said Edward, stooping to retrieve his cards from where they had fallen.

'Forgive me,' began John, 'but I think it is because he is plagued by a troubled conscience. He is young and impressionable, exposed to all manner of temptations,' he continued, his clear eyes switching between Lucy and Edward. 'He has fallen under the influence of those he refers to as "friends", though I suspect they have only their own interests at heart and they have filled his head with all manner of gossip and untruths. He feels the need to belong, like all his contemporaries, to this group of men. He feels threatened and I'm rather afraid that our presence at Hopton has antagonised him.'

Lucy smoothed her gown. Her eyes were downcast. She looked as though she was about to say something but then hesitated.

'But I do feel for him,' John went on, 'for he knows in his heart of hearts, that these so called "friends" are false. It is Edward who speaks the truth when he refers to the Catholic faith as being the one, true faith.'

Lucy looked up. She was smiling but there was a troubled expression on her face. 'Master Beale and my brother are most persuasive when they explain the doctrine of Calvin. And they are most vociferous in pouring scorn on your faith, as you have just witnessed. I have read *Institutes of the Christian Religion* and found its reasons and arguments to be most compelling. There is much that is contrary to your Catholic way.'

'I am familiar with this book,' replied John, 'and can show you many misrepresentations of fact. You must not let your judgement become confused by such principles; rather you should trust what you know to be right. How can we, who are mortal, question the teachings of the divine Scriptures?'

Lucy considered for a moment. She was far from convinced. 'Then I am afraid we must disagree, Master Staunton,' she said softly. 'But perhaps we can discuss these matters later, and maybe I could persuade you to see my point of view?'

'At a more convenient hour, perhaps?' said John.

'Quite so! Now if you will excuse me, I will retire to my chamber. It has been a long day.'

As she left the room, she glanced at Thomas. 'Do not think of me as altogether bad, Master Tanfield,' she said. A tender smile played on her lips, and her eyes were filled once more with that youthful vibrancy that enhanced her natural beauty.

Thomas sat for several moments with his hands folded in his lap, a strange look on his face. Confused by his feelings for Lucy; his secret cravings and desires. 'What about Jack?' he enquired, looking up. Though distracted, he was still concerned over the younger brother's tempestuous departure.

'Oh, he will calm down eventually as he always does in these situations,' said Edward. He turned to John. 'Perhaps, when Jack's temper has subsided, you will try and speak with him?'

'By all means,' replied John. 'But can you convince someone who won't listen.'

† 

As they climbed the wide oak staircase and went along the empty passage to their rooms, the brothers reflected on the day's events; while John contemplated in silence, Thomas gave vent to his thoughts.

'Jack … Robert. Neither is to be trusted, I tell you! Jack is lost, beyond hope! He is so blinded by his zeal that no amount of reasoning will persuade him to take a different view. And he seems prepared to sacrifice all his principles for his ambition to enter court.' He spoke rapidly. 'As for Master Beale, it is clear that he loathes all Catholics as much as his odious brother-in-law, Sir Francis Walsingham! I confess that I find him repugnant!'

'Be quiet cousin!' retorted John angrily. 'This is not the place for such loose talk.' He opened the door to his chamber. Thomas pursued him, only half closing the door behind him.

'Sometimes … cousin …' he stuttered; 'I confess I don't understand you! Are you not of the same opinion?'

John sighed but made no reply, stirring up the few remaining embers in the large fireplace instead. Thomas looked about him. A single rushlight fixed at an angle on the panelled wall cast a dim, shadowy light across the small room. Beneath a small latticed window there was a chair and a sturdy-looking table with a wash basin placed upon it. An embroidered coverlet lay across the bed.

'Anyway, you should have good reason to be content,' continued Thomas, changing mood slightly. 'I believe you have made quite an impression on Mistress Lucy. But whether she can be reconciled, I am not certain. She seems quite set in her beliefs.' There was a weariness on his face as he spoke.

'I will pray that her soul can be saved, but without His grace we can achieve nothing, for what is done is done by God.'

'Ah! You should not be so bashful!'

John looked intently at his brother and smiled ruefully.

'I am sorry that I disappoint you,' said Thomas repentantly. 'I wish I was more like you. I know there is much I have to learn but I am a poor student and I don't know how to begin.'

'But you already have. You have a good heart but you have a long road before you. Now it is time to rest,' John said, beginning to remove his boots. 'Saving souls is an exhausting business!' he added with a sparkle in his eye.

At that moment they heard footsteps retreating down the passage and a few seconds later, a door slamming shut.

Thomas poked his head round the door, then looked back at John and shook his head. The passage was deserted and quiet.

'We have been careless,' said John, his brows knitting together. 'We must take greater care. Now, Thomas, I bid you good night.'

Thomas returned his brother's weary smile and left the room for his own. As he did so, he failed to notice the shaft of light escaping from beneath a door at the far end of the passage.

# CHAPTER 15

Sir Francis Walsingham, dressed all in black as was his preference, sat in the office in his town house in Cheapside staring in amusement at the opened letter on the table before him. Now the distractions of Christmas had ended it was good to return to the business from which he derived his greatest satisfaction.

He fingered the edges of the parchment as if it were some invaluable treasure, wholly oblivious to the unremitting din from the busy streets outside: the tramp of hooves, the rumble of coach wheels on the cobbles, the shouts of traders and the rowdy brawling of apprentices. He stroked his neatly trimmed beard and moustache, picked up the letter again and began re-reading it.

*My heartiest commendations to you, Master Secretary. I have made bold to write you this private letter, the content of which I beseech your consideration.*

*The preservation of the Protestant religion throughout the realm of Her Most Glorious Majesty is the lawful duty of all her true subjects. Accordingly, as one such loyal and devoted servant, and in order to keep a good conscience, I am obliged to report on the recent goings-on at the Hopton estate in Suffolk.*

*There are two belonging to the Catholic faith currently in residence there, as guests of the recusant, Edward Hopton. They give me considerable cause for distress and I am far from satisfied that they are the innocent gentlemen they claim to be. I have heard them talk late into the night of saving souls.*

*More recently, they have taken to visiting other households in the area and I have heard rumours that, at the house of Edward Hopton's married sister, the younger of these two Catholics, he with the little beard, performed strange deeds, anointing so I am told, as though he were a priest!*

*They accept all hospitality which is freely given and they are able to impose their own will at Hopton more and more. They are at liberty to come and go as they please whilst my acquaintances, good Protestants all, are prohibited.*

*It appears that as fast as one enterprise faileth, these Papists and Recusants, take another in hand, hoping at last to prevail – but they must not be allowed to.*

*I am no spy and I seek no gain but to serve my Queen but if you were to send for a search of Hopton, you will discover all manner of popish trinkets and symbols of their Catholic blasphemy: sufficient evidence indeed of their abhorrent crimes.*

*I most eagerly await your agent's arrival and assure you of my continued assistance in this matter.*

*Your most dutiful bound obedient servant,*

The scribbled signature at the foot of the letter was that of Jack Hopton.

Sir Francis replaced the letter on the table, taking great care not to disturb his glass of claret, and then leant back in the chair to meditate. While the letter provided him with reasonable grounds to carry out a search, it was the reference to 'priestly acts' that intrigued him. What a find it would be if one, or even both, of these parasitical Catholics was a priest, he thought to himself.

He was only too well aware of the challenges posed by 'another Edmund Campion' and resolved to act quickly and decisively; after all, his Queen depended on him. Dipping his quill into a small pot of oak-gall ink, he began to write on a blank piece of parchment the orders that would dispatch the necessary men to Hopton the very next day. He paused for a moment; he must also send word to Richard Topcliffe so that he could prepare himself to extract any confessions that may be required.

A smile crept over his lips; it is always the most gratifying when a young tree provides such early fruit, he thought.

† 

An increasingly hostile blizzard whipped up the falling snow as it swirled around the courtyard at Hopton Manor. Jack, shivering and exasperated, was about to return indoors when he saw a group of six or seven horsemen galloping towards him.

'It has been over a week!' he raged and, without waiting for a response, turned his back on them and retreated inside.

The officer in charge, a portly man of about forty years of age, hurriedly dismounted and with his long black cloak billowing behind him, ran after Jack into the Great Hall.

Jack made his way to the fireplace where a blazing fire began to thaw his frozen body. His temper, though, remained raw. 'A pox on this foul weather!' he snarled through gritted teeth, brushing the damp snow from his clothing and stamping his boots loudly on the hearth. He swung round and addressed the officer. 'Your arrival has come too late!' he snarled, with obvious irritation.

'Sir!' the officer exclaimed indignantly. He was breathing heavily and his forehead was streaked with sweat. With the back of a gloved hand he wiped dew from the end of his long nose. 'We have come as swiftly as possible but the weather has deteriorated to such an extent it made our journey near impossible. One of my men even complained of frostbite in his toes!'

'Excuses! Excuses!' Jack hollered. 'Because of your feeble efforts … and be aware that your master will be duly informed of your miserable failure…'

The officer made to object but Jack would not be interrupted.

'… because of your feeble efforts, the Catholic scum have already moved on, no doubt to practice their evil heresy elsewhere.'

'May I assure you, sir...'

'Enough! Get out of my sight!' Jack waved dismissively. 'I don't want to listen to any more of your pitiful excuses!'

'Gentlemen, gentlemen, please…' Robert Beale, who

had crept unnoticed into the Hall, spoke condescendingly. Both Jack and the officer fell silent as if commanded by a higher authority.

Beale possessed his usual confident swagger as he sauntered across the Hall. He stopped next to Jack and warmed his outstretched hands in front of the flames.

'You and your men may rest here for the night,' he announced presently. 'I am certain Master Hopton will have no objections.'

'What?' exclaimed Jack.

'With your brother away in Norwich, I assume you would only be too pleased to show your hospitality to such dedicated servants of Sir Francis, to provide them with some respite against the worst of the weather.' He flashed a yellow smile at the officer. 'And come the morning,' he stepped forward so that he was only a few inches away from the officer's face, 'when you are fully recovered, with fresh horses and supplies, you may continue your pursuit.'

'You know where they are?' asked Jack, raising his eyebrows. Maybe the blizzard had not swallowed up his chance of gaining Walsingham's gratitude and the respected position in his retinue that he craved. Only when that had happened would he be in a position to exert his influence on Sir Francis and bring weight to bear on his older brother to oust him from Hopton completely.

Beale smiled and nodded; he understood Jack's motives and ambitions only too well. 'They were bound for the Midlands,' he revealed calmly. 'To be precise, they are heading for the village of Rowington in the county of Warwick.'

# CHAPTER 16

Thomas and John Rufford had, in fact, arrived in the small village of Rowington on the very same day the pursuivants reached Hopton. The brothers had journeyed to the home of the Catholic Reeve family in the Forest of Arden. The manor house, built of local honey-grey Warwickshire sandstone, surrounded by a moat and sited in a secluded clearing, was now leased to two sisters, Anne Ferrers and the widowed Eleanor Sheppard. It was the perfect setting to convene the Jesuits' annual conference.

John, by way of a coded letter he had received at Hopton, had been summoned by his superior to attend Rowington to discuss the current state of the mission in England.

On their arrival at Rowington, they were warmly welcomed by their hosts. Mistress Anne Ferrers, a few months younger than Thomas, was a strong willed and pious Catholic. A maid by choice, she dedicated her entire life to the service of God and used her considerable fortune to rent the house at Rowington for the sole purpose of providing a safe refuge for the Jesuit priests. Anne's widowed sister, Eleanor, two years her senior, was equally devout but of a much more timid disposition.

The brothers were presented to two other priests who had preceded them. The first, Thomas Lister, a distinguished and learned individual, had only recently joined the Society and was unfamiliar to John. The second, however, required no introduction.

'Ah! It is good to see you again, my friend,' said John affectionately and the two priests embraced each other warmly. 'May I introduce you to my brother,' he added.

A thin smile emerged from beneath a neatly trimmed beard and the priest greeted Thomas with a reticent politeness.

'Thomas, this is my travelling companion from Rome, Father Edward Oldcorne.'

Thomas was struck by the gaunt, anaemic appearance of the priest; this was not the strong and indomitable character he had imagined from John's earlier anecdotes. Indeed, if this was the calibre of all the priests on the mission, then it was doomed to fail. Thomas believed that the mission's success was reliant on brave, heroic men not weaklings like the one standing before him. But as he contemplated Father Oldcorne's frail appearance, he became aware of John's piercing gaze. It seemed that his brother could read his thoughts and Thomas shifted his feet awkwardly. He knew he should not make rash judgements; rather, he should take stock of his own shortcomings. He sighed heavily. He still had much to learn.

In the days after Thomas and John's arrival, they were joined by Father Henry Garnet, the Jesuit Superior, Father Robert Southwell and some dozen or so other priests and laymen. Soon, the house was filled with the murmur of prayers, together with more practical conversations about the strategy and future plans of the mission.

To begin with Thomas felt awed by such a large number of learned men gathered together in one place. He was amazed by the articulate manner they displayed during their frequent theological debates. He listened politely to their reasoning, their philosophy, their rhetoric; all were flawless, while their command of languages, Greek and Latin in particular, was astounding. He felt very small and out of place but John, as a conscientious brother always does, ensured that he did not feel excluded from their circle. It wasn't long before Thomas began participating in these discussions, airing his views with youthful enthusiasm and candour. Though his style was somewhat awkward and less eloquent than the priests', he quickly ingratiated himself with them all.

In the evenings, those assembled for the conference split into three distinct groups. The younger novices congregated in the Great Hall with the Jesuit Superior, Father Garnet, at their centre, all ears to his words of wisdom. In another room, the rather dour Father Edward Oldcorne, along with three or four of the older priests, earnestly studied scripture. In the third group were Thomas and John, their hosts Anne Ferrers and Eleanor Sheppard, Father Robert Southwell, a tall, slight man who was well known to both sisters having stayed with them upon his return to England in 1586, and Nicholas Owen, the diminutive lay brother, who had devised and constructed various priest holes at Rowington.

After a communal supper on the Feast of the Epiphany,

everyone moved to their various rooms as normal. Father Robert Southwell was amongst the third group in one of the many upper chambers, reciting his latest poem. The priest's oratory was clear, his manner self-assured.

*'As I in hoary winters night stood shivering in the snow,*
*Surprised I was with sudden heat which made my heart*
*to glow;'*

The others listened intently, enraptured by Southwell's charm; everyone, that is, except Thomas. He seemed distant; his eyes were dull and remained downcast the whole time. He didn't hear the words; in his head he was replaying the previous evening's debate when Southwell, having delivered a stirring rendition of another of his poems, 'Decease, Release', commemorating the death of Mary, Queen of Scots, had gone on to condemn Anthony Babington's treachery. Thomas had rallied to his friend's defence but the priest stated that although he remained convinced the plot was the work of Walsingham, Babington's actions had heaped further hatred on English Catholics.

'It is not our mission to be rebels and assasins,' Southwell had said.

Even John had begged Thomas to see that Babington's way was a false one. 'His head was turned; his way was madness. It is through the strength of our faith and the force of our argument that we shall prevail.'

Thomas still found this a difficult truth to accept.

The gentle yet sincere applause that greeted the end of Father Southwell's poem brought Thomas back to the present.

'What a wonderful poem!' Eleanor remarked.

'I think Father Southwell possesses a rare talent,' said Mistress Anne, placing her hand on her sister's arm. 'To write such inspired verse is a gift not shared by many.'

'Please … I would dearly like to hear some more,' begged Eleanor.

Everyone nodded and even Thomas forced a smile. He still felt sour towards Father Southwell and couldn't forgive his comments about Babington, but he acknowledged that the tribute to the dead Queen of Scots had moved him and that Southwell's work could grace the stage of any of the new London theatres.

At that moment the door to the room swung open and the Senior Jesuit, Father Henry Garnet, entered. His countenance, which had always been lively and cheerful, was anxious.

'Forgive my intrusion,' he began, his low voice still betraying a hint of a Derbyshire accent. 'I need not remind you of the dangers of so many of us congregating under one roof and the risks taken by those who provide us with safe refuge.' He crossed the room and laid a hand on Anne Ferrers' head.

Thomas was surprised. He had become so engrossed in the intellectual debates of the past four days that such an obvious thought had not even occurred to him.

'But, now that you have renewed your vows,' Garnet continued, his gaze resting on the two priests in the room, 'you must not remain here. As I speak, some of the others are saddling their horses and preparing to leave. Father Oldcorne has decided to go on a pilgrimage to St Winefred's Well. I will return to London in the morning.'

Thomas stared at his brother and Father Southwell, both of whom appeared indifferent to this sudden and alarming directive. Thomas, however, felt the stirrings of a familiar rage. That old feeling of being hunted returned. He was not going to remain silent. 'It is an abomination that we are forced to run and hide!' he erupted, rising to his feet.

For a few moments, no-one stirred. Then Father Garnet cleared his throat, crossed his hands on his chest and smiled his gentle, fatherly smile. 'Yes, it is an ugly fact of life, Master Rufford, but one we must be happy to endure,' he replied.

'Father Garnet is right,' said John, getting up from his seat. 'The longer we remain here, the greater the risk. We do not wish to hasten any retribution on our hosts.'

'Nor do I wish any harm to befall them,' said Thomas, glancing from Anne to Eleanor. 'But to persecute a man, to deny him his beliefs–!'

'And what do you believe?' asked Father Southwell abruptly. He remained seated with his hands neatly folded on his lap.

'What?' said Thomas, flushing.

'We are all servants of God and we must submit to His will,' asserted Father Southwell. 'I am pleased to suffer in God's name and without complaint.'

Thomas gazed into Southwell's face. 'That is all well and true,' he said. 'But surely, if our mission in England is to succeed, we must confront our oppressors with something a little more effective than prayers and the celebration of Masses.'

'What would you recommend?' retorted John, looking

intently at his brother. 'Armed uprisings, perhaps?' He shook his head disapprovingly. 'To embark on such a fiery course would lead only to the mission's immediate and catastrophic downfall. It would betray the trust not only of those who depend on us for their spiritual guidance but also the very principles upon which our Order – and indeed our entire lives – is governed. God's will is one of peace, not violence.'

Thomas shifted uncomfortably and glanced around the room, at the sympathetic eyes. He flushed. He felt like a young pupil when scolded by a learned teacher for failing to grasp a simple truth.

'Come, Thomas,' laughed Father Southwell, finally getting to his feet. 'If we are called upon to be martyrs, then we should be so cheerfully and with faith in our hearts.'

'Your zeal is most commendable, Father, and is to be greatly admired, but I'm afraid we may not all share your bravery.' Father Garnet sounded apprehensive. He was not afraid of death but perhaps the manner of it.

'Oh, I do wish you wouldn't speak of martyrdom in such a nonchalant manner,' Eleanor said, her dark eyes wide with fear. 'Such talk makes me very afraid.' Her lips began to tremble and the sad expression which rarely left her plain face made it appear that she was about to burst into tears. She gulped and turned away.

Anne placed her delicate but reassuring hand on her sister's lap. 'Dear Eleanor, you must not alarm yourself,' she said softly, her face illuminated by a tender smile.

'I cannot understand why a man would desire such a painful death,' Eleanor whispered timidly.

Thomas looked at the two sisters huddled together. He moved closer. 'Please, don't upset yourself, Mistress Eleanor. I assure you I do not crave such a … I have seen… I mean… I too am afraid,' he stammered. He glanced desperately at John.

John's mouth widened in a comforting smile. 'Bravery manifests itself in many different guises,' he began thoughtfully. 'The courage and strength which you and your sister possess far exceeds any that we may have. Your humility and gentleness is a true gift from God and is an example to us all.'

Eleanor smiled nervously. She tried to say something but could not get out a single word. It was clear that her fear prevented her from appreciating the truth in what John had just said.

John's attention fell on his brother, his smile faded and his voice became solemn. 'The very survival of our faith in England is dependent on such courage and dedication. Father Garnet is right; every day we remain here places us and the mission in even greater jeopardy.' He paused for a moment. 'Our presence at Mythe Hall is long overdue,' he went on. 'So, brother, we too shall gather our belongings and leave immediately.'

Anne Ferrers was aghast at such a suggestion. 'But to depart on such a long journey at this late hour is pure folly,' she said, rising to her feet. 'If you go through the villages and towns, you will arouse suspicion. And to travel across the countryside in darkness, well, you will get hopelessly lost! No! You will stay the night! I insist!'

John smiled in admiration of Anne's stubbornness and at her logic. He was, nevertheless, about to raise his objections but was cut short.

'We will have the servants prepare some horses ready for your departure in the morning,' Anne continued, starting for the door. 'You are quite safe in this house for one more night. Come, Eleanor, let us see to it right away.'

Eleanor rose and followed her sister, curtseying clumsily as she passed Father Garnet.

# CHAPTER 17

THE HOUSEHOLD WOKE early the following morning and by the time Thomas came downstairs at five o'clock, the servants and maids were already going about their duties preparing breakfast, cleaning boots, putting out cloaks and packing their guests' belongings in readiness for their departure.

As Thomas entered the Great Hall, the tranquillity of the early morning, was abruptly and terrifyingly shattered. The heavy oak entrance door crashed open and in rushed a youthful terror-stricken servant, red-faced and perspiring, his chest heaving as he gasped for air. Slamming the door behind him, grinding the key in the lock and clumsily manhandling the cross-bar into position, he turned on his heels, ran straight past Thomas and left through the kitchen door.

A few seconds later Mistress Anne, still in her nightgown and her face a little more flushed than normal, entered the Great Hall by way of the same door. She hurried over to Thomas. 'The pursuivants are here!' she said quietly.

Thomas's mouth fell open and the hairs on the back of his neck stood on end. 'What? I don't understand. How did they find…' he spluttered.

CHAPTER 17

'It doesn't matter! They're here now!' Anne said, her voice unwavering. 'We have very little time…'

As she spoke, Thomas was distracted by the growing commotion outside. He heard hurried footsteps on the cobbles and angry voices threatening the servants who had come running over from the stables in an attempt to confront the intruders.

The door shuddered as fists pounded against it. Thomas felt his whole being shake. Instinctively, he felt for his sword; the desire to do something had taken hold of him and he was powerless to resist. But the sword wasn't there; he had left it by the side of his bed. In an instant, his mind was flooded with images of capture, torture and executions. For a moment he thought about making a run for it.

He stared into Anne's serene face. What about the women? What about his brother and the other priests? He couldn't abandon them. It was hopeless; they were trapped. He stood, rigid, waiting for the inevitable.

A maid brushed passed him.

'How dare you create such a disturbance,' she hollered through the closed door. 'The mistress of the house, a widow to be sure, is still in her chamber but will be down presently – and I warn you she will not stand for any nonsense.'

Feeling a tug at his sleeve, Thomas swung round and found himself staring down into the restless dark eyes of Nicholas Owen.

'Follow me … come quickly,' Nicholas urged and he tugged again at Thomas's elbow.

Thomas went towards the stairs at the far end of the Great Hall, the same stairs which he had descended only a few minutes earlier expecting nothing more than a hearty breakfast prior to his departure. He glanced anxiously over his shoulder at Anne and at the maid who was still barking at the pursuivants through the bolted and barred door.

'Go!' implored Anne frantically. 'We shall delay them as long as possible.'

†

Upstairs in a small room in the west wing that served as an improvised chapel, Father Southwell had been saying Mass. He had guessed the reason behind the commotion and had already removed his vestments, extinguished the candles and stripped the altar bare, throwing everything into a sack.

Nicholas and Thomas sprinted along the corridor towards him. John, together with Father Garnet and one of the trusted household servants, appeared from an adjacent room.

'We must gather all our personal belongings,' instructed Father Garnet. 'Boots, cloaks, swords – anything that may betray our presence in the house – and hide them away with us.'

Immediately, Father Southwell and John hurried away.

'The beds!' exclaimed the servant suddenly in a high-pitched voice. Thomas shot him a bemused glance.

'The beds!' the servant repeated. 'They'll still be warm! We must turn them, place the cold side uppermost.' Then he also scurried off, retreating back towards the bedrooms.

Meanwhile Mistress Anne had assumed Eleanor's role, for her sister had already been taken to a hiding place at the top of the house to avoid facing the aggressive searchers.

Anne was playing for time. 'Does it seem proper that you should be admitted into a widow's house before either she or her maids have risen?' she said, with calm authority.

'We are on the Queen's business!' came the immediate reply from the other side of the door. 'And we demand entrance at once.'

'I am sure the Queen's business is not of such importance that it would have you disturb our slumber! If you are able to wait a while we will make ourselves sufficiently decent to receive servants of Her Majesty in a proper manner.'

'We are to search the house immediately!' snapped the voice.

'Search the house? And pray, what do you hope to find?'

'Jesuit priests! Now, open the door or we shall force our way in!'

Anne took a step back and peered nervously towards the top of the stairs. Had she managed to gain enough time for the priests to hide themselves? She could not be certain but neither could she hold the pursuivants at bay any longer. Reluctantly, she gestured to the maid to open the door.

The maid tentatively turned the key. Barely had the last remaining iron bolt been pulled back when she was thrown to one side by the violent force which flung the door wide open.

Anne stiffened as the cold, damp air came rushing in, taking her breath away. Staring defiantly at the well-dressed officer standing before her, and contemptuously ignoring the warrant he thrust at her, she offered her assistance to the stricken maid. The young girl, visibly shaking, forced a half-smile and gratefully reached for her mistress's outstretched hand.

'What kept you so long?' the officer raged. He screwed up his eyes and glared around the room as if hoping to catch a glimpse of a forbidden priest making his escape. His sharp eyes softened a little as he became aware of the trembling, half-dressed women before him; looking somewhat embarrassed, he diverted his gaze.

'This is the necessary warrant,' he said almost apologetically, pushing the crumpled piece of parchment into Anne's grasp.

Anne's attention was momentarily distracted by the two grubby individuals flanking the officer. They were almost identical, dressed in black tunics and wielding long swords. Their faces were covered with thick black bristles and their small mouths fixed in permanent sneers. They looked like carrion crow impatiently waiting for their turn to scavenge. Four more soldiers did not enter but stayed behind in the courtyard.

'By all means, proceed with your search if you must,' said Anne, her gaze once more falling upon the officer. 'But I assure you it will be in vain.' She returned the warrant without looking at it.

Within minutes, the entire household had been rounded up and were being held in the hall. Cowering together with Anne, they could only watch in horror as the priest-hunters tore through the house in a frenzied pursuit of their quarry, searching each room in turn, overturning tables and chairs, emptying chests and scattering clothes, pounding the walls, prying into the darkest of corners with their candles. And above the pandemonium could be heard the officer's constant harsh bawling.

The sight of such vandalism was too distressing for some of the younger serving girls to bear. Anne requested that they be allowed to go about their daily routines. The officer, preoccupied with trying to control his over-zealous men, promptly agreed.

Still in her nightgown, Anne steered some of the maids into the kitchen and they began preparing breakfast. 'They are like children playing blind man's bluff,' she remarked. 'Covering their eyes and then trying to touch and grasp everything about them.'

After nearly two hours, and with the soldiers frustrated at their lack of success in finding any incriminating evidence in the house, let alone a live Jesuit priest, Anne offered them something to eat and drink. Ravenous, they accepted her hospitality without a second thought.

Anne presided over the table with deliberate courtesy, encouraging them to linger. The more distraction and disturbance to their search, she reasoned, the quicker they would grow tired and give up.

'I trust you are finding the food and drink to your satisfaction,' she said to the officer, whilst serving up some cold meats, cheese and bread.

'That's more like it!' one of the searchers said impatiently, grabbing a flagon of beer, clumsily pouring some into his cup and spilling most of it.

'I've got a thirst for something!' snorted the other, drooling.

Anne's eyes turned to the two grubby soldiers sitting at the table. She winced at the ugly way they were stuffing their faces and swilling her beer. Silently, she prayed that this whole nightmare would soon be over. The officer glimpsed the look of revulsion on her face.

'Filthy swine! Have you no manners!' he yelled at his two accomplices, thumping his fist on the table. He looked up at Anne grinning, baring his straw-coloured teeth.

Anne smiled insipidly back.

'Come on you layabouts!' he snapped abruptly. 'We have work to do!' He pushed back his chair, drawing himself to his full height. Facing Anne, his eyes narrowed to little more than slits. 'Help us to find what we are looking for and I will put in a good word on your behalf, make it easier for you,' he said.

'I cannot do that which you ask, sir and neither do I care for your false promises.'

The officer seethed. 'You try my patience. Tell us where the priests are hidden!' he demanded angrily.

'You have been misinformed, sir. There is nothing for you here.'

'Well, we shall see what we shall see!' And he turned his back and stamped away, kicking over his chair in the process.

Despite having searched the rooms on the upper floor several times already, the two men were dispatched to try their luck again. Another two hours later, and still without any success, they were finding it difficult to maintain their earlier enthusiasm.

'Fools! Idiots!' the officer shouted. 'You won't find them by gawping through the windows!' He swung at them but they jerked instinctively to one side and evaded his blow.

Sniggering like errant school boys caught by their master, the two searchers slithered past him and disappeared into an adjacent room where they immediately began hammering violently on the oak wall panelling with their bare fists, listening for any tell-tale hollowness.

The officer stared vaguely at the three small windows in the wall opposite and cursed his men for their laziness. He strolled across the room. Their lethargy was hardly surprising though, he thought to himself, gazing out of the two lower windows into the still water of the moat. Unlike him they were ignorant folk without any principles, and while they would carry out whatever tasks were asked of them, their only real concern was the meagre pittance they received in payment. His own reward for all the honest commitment and devotion to duty which he demonstrated was not that much better – and he would have to endure the wrath of an outraged Master Secretary if, as was becoming ever more probable, the search failed to produce the required priests. He shrank visibly at the thought of such a wretched prospect. He resolved that he would not leave Rowington empty handed.

But without realising it, the officer had just left the very same room where Father Southwell had been celebrating Mass; though no hint or suggestion now remained of this treasonous event. Had he remained focussed on the job in hand and not unwittingly been distracted by the curious position of those three small windows, he may have instead chosen to cast his eyes downwards where he would undoubtedly have detected another curiosity and one which held far greater significance.

# CHAPTER 18

STOOPING TO LIFT a camouflaged trapdoor in the thickness of the outer wall, Nicholas Owen forced Thomas down into the old garderobe shaft beneath.

'Go on … go on! Hurry!' he urged.

For once, Thomas didn't hesitate and immediately squeezed into the narrow shaft. Unable to see a thing in the darkness, he descended rapidly, scraping the skin from his elbows before eventually tumbling into a narrow tunnel. The air in the tunnel was thin and dank, and the low ceiling compelled Thomas to squat awkwardly. The only light came from thin slits at intervals along the outer wall.

As his eyes gradually adjusted to the gloom, Thomas realised he must be standing in the old sewer. The water from the moat beyond lapped at his ankles. Feeling the cold creeping up his legs, he began shuffling his way along the passage.

Hearing a scuffling noise from behind, Thomas was relieved to see he was being closely followed by his brother. He glimpsed, Father Garnet and several other crouching figures immediately behind John, groping their way through the darkness. He thought it impossible that anyone else could cram into the narrow tunnel.

Thomas's heart thudded and his throat felt swollen and dry. His chest was tight and he gasped for what little air there was. Standing in the freezing water, he realised the danger they were all in.

For four desperate hours Thomas and his companions stood in silence; alert, listening to the pursuivants overhead, their search growing ever more frenetic. Thomas flinched at each dull thud of a chair or table being overturned. With the intense, relentless hammering on the oak panelling, the trapdoor seemed like scant protection and Thomas feared that an enraged searcher would come bursting through it at any moment.

He peered along the line of priests, huddled together and motionless. Father Garnet stood on the other side of his brother, weary and exhausted, the strain of the ordeal clearly etched in his leathery face. He believed that his decision to delay their departure from Rowington had placed the entire mission in peril. Next to Father Garnet was Father Southwell who, on observing Thomas, flashed a wide smile as if the terrifying experience were actually an enjoyable one. Next to him the wraithlike figure of Father Oldcorne held a rosary between his long fingers, his lips twitching in inaudible prayer. Then there was one of the younger priests, whose name Thomas couldn't recall, and the servant whom he had seen rushing away to turn the beds; both were wearing the same terrified expressions. Finally, furthest away and only just discernible in the gloom stooped the tiny, crooked figure of Nicholas Owen.

Suddenly there came silence, an ominous calm, a stillness more threatening than all the raucous clamouring that had preceded it. Thomas had not heard the searchers leaving and wondered whether it was safe to come out of hiding. He shot an enquiring glance at his brother and saw that he too was straining every muscle, listening for a sound or a voice, any inkling as to the reason for this sudden lull. The suspense of not knowing was the worst part of all.

†

'Ah! There you are!' snarled the officer, thrusting his head around the parlour door before barging his way in. Anne was comforting two distressed maids who had been unable to restrain their tears any longer.

'I must object most strongly to the bullying conduct of you and your men…' Anne began angrily.

'No!' the officer shouted, cutting her short. 'You may not object!' His nostrils flared, his face turned a deep shade of purple and a vein pulsed in his temple. 'You protest your innocence while all the time you harbour traitor priests in your large, splendid houses…'

'Be careful what you say! You have no proof!'

'Why, everybody knows you Papists are all the same,' the officer went on vehemently. 'Every ale house in the country is ripe with tales of old Catholic manor houses and their secret priest holes. The country is riddled with scheming, lying wretches like you, who will stop at nothing to shelter these traitors. There is not an honest one amongst you. You cannot be trusted, that much is certain.' Leaning forward, his eyes glinting with malice, he added: 'I despise the like of you for you are the cause of all my troubles!'

'In the name of God, leave us alone!' retorted Anne, recoiling from the stench of the officer's foul breath.

'Well,' said the officer pensively, his wily gaze still fixed on Anne. 'What would convince us to leave? Not so much God, but the sweet voice of an angel perhaps!' He raised himself to his full height, his back as stiff as a ramrod.

Anne was indignant. 'As if we had not enough to endure, we are to be charged for our suffering too!' she said furiously.

The officer waved a petulant hand. 'Cease your whining, woman. You bring it upon yourself.'

It was an impossible situation. Pay up or face yet more frenzied searching, all the time with the possibility that her hidden 'guests' would be discovered. Anne held the two distraught maids closer. She had no choice. Absently, replacing a loose strand of hair behind her ear, she turned to the younger maid, and instructed her to bring the heavy leather purse from the left-hand drawer of the dressing table in her bedchamber.

'Calmly!' she added, smiling after the young girl, who bolted from the room, colliding with the officer in her haste.

Moments later the girl returned and stood in the doorway clutching a bulging leather pouch in her tiny hands. Anne smiled her thanks and bid both the maids rejoin their colleagues in the kitchen.

'Well, what is the going rate these days?' she said, glaring at the officer, while she untied the drawstring around the top of the purse.

'Going rate? Well, there's a clumsy phrase. No, I prefer to say, "gift". Yes, a gift for services rendered,' the officer said, trying to suppress his glee. 'I think a gold angel should suffice … for each of my men, you understand. They still have to be paid, do they not? And for all the trouble you have caused me … let us say two gold angels.'

'That is outrageous!' snapped Anne.

'I would think it a small price to pay for being left in peace.'

'Yet, somehow I fear you will never leave us in peace,' said Anne, pulling out some gold coins with trembling fingers. She drew a steadying breath. She must remain focused. She must not let her defence down now, not now they were so close. It was nearly over.

'Good, good … that's better. I knew you would see reason,' said the officer, counting out eight gold coins from one clammy hand to the other. A wide grin spread over his face and for a few moments he caressed the coins with his stubby fingers, relishing their sound and the way they shimmered in the light.

'I trust that your master's displeasure at your failure is now made more tolerable,' said Anne.

The officer's face suddenly showed deep irritation. For a moment he did not speak and his wild eyes stared in contempt at Anne, who looked away, angry with herself for having provoked his anger.

'Your priests may have eluded us on this occasion,' the officer began through gritted teeth, 'but believe me, neither they nor you will be so fortunate next time.'

Anne made no reply.

Moments later, the pursuivants had gone.

Leaving just sufficient time to ensure that there was no danger of them turning back suddenly, as they were known to do, Anne called down through the trapdoor into the darkness below. Slowly, and with painful, laboured movements, those in hiding began to emerge from their place of safety.

'Not one but several Daniels appearing from their den,' beamed John, as his head popped through the trapdoor. He clambered back into the room and stretched his tired body.

The relief was tangible. Some of the priests gave thanks to God for ensuring their safety, saying that providence had proved beyond all doubt that their mission was a just cause. Thomas, a weary yet pleased smile on his dry lips, chose to reflect on a more secular explanation for their continued liberty. His eyes wandered the room, searching for that reason; huddled next to one another in one corner were Nicholas Owen and Anne Ferrers.

'Thank you, thank you. We owe you our lives,' he said, smiling, forcing his way through to them. He gazed at Nicholas, who in turn looked first at Anne, as if he was unsure at whom the compliment was being directed, and then back at Thomas, before responding with a self-conscious smile and a shrug of his shoulders.

'Your modesty is a virtue,' said Thomas. 'But it cannot hide the ingenuity and skill that created our hiding place and which provided us with safe sanctuary.' At the outset, he had been ill at ease in Nicholas's presence; now, he bitterly regretted his early prejudice. He felt humble, tiny.

He turned to Anne. 'Then, of course, there is Mistress Anne.'

Anne's eyes shone with joy, lighting up her exhausted

face and making it more beautiful than ever. Thomas held her hand. 'You are deserving of my greatest admiration and respect,' he said. 'You take such terrible risks, without a hint of complaint and without any reward. Your strength and courage are immeasurable … greater than most men, in fact.' As he spoke, he reproached himself for his own weakness of will. 'Not at all the weaker vessel!' he added with a wry smile. As he looked at her, an image of his sister, Jane flashed across his mind.

'You're most generous, Master Rufford, but I'm not worthy of your kind words,' said Anne, lowering her eyes.

Father Garnet approached apprehensively, as if he were half expecting the pursuivants to return at any moment. Gently kissing Anne's bowed head, he said softly, 'God will reward my sister in Christ.'

# CHAPTER 19

'What is it this time?' Walsingham snapped tetchily. 'How am I to concentrate on my work with these continual interruptions?'

'Begging your pardon, Sir, but Master Topcliffe offers his heartiest commendations and requests an audience!' declared his head steward, a sprightly man of about forty, with intelligent eyes and a smooth dark beard. He was not in the least disconcerted by Walsingham's abrupt tone.

'What! He is here now?'

'Yes sir, and he is most insistent.'

Walsingham was sitting at his desk in the office in Cheapside, the light from two candles flickered in the draught. 'Oh, very well, show him in.' He began hastily gathering up the papers which he had been studying ever since they had arrived earlier that day and which were the source of his ill temper.

Walsingham disliked Richard Topcliffe intensely, though he had to indulge him, being well aware that the Queen's Pursuivant, as Topcliffe had become known, held considerable favour with Elizabeth. Moreover, while being far from squeamish, Walsingham often shuddered at the grisly methods Topcliffe deployed in the dungeon under the White Tower, and more recently in his house in Westminster, even if they proved successful in extracting confessions from his victims. Topcliffe had undeniably earned his reputation as a cruel yet efficient torturer. Walsingham, recognising that he was a necessary evil in the hunt for traitors, continued to suffer his vile company whenever he called.

'It is good of you to see me at such short notice, Master Secretary,' began Topcliffe, slipping briskly into the room.

In contrast to the sombre appearance of his host, Topcliffe was dressed in the manner of a rich courtier, though no amount of extravagant trappings could disguise the hoary features of a man rapidly approaching fifty years of age. Removing his hat and sword and thrusting both into the outstretched hands of the steward, he took the seat at the other side of the desk.

'There is much profit in your work, Master Topcliffe,' said Walsingham dryly, a smile creeping across his face. 'Though I deduce from your grave expression that you have some other news for me – perhaps from the old priest you presently examine?' His keen eyes fixed on Topcliffe.

'His tongue has not yet been loosened, Sir Francis, but it will not be long,' replied Topcliffe, gently stroking his dagger-shaped beard.

'Something else, then?'

'It is a grave matter, Sir Francis,' said Topcliffe. 'Her Majesty has expressed her deep concern that the Jesuit traitors are still at liberty despite your best efforts …

I mean, our best efforts,' he corrected, 'and that they continue to spread their lies and corruption throughout the realm.' There was a deliberate pause. 'She fears the trail has gone cold and wishes that I take a more prominent role in the matter.'

There was a tremor in the lower part of Walsingham's face. 'What's this?' he growled. 'Be mindful of your position, Master Topcliffe. Remember who it is you serve!'

Topcliffe seemed to relish the anger on Walsingham's face. 'Why, I live only to serve Her Most Glorious Majesty, Queen Elizabeth,' he said with feigned indignation.

'There is no need to pretend on my account,' replied Walsingham, recovering his composure. 'You serve only what is in your own best interests.'

'Not so, Master Secretary!' Topcliffe protested. 'There is no man alive, save your good self, more devoted to his duty than I. As a loyal subject, I swear that I will not rest until every Catholic has either departed our country or is dead!'

Walsingham stared back at him coldly. 'Do not confuse loyalty, that is, true loyalty to the Sovereign with selfish ambition and your insatiable desire for Catholic blood.'

'Harsh words Master Secretary!' retorted Topcliffe, stirring in his seat as if about to rise.

Walsingham nodded his head and gestured at Topcliffe to remain seated. 'Maybe so,' he said in a conciliatory tone.

'You and I share the same purpose, Sir Francis.'

Walsingham leaned back in his chair. 'And in order to achieve that purpose?' he said, measuring his words carefully.

'I am the Queen's faithful servant but I am also yours, Sir Francis; perhaps there is some task you would have me perform?'

Walsingham, observing that Topcliffe's arrogance had now been replaced with deference, permitted himself a brief smile of satisfaction.

'We must not underestimate our enemies' abilities,' he said. 'They devise many ingenious ways in which to evade our grasp. We know that they use false names and disguise themselves as country gentlemen as they go about their treason. And, as always,' Walsingham leaned forward, resting his elbows on the table, 'these Jesuit priests depend on the assistance provided by friends and accomplices. They are as sly and cunning as foxes, moving from house to house, relying on this network of wealthy Catholic families.'

Walsingham leaned back again in his seat, his eyes and hands resting on the folded papers on the table in front of him, as if guarding their content. 'But we have taken infinite pains and have garnered much information…'

'That is your talent, Sir Francis.'

'One family in particular persists in attracting my attention,' Walsingham continued, ignoring Topcliffe's shallow attempt at flattery. 'The Molynieux family from the Broad Oaks estate in Essex.'

'If you know them, arrest them!' Topcliffe cried angrily.

'Indeed, I am acquainted with Lord Molynieux … over the Babington affair. But alas, it is not that straightforward. They are a much respected family who have prominent connections at court. And there is a lack of proof of their complicity … although they are undoubtedly guilty of sheltering and helping priests.'

'Then I will help to obtain such proof, Sir Francis,' Topcliffe said. 'I will leave at once.' Pushing back his chair, he rose from the table.

Walsingham smiled but said nothing, simply pointing Topcliffe to the chair which he had just vacated. He was now in full control. Topcliffe returned to his seat.

'The enthusiasm you show for your work knows no limit,' said Walsingham dryly.

Topcliffe was unable to hold back a vague smile at this last remark, as if proudly recalling some cruel torture he had recently performed.

Walsingham moved towards a small sideboard at the back of the room. 'I understand the lady of the house has acquired quite a reputation for charity, showing great generosity and benevolence to the poor, giving alms and tending to their needs.'

Topcliffe looked puzzled. It was not uncommon for such people to act in these ways he thought to himself; they believed it to be good for the soul. Why would Walsingham wish to inform him of this fact? It was of no interest to him. For Topcliffe, any display of kindness to those less fortunate than themselves was a sign of weakness. Compassion was completely foreign to him.

Walsingham returned with two cups of wine. 'Above all, I hear that she tends to their injuries, preparing poultices for their wounds, that sort of thing.' He offered Topcliffe one of the cups. 'Perhaps you know of someone who requires her help, her healing powers?'

Topcliffe was perplexed by the obscure nature of the question. 'I'm not sure I understand,' he muttered.

'It is not a trick, Master Topcliffe. Think!'

Topcliffe racked his brains. He brought the cup of wine to his lips. 'I know of no good Protestant who would dare go near the place ... only Catholics and priests ...' He broke off suddenly. A smile crept slowly across his lips. Jones! Father Henry Jones! The priest he was currently ... examining ... in his house at Westminster.

There followed a few moments of silence as Topcliffe's mind set to work.

'You are an ambitious man and desire success,' said Walsingham, stooping low over Topcliffe. 'Then do as I bid! Bring me the evidence that will deprive the Jesuits' of their support and their mission will crumble and fail! That is our purpose!'

# CHAPTER 20

FOLLOWING THE RAID at Rowington, those who had come so close to discovery dispersed. The Jesuit Superior, Father Garnet, returned to London where, overcome by doubt about his leadership, he promptly wrote to Rome and tendered his resignation as head of the mission in England. John, considering that at the present time it would be too dangerous to visit his parents at Mythe Hall, announced that he would go on the pilgrimage to St Winefred's Well together with Father Oldcorne and Father Southwell.

The two sisters, Anne and Eleanor, also decided to travel to Holywell. Anne, who was troubled by female disorders, hoped for some miracle cure; together with a small number of servants, she travelled by a different route to that taken by the priests.

Nicholas Owen, whose vocation was to build safe hiding places for Jesuit priests, declared that he had to complete some 'important work' at a Catholic house near Worcester but then he too would join them at Holywell. Thomas, who still viewed stories of 'miracle cures' at the shrine with great scepticism, dismissing them as superstitious nonsense, and looking for a convenient excuse to delay his going there, invited himself along as Nicholas's travelling companion. It was agreed that they would all meet again at Holywell in one month's time.

Thomas Rufford and Nicholas Owen travelled all day and it was dark by the time they arrived at their destination, the home of the Habington family, four miles to the north of Worcester.

The day after their arrival, Nicholas immediately set about his 'important work': to construct a hiding place at the house. Thomas discovered from the young owner that it was the sixth hide Nicholas had built there in as many years, each one completely different. Desperate to take his mind off the impending visit to Holywell, Thomas offered to assist but Nicholas refused his help, asserting that the hide he was working on behind the wainscot in the gallery was so narrow and cramped that it would be impossible for two men to work side by side.

Thomas, therefore, spent his days in conversation with his genial young host. The topic of discussion was always the same: the unjust and relentless persecution of Catholics. Thomas thought that his young host possessed a strong resemblance to Anthony Babington, not only in his dapper and stylish appearance but also in his impulsive temperament.

Before long, Nicholas's work was done and the two men bade their farewells and departed for Holywell. As they galloped away, Thomas could not help wondering about the young man they had just left, his house and its many hides – and what drama might be enacted there at some future date.

†

As planned, it was exactly one month after leaving Rowington when Thomas and Nicholas finally arrived in Holywell on the north coast of Wales. It was still an hour or so before noon when they passed through the village and started to descend the gentle slope towards the shrine. The sun was low and directly behind them. Thomas dismounted and walked to the top of a rocky outcrop from where he stood and gazed down at the almost biblical scene which greeted him.

Below him, at the foot of the hill was the chapel, its stone ramparts splashed in weak sunlight, like an ancient castle standing sentinel over the sacred shrine, unyielding, everlasting. Some thirty or forty pilgrims were gathered around; some were bathing in the icy spring water gushing forth from the well, some were crossing themselves and reciting prayers of devotion, while others were singing softly, with arms outstretched and eyes upraised to heaven. Thomas noted that many of them were barefoot; he watched a short, dark haired young woman treading carefully along a stony path towards the stream. A group of three elderly men were kneeling on the ground, heads bowed, beating their breasts and sighing. And everywhere he looked the pilgrims' faces were fired with the same solemnity.

The shrine was inspired by the legend of a seventh-century virgin princess, a saintly and beautiful girl, who was brutally murdered by the son of a chieftain after she resisted his advances. Overcome with rage, the suitor cut off the girl's head with his sword. Legend had it that when her severed head hit the ground, a powerful spring instantly burst forth.

Thomas sighed and shook his head. In his heart he still remained sceptical. He stole a sideways glance at Nicholas and wondered if his companion believed; from his friend's serene expression it would seem that he did.

Thomas's gaze returned to the path which led to the stream as he searched again for the dark haired young woman. She had vanished and in her place there was a shrivelled old woman, bent with age, shuffling along with bare feet. When she stumbled, Thomas wanted to rush forward but he seemed unable to move. Nicholas raced ahead in his place and came to the old woman's aid.

'Let us go and find the others!' Thomas said, when Nicholas rejoined him.

As they continued the search for their companions amongst the mass of pilgrims, Thomas grew more and more impatient. 'I don't understand,' he said irritably. 'Of all places, why did they have to arrange to meet here?'

They made their way down towards the stream, which had risen a foot above its normal level following a period of persistent rainfall and which was now in danger of overflowing onto its banks. Nicholas was a little ahead of Thomas when he suddenly turned round and called to him. 'There they are!' he cried, pointing to a cluster of people gathered further along the shore.

Thomas saw three cloaked figures huddled together, perched on the very edge of the steep bank, clinging tightly to one another so as not to tumble headlong into the water. Thomas recognised them as maids of Mistress Anne Ferrers. He also recognised Father Southwell and Father Oldcorne standing slightly apart from the maids; they looked rather odd dressed in their country gentlemen's clothes. He found it quite alarming that priests, men of God, men of great knowledge and wisdom, should have to wear disguises in order to survive.

As he drew nearer, Thomas scrutinised each of their faces. Where was John? His heart sank and his pace instinctively quickened. Immediately, he imagined the worst; perhaps his brother had been taken. No! Impossible! But if he had, surely they would have got word to him. No, there must be a perfectly rational explanation. Perhaps John had been delayed or had taken a detour. Yes, that was it! He must have decided to visit Mythe Hall, gone home after all! That must be the reason for his absence. Satisfied, Thomas relaxed and his footsteps slowed again. Thomas shook his head at the tricks his mind could play.

As he followed the footpath, his attention was diverted by the sound of splashing. Staring into the stream below, his eyes grew wide in disbelief. There, up to their waists in the water, were Mistress Anne Ferrers and his sister, Jane.

Anne was standing upright, defiant against the strong current. Her face was turned towards heaven, her eyes were closed and her lips moved in silent prayer. Jane, her head bowed and her hands clasped, looked pale and trembled with the cold.

'What are you doing? Have you no sense at all? You'll catch your death!' Thomas shouted. And yet, as he spoke, something stirred inside him. He looked about. The unshakeable conviction of such people, who happily gave themselves, heart and soul to their faith, impressed him more strongly than anything he had yet seen or heard. He thought about the question Father Southwell had posed to him at Rowington: 'What do you believe?' Back then, he had been unable to answer; now, as he gazed at the two women before him, he was a little closer to understanding.

'Oh, Master Rufford, Master Owen!' exclaimed the maid nearest him, startled at his and Nicholas's sudden appearance. Father Southwell, Father Oldcorne and the other two maids all turned towards them.

'Thomas! You have no sense of the place!' cried Jane, raising her head and glaring disapprovingly at her brother's clumsiness. Anne, her meditation interrupted, also looked towards the bank.

Thomas immediately regretted his lack of piety. 'No, sister, I didn't mean to ... I mean ... the water must be freezing!' he stammered. 'I only have your and Mistress Ferrer's good health at heart,' he added, desperately trying to remedy the situation.

Father Southwell, observing the look of genuine contrition on Thomas's face, stepped forward. 'Your devotion sets an example to us all, ladies, but I believe Master Rufford is right. You have been in the water long enough.'

Jane and Anne obediently waded to the side and scrambled onto the bank where the maids smothered them with thick woollen blankets.

'May Almighty God save you in spite of yourself,' cried Jane, panting and shivering uncontrollably. She crossed herself and then, smiling at her brother, she threw her arms around him. 'But I am very glad to see you, Thomas.'

'And I you,' replied Thomas hoarsely, embracing her and kissing her on her forehead. 'Though I am somewhat surprised for I understood you to be at Mythe Hall.'

Before she could answer, he turned to Anne. Droplets of water trickled down her kindly face and he gazed into her eyes, which appeared even more radiant than he remembered. She possessed a beauty which he had not noticed before, which seemed to radiate from her whole being.

'I am truly sorry, Mistress Anne. I did not mean to interrupt your devotions. I have heard stories about this place that I must confess I didn't believe, but now I see it with my own eyes. I have never witnessed such compassion and power as that which I have seen here. It is indeed a wonderful and holy place.'

He paused and looked about him. On his arrival at the well, he had shrunk from the sight which greeted him, unable to comprehend it, still clinging to his own way of life. Now new feelings stirred in his soul, feelings of peace he had not known before. But as soon as he became conscious of them, they vanished again; he did not know how to hold onto them.

Anne looked at him intently and a smile played over her lips. 'We are all pilgrims, each seeking perfection,' she said. 'You are a kind man, Master Rufford and I know your heart is true.'

'And I am most fortunate to have a brother who shows such concern for my health!' Jane added, smiling ironically at her brother.

Thomas regarded his sister's mockery with feigned injury and averted his gaze. Looking past her towards the opposite bank, he saw a group of three gentlemen who were preparing to step into the water. The youngest of them, about the same age as himself, had stripped to his linen shirt and woollen breeches and was sitting on a small outcrop of rock. The other two were encouraging him to be the first to take the plunge. The tallest of these, an older man with close-cropped hair and a neatly-trimmed beard, stooped over the young man, offering advice. As he did so, Thomas glimpsed a silver chain with a crucifix hanging from around his neck.

Immediately Thomas's brow furrowed. 'Where is John?' he inquired suddenly.

'Your brother has already departed for Broad Oaks,' replied Father Oldcorne. 'Lord Molynieux sent for Father Rufford to hear his confession.'

'What is it? Has something happened?' asked Thomas.

'Oh! Forgive us,' began Jane, taking her brother by the arm and leading him away. 'You will not have heard. The sad news reached Mythe Hall last week that Lord Molynieux has taken gravely ill, so ill that it was feared he would not last more than a few days. I wasted no time in coming here and relaying the news to John.'

'Lord Molynieux!'

Thomas's face turned ashen and he covered his mouth with his hand as if to smother the words. He remembered Lord Molynieux as he had looked when he had last seen him, so energetic, so full of life. What terrible illness could have suddenly befallen his friend and mentor? Was his condition so critical that a priest had to be sent for? And what of Lady Molynieux and the children?

He turned to his sister and took her hand, drawing her closer. 'Then we too should leave at once,' he said impatiently. 'Every minute is precious. Let us pray to God we are not too late.'

He swung round and marched along the bank away from the shrine. The others immediately set after him, running to keep up. As they climbed back up the hill, Anne touched Thomas on the arm. 'Have courage, my friend,' she whispered. 'God is merciful.'

Thomas nodded silently but didn't look at her.

Behind them at the shrine, the hesitant young man, having eventually removed his boots and evidently taken his companions' advice, had immersed himself in the water and was praying for his soul.

# CHAPTER 21

THE TIRED SUN had long since shared the last of its meagre warmth. Now there seemed to be no sky at all, only the bleak grey half-light of a late winter's afternoon. In the woods at the edge of the Broad Oaks estate, abandoned birds' nests littered the bare branches; across its parkland, deer and rabbit tracks darted this way and that in the soft wet ground. The chill air was lifeless, without a breath of wind.

This atmosphere of serene tranquillity was disturbed by the rhythmic drumming of galloping hoof beats and grunts of protest from exhausted horses. Wood smoke, drifting upwards from a chimney, tickled the nostrils of the three riders as they approached the house. Moments later, Thomas, Jane and Nicholas Owen entered the empty courtyard to the front of the house.

Thomas reined in his horse and dismounted in front of the porch. He looked about him. The house appeared to be in complete darkness: no lights were showing from any of the windows and no-one came rushing out to greet them. He thought he glimpsed a face peering at them from a first floor window but when he looked closer, the figure shrank back into the shadows.

Nicholas dismounted and offered to lift Jane from her

horse but despite aching after the long ride, Jane slid wearily from her brown palfrey without assistance. The hard stone cobbles jarred and her legs trembled from too long in the saddle.

Thomas tried the handle of the huge door. The door was locked and barred from inside. He pounded on the oak boards with his fist. Nothing. He hammered again. Still nothing.

The three visitors waited anxiously.

A few minutes passed, though Thomas imagined it to be much longer. Suddenly he heard the sound of feet scurrying across the stone floor within. A key turned in the lock and the heavy bar rattled as it was withdrawn.

'Forgive us Master Rufford, we thought at first it was the pursuivants returned,' came the trembling voice of a young maid as she pulled open the heavy door. Her face had a meek, mournful expression. She held up a candle and beckoned them in.

'The Pursuivants have been here?' exclaimed Thomas.

'Yes, but how their suspicions were aroused, we do not know.'

'Have they been gone long?' demanded Nicholas, looking nervously about him.

'They departed three days ago after four days of tearing the house apart. But we must be on our guard; we fear the house may still be under close watch.'

Jane brushed aside Nicholas and her brother and went up to the young maid. 'Is everyone alright, my dear?' she asked, laying her hand on the maid's arm. The maid's eyes filled with tears.

'And my brother?' interrupted Thomas.

'Your brother is safe,' replied the maid. 'By God's grace

… and my Lady's fortitude, he was not discovered.'

'He is still here?'

'No, Master Rufford. Your brother departed for London immediately after the search finished.' She turned to Jane. 'Please come, my Lady is in her room and will be pleased to see you.'

She led them through the Great Hall towards the main stairs. Thomas frowned as he saw the ripped tapestries hanging loose on the walls. Halfway across the room, a young stable boy came running towards them, carrying a pail, his boots clattering. He stood to one side to let them pass and then, without a word, dashed off to attend to the horses. At the top of the stairs they passed hurriedly down a dimly-lit corridor until they reached the last door on the right.

The maid paused. 'I fear you will find my Lady somewhat frail in body,' she whispered. 'She tires easily, what with the ordeal of the search following so closely after the sad death of Lord Molynieux. But her mind is as sharp as it has always been and she will be glad of your company.'

She knocked politely and without waiting for an answer, entered the chamber. Thomas, Jane and Nicholas stared numbly after her. Lord Molynieux … dead! They could scarcely take it in. With slow, hesitant steps they followed the maid into the room.

On one side, there was a tall carved and inlaid oak bedstead with fine velvet hangings and on the other a long table covered with a carpet, upon which there was an assortment of highly decorated wooden caskets. The panelled side walls were hung with Flemish tapestries depicting landscape scenes. The room's melancholy gloom was somewhat brightened by a vast gable window, under which there was a high-backed chair. Lady Molynieux sat in this chair, propped up by some embroidered cushions, her head lowered, reading a small, leather-bound book. In one hand she clutched a shrivelled handkerchief and, as usual, the forbidden crucifix hung from her neck.

As her visitors entered, she raised her head. Her face was pale and her eyes were red from the constant wiping away of tears. She had aged greatly since they had last seen her. The Gentlewomen of the Chamber stood around her chair. Slightly to one side was an elderly gentleman with long grey hair whom Thomas recognised as the family's chaplain, one of the old Marian priests ordained before Elizabeth had come to the throne. He smiled at them.

Jane glided silently up to Lady Molynieux, her eyes shining with pity and tenderness. 'Forgive us, Lady Molynieux. We have just this minute been informed of your beloved husband's death and we are truly saddened. Please accept our deepest sympathy. Lord Molynieux was a wonderful man, kind and generous. He must be a great loss to you.'

Lady Molynieux managed only a feeble smile and dabbed her eyes with her handkerchief.

'We spared neither our horses nor ourselves in order to be here,' Thomas added.

'My dears, your presence at Broad Oaks gladdens my heart,' said Lady Molynieux. She presented an outstretched wrinkled hand which Jane and Thomas dutifully kissed. 'Come, Master Owen!' She beckoned to Nicholas who had remained at the door. 'You are most welcome. Forgive me for not rising to greet you but I am getting old and the past few weeks have sapped my strength.'

'I can hardly believe it's true,' Thomas said, his voice barely a whisper.

Lady Molynieux squeezed his hand gently. 'It is true,' she murmured. 'He is no more. The sweating sickness claimed him. He was very fond of you, you know; he regarded you as his own son.'

Thomas choked back tears as he looked at her. He wished he could offer some words of comfort but didn't know where to start.

'There is no sorrow like separation but in my grief I am sustained by the scriptures and the loving kindness of those around me,' said Lady Molynieux. 'And I console myself with the thought that he is no longer suffering and is at one with Our Divine Saviour.' She crossed herself, brought the crucifix to her lips and kissed it. 'Now, you must take some refreshment before you collapse, my poor dears. My steward will look after you for now. This evening, we shall dine downstairs and I shall tell you more – it relieves the pain to talk openly.'

Thomas, Jane and Nicholas took their leave and retired to their rooms. Later, they gathered in the ground-floor dining room for supper. When Thomas entered he was horrified by the devastation which met his eyes. The oak table in the centre of the room was almost the only thing that had not been damaged. The silver candlesticks also remained untouched, but the rest of the room was in complete disarray. Most of the plasterwork had been hacked off the walls; the wooden panelling had been smashed out of its frames and splintered. Paintings were slashed, and broken wood and plaster and fragments of earthenware pottery lay scattered on the floor, although someone had made a clumsy attempt to brush them into a corner. In their desire to find their quarry, the pursuivants had left only a small section of wall immediately adjacent to the stone fireplace untouched.

Thomas continued to gaze at the destruction as two servants rushed in with chairs from another room. He wanted to scream, to vent his fury, but when he glanced at Lady Molynieux and saw how gaunt and thin she had become, he was so overwhelmed with pity and compassion that he forgot his anger.

'You mustn't concern yourself with all this,' he said to her. 'Nicholas and I will see that everything is repaired.'

During the course of the evening, Lady Molynieux told them more about her husband's illness. 'He became delirious. He was not aware of his surroundings and he did not recognise me,' she said. 'His face was so thin; it seemed to just shrivel away. He was in so much pain. The doctor bled him, of course, but it was no use; there was no hope of recovery. And yet the day Father Rufford arrived, he seemed a little better. Though he could barely speak, you could tell by the peaceful look in his eyes that he was pleased to see him. I thank God your brother arrived in time to hear his final confession.'

Thomas, Jane and Nicholas found it heartbreaking to listen to her and could not suppress their tears. Thomas, in particular, struggled to control his grief and sobbed uncontrollably at the loss of his cherished 'uncle'.

'My dear Thomas, do not distress yourself,' said Lady

Molyneux, smiling through her tears. She took his hand and kissed it. 'Lord Molyneux lived his life with dignity and a good conscience. He was not afraid of death. Indeed, he is not dead and we should not be sad, for he will be forever in our thoughts and in our hearts.'

Thomas wiped away his tears. He thought about his 'uncle', remembered his voice, the laughter wrinkles on his face, his bright eyes. He smiled as he recalled that peculiar gait.

The firelight reflected in Lady Molyneux's face. He thought about her patience and understanding, her ability to put others first, her simple wisdom, her faith in God. And in that moment he was conscious of God; the everlasting, eternal God.

†

As the evening wore on, Lady Molyneux recalled the pursuivants' search and how Father Rufford had miraculously evaded capture. She said that afterwards, though he was wasted and weak with hunger and lack of sleep, he had insisted on leaving Broad Oaks without delay. His mind was set on London, perhaps to meet up with his Superior, so she had offered him the use of her house in Holborn while he sought his own lodgings. He had left Broad Oaks that same night under cover of darkness.

Thomas and Jane were completely absorbed as Lady Molyneux described her experiences of the past week. She would have continued talking had one of the maids not interrupted her. 'Why, it's past one o'clock!' the maid exclaimed disapprovingly. 'It is time my Lady retired to her chamber and her guests to theirs.'

'Forgive me!' said Lady Molynieux. 'I forget myself.' With considerable effort, she rose slowly from her seat and started towards the door. Then she stopped, turned and looked at them.

'It is so good to see you,' she said softly. 'And I am content for you to remain at Broad Oaks as long as you wish.'

Jane smiled. 'We are indebted to you, Lady Molynieux and we shall be only too pleased to stay,' she replied.

# CHAPTER 22

THE FOLLOWING MORNING, Thomas sat alone in the attic chapel. It was early and the house was quiet and peaceful.

At the far end of the room was an altar table covered with a gold-embroidered cloth. Six candlesticks, a crucifix and a gilt-silver chalice were set upon it. There was an ornate reliquary casket decorated with images of saints and the Lamb of God on a bench next to the altar, a statue of the Virgin in a little carved niche in the wall behind it. All the treasures had been hidden away and survived the recent search and were immediately brought out again afterwards.

Thomas's gaze was fixed on the brick fireplace in the centre of the outside wall. As he looked, a wry smile played across his features. He stood up, crossed the room and crouched down in front of it, staring at its tiled hearth. For several minutes he stayed there, occasionally running his fingers through the fine layer of wood ash at the bottom of the grate.

The sound of the latch being lifted on the door behind him startled him. 'Ah, there you are! Good day to you, Master Rufford,' the head steward said.

Thomas got to his feet and turned to face the intruder.

He was a short, rotund man with a ruddy complexion and sly eyes. On Thomas's previous visit to Broad Oaks, he had dismissed the steward as a stupid man who disparaged the lower servants and took advantage of his position. But he had expressed great sympathy for Sir William's plight when he was imprisoned in the Tower and had offered to deliver his master's petitions to Walsingham. For this reason alone, Thomas was prepared to overlook the man's shortcomings.

'Good day to you, steward,' Thomas replied. 'You were not here when we arrived yesterday. You have been away from the house?' Without waiting for a response, he turned back to face the fireplace.

'I have indeed, Master Rufford.' The steward stepped into the middle of the room. 'I neglected my duties during the search and our meat provisions were depleted, so I called at Dyson's in Saffron Walden. They are purveyors of the finest beef and mutton in the county, you know! Had I known that you and your sister had arrived, I would have returned to Broad Oaks straight away.' Observing Thomas's inspection of the empty grate, he moved closer. 'What is it?' he asked.

'It's incredible!' said Thomas. 'I am not surprised they didn't find it. Had Lady Molynieux not revealed its precise location, I would never have believed it possible.'

'What is incredible and who are they? And find what exactly?' pressed the steward. His voice was eager and his face had an unnatural smile about it.

'Look closer, steward, and tell me if you can see anything unusual.'

The steward's eyes surveyed the fireplace impatiently.

'I can see nothing unusual.'

'The pursuivants searched for four days,' Thomas began. 'They found the hide in the dining room with some untouched biscuits and a full bottle of wine – but no Jesuit priest! All their measuring and sounding, all their lifting of floorboards and ripping off of plaster and wall panelling was in vain. All the time, my brother was here!' He pointed to the fireplace. 'Beneath this false hearth is the entrance to a hide in the thickness of the wall. This is where my brother lay undiscovered for all that time.'

The steward's mouth twitched with satisfaction. 'So it was there!' he said. 'My mistress did not breathe a word.'

Thomas glanced up and suddenly he became uneasy. He had forgotten that although most of the servants at Broad Oaks were of the old faith, the steward was not. A horrible thought flashed through his mind: why had Lady Molynieux not revealed the location of the hide to him, a man who had served her for countless years, who knew every nook and cranny of the place. Surely such a man was worthy of her trust.

'And for your mistress's sake, you will not breathe a word either!' Thomas demanded threateningly.

The steward stared at him in amazement. 'Bless you, Master Rufford. Why, you don't suspect I would do such a thing?' he said, laughing. 'You have no cause to fear on my account. I've only ever done what is right – you can trust me! Now, I bid you, come downstairs, have something to eat and enjoy Lady Molynieux's generous hospitality.'

The steward seemed far too smug for Thomas's

liking but his irritation was stifled by his elation at his brother's escape. And besides, he was ravenous.

† 

Some days later, Lady Molynieux was dozing in the drawing room, an unfinished piece of embroidery resting on her lap, when her slumber was disrupted by the head steward.

'Forgive my intrusion, my Lady, but if I may have a word,' he said.

Lady Molynieux glanced up sleepily, rubbing her eyes. She never refused her servants and gestured that he enter the room.

'I know that it is an inopportune time, but if I may seek your permission to leave Broad Oaks for a few days,' he began tentatively, rubbing his hands together nervously. 'I have a sickly cousin in London and I wish to pay him a visit – it is feared it may be the same…'

'Pray to God, not the sweating sickness?' Lady Molyneiux clapped a hand to her mouth.

'I fear so,' the steward said, lowering his gaze.

'Then, of course, you must attend your cousin at once.' Lady Molyneiux rose to her feet, and in doing so, the embroidery on her lap fell to the floor.

Disregarding it, she went over to the steward and took his hands in hers. 'I will go to the chapel immediately and pray for his swift recovery,' she said and made to leave the room.

'I am indebted to you, my Lady.'

Lady Molyneiux paused and looked back. 'While you are in London, perhaps, you will do me a favour.' She produced a small leather pouch from a pocket in her dress. 'Will you take this and deliver it to a friend?'

Without speaking, the steward obediently took the pouch, felt that it contained numerous coins and placed it carefully inside his doublet.

'He is staying at my house in Holborn while he looks for a place more suitable to his needs,' Lady Molynieux added.

As they left the room together, the corner of the steward's mouth rose in a barely discernible smile.

# CHAPTER 23

DURING THE DAYS that followed the steward's departure, and for the first time since Lord Molynieux's death and the pursuivants' search, a semblance of normality began to return to Broad Oaks. Lady Molynieux, deriving reassurance and consolation from Jane and Thomas's companionship, busied herself once more with everyday domestic tasks. She had always taken a keen interest in such matters and it was a relief that she was able to do so again. On this particular morning, she was in the kitchen overseeing the making of bread.

'Now, set the dough aside. We must let it rise for half an hour,' she said, leaning over the shoulder of the chief cook and clearing away the wooden kneading trough.

The chief cook, a skilled man who had been employed in the kitchens of several great houses during the past twenty years and who was thoroughly conversant with bread-making, carried out his mistress' wishes cheerfully and with a respectful nod of the head.

As always, the kitchen was hot and noisy. Servants and maids bustled between the pantry, the larder and the main kitchen. Two bronze cooking pots, full to the brim with a thick simmering pottage, hung from chains over an open fire. A ruddy faced servant was preparing to rake the coals from inside the brick bread-oven and a young scullery maid was standing over a sink, cleaning the pewter dinner service with hot water and bran.

Satisfied that her instructions for the bread were being adhered to, Lady Molynieux turned her attention to the scullery maid. Disapproving of her slovenly technique, Lady Molyneiux had just started to demonstrate her own more efficient method when the kitchen door suddenly burst open and the principal receiver entered, flushed and clearly agitated.

'My Lady! I am so sorry but I could not prevent them entering the house!' he gasped.

'There, there, Samuel. Compose yourself. Now, tell me calmly, what has happened?' demanded Lady Molynieux.

'Forgive me, my Lady,' the old man apologised. 'These two gentlemen, if you can call them such, were outside the main entrance … and another figure behind them, skulking about in the shadows. It was the bearded gentleman who did all the talking. Cooper, he said his name was, bold as you like. He told me that his young companion has a painful wound on his leg that needed immediate attention before infection set in. Naturally, I told him to seek out the apothecary in the village but he ignored me and pushed straight past into the Great Hall, demanding to see the lady of the manor. Such rudeness! Such bad manners…'

'And has his friend such a wound?' interrupted Lady Molynieux, moving swiftly across the kitchen.

'Oh, yes, indeed he has! When the bearded one … I mean, Master Cooper … had forced his way in, the second gentleman summoned the other fellow out of the shadows. As he did so, I could clearly see that this man's breeches were muddied and ripped and his arm was broken too, by the look of things. He clasped his thigh with his able hand, yet he was barely able to move! It finished up that he had to be dragged into the Hall by the other two ... and very brutal they were!' A frown creased his brow. 'They showed no compassion at all!'

'Then of course I will attend to his injuries,' Lady Molynieux snapped, rather more fiercely than she had intended. Despite the principal receiver's attempts to dissuade her, she ran out of the kitchen to the Great Hall where she was greeted by the bearded Master Cooper.

Mumbling something about a riding accident in the nearby woods, Cooper pleaded on behalf of his companion. Lady Molynieux glanced past him at the injured stranger and beckoned that he take a seat by the window where she promised to examine the extent of his injuries. But the near-crippled figure, his hair matted and tangled, his young face streaked with dirt and sweat, stared at her in terror.

'Please, do not trouble yourself. Your man is right: we should go and see the 'pothecary!' His voice cracked with pain.

'Nonsense! Here take hold of my arm. I will need some hot water, my ointments and some bandages,' she added, turning to her maid. 'Now go! Hurry!'

Horror flashed across the injured man's face as if her reply had sealed some tragic fate that now awaited them, but Lady Molynieux didn't notice. Reluctantly, his whole body shaking and convulsing with the effort required, the injured man shuffled towards the window seat.

The maid returned and Lady Molynieux began cutting away the bloodstained breeches to reveal several deep lacerations in the young man's right thigh. Blood still oozed from the wounds and the surrounding flesh was swollen and angry. Examining further, she discovered that the man's upper body had suffered multiple cuts and bruises and that his right arm was twisted at an angle where it had been broken.

Lady Molynieux was soon fully absorbed in her task, her hands steady as she bathed and bandaged her patient. She didn't speak except to ask her maid for things that she required.

'It is a treat to watch you perform with such skill, my Lady,' said the bearded man. 'You must have comforted many over the years.'

Lady Molynieux gestured for another bandage. 'I fear my simple medications and dressings are quite inadequate for such serious wounds and are no substitute for those of a good apothecary,' she said.

'You are too modest, my Lady. You have a gift for healing that is better than any apothecary I've ever come across,' Cooper asserted. 'Besides, no good apothecary would want to be seen treating my companion here for he is of the Catholic faith. But there again, perhaps you too are of the old faith,' he added, nodding at the rosary and crucifix Lady Molynieux was wearing.

At that moment, a door which led to one of the inner chambers burst open and Jane came rushing in. Seeing the group gathered around the window seat, she stopped half-way across the floor. Conversation ceased and all eyes immediately fastened on her.

Heavy footsteps could be heard approaching from the open door behind her and the next instant Thomas marched in. His eyes scanned all those present before he stopped abruptly next to his sister. His eyes met those of the young man on the window seat. At first, Thomas saw sadness and desperation, but something else that struck him: behind his forced smile, the stranger looked frightened. Thomas's gaze fell on the bearded man. His haughty air and the sneering countenance warned Thomas to be wary of him. The man stared back at him as though he were mocking him, challenging him. Thomas was about to quiz him when his sister interrupted.

'I have just been told!' she exclaimed crossly, addressing Lady Molynieux. 'What are you thinking of?'

Lady Molynieux gave a deep sigh and struggled to her feet. 'I have done what I am able,' she whispered to the injured man. 'I pray you now seek out a good bonesetter.'

'May God bless you and keep you from harm,' murmured the young man, closing his eyelids as he spoke.

Agitated, Jane turned to face Cooper. Something about him made her feel strange and ill at ease. 'I do not wish to give offence, but it is difficult to know who to trust these days,' she said, almost apologetically. 'My Lady is well known for her charity but I fear there are some who would take advantage of that kindness. We must be careful we are not fooled by such imposters. You are welcome to take some refreshment but then I shall be obliged if you take your leave.'

'Your charming daughter, I presume?' enquired Cooper, shifting his gaze from Lady Molynieux to Jane.

'No, sir, I am not!' said Jane, feeling uncomfortable under his hungry stare. 'I am Mistress Jane Rufford and this is my brother, Thomas.' Her eyes petitioned Thomas for support.

'Rufford?' the man repeated pensively. His mouth turned up at the corners and his fingers began gently caressing his beard. 'Your concern for Lady Molynieux is admirable, Mistress Rufford. But you too should take care, great care.'

'And you, sir, should not burden the home of a grieving widow with aggravation,' retorted Thomas, stepping forward.

Cooper laughed, but there was no mirth in his eyes. 'His fate is already assured,' he said dismissively. He moved closer to Lady Molynieux, his eyes fixed on her face. 'It is as we suspected,' he went on. 'By your actions Lady Molynieux, you have shown where your true allegiance lies. Now, your fate is secured.'

'I do not understand you, sir!' said Thomas. 'Why do you bandy such words? Who the devil do you think you are?'

'My name is Richard Topcliffe. No doubt you have heard of me?' The tone was boastful and, as if to enhance the effect, as Topcliffe spoke he slapped his sword onto the table, scattering bottles of ointment and bandages onto the floor.

'What!' cried Jane. She turned in alarm to Thomas; the very name of Richard Topcliffe struck terror and fear into the heart of every Catholic in England.

Thomas stood rigidly for a moment. The man's

reputation preceded him; everywhere there were reports about his hatred for Catholics and his penchant for cruel interrogations. It was rumoured that he was the greatest rack-master in England. Thomas felt sick to his stomach; it was as though he could smell the sweat and fear of that horrible dungeon under the White Tower where Topcliffe performed his grisly work.

Topcliffe stared back at them, delighted by the terror in their faces. He stepped closer still to Lady Molyneiux, his face alive with anticipation. There was a dribble of saliva from either side of his mouth.

'Lady Molyneiux, in the name of our most glorious majesty Queen Elizabeth I am arresting you for receiving, comforting, helping and maintaining a priest of the old faith. And it is my duty to bring you to London …' He broke off, as she cast a fleeting glance at the young man whose wounds she had tended and who was sitting helplessly next to his burly associate.

'Ah, yes!' Topcliffe went on, waving at the young man. 'This pathetic creature is Father Henry Jones, a traitor, a Jesuit priest, on a political mission to pervert the Queen's loyal subjects and to seduce them from the Queen's allegiance.'

'Lies! It is all lies!' cried Thomas, rushing forward to confront him.

Topcliffe raised an authoritative hand to silence him. 'Master Rufford, be careful of what you say,' he said. There was an undertone of anger in his voice and he was shaking his head from side to side in reproach.

But Thomas continued, undaunted. 'It is not true! The Jesuits are loyal subjects and they are forbidden to meddle in state affairs. Their only mission is to bring back souls to the love of God.'

'Why, you even speak like one of them,' mocked Topcliffe. 'Are you a priest too, perhaps?'

'I am a Catholic,' answered Thomas, staring back at him. 'And therefore, in your eyes, I am guilty also.'

'And it is my sworn duty to rid England of the Catholic scourge!' spat Topcliffe. He paused, wiping his mouth with the back of his hand. 'But for now, I will satisfy myself with Lady Molynieux. We have long suspected her of connivance with the Jesuits. This house is well known as a haven of refuge for them – and that is a treasonable offence.'

'Lady Molynieux has committed no offence other than to tend the wounds of an injured man – as any good person would,' Thomas raged. 'She did not recognise him as a priest. These charges are false! This is a travesty.'

'You have tricked us, deceived us!' Jane hissed.

'You deceive yourselves!' Topcliffe cried impatiently. 'It is foolish to believe you can harbour traitors.' He gestured to his accomplice who responded immediately by hauling the priest to his feet. Topcliffe stepped forward, barring the way and preventing Thomas getting any closer.

'You will accompany me to London, my Lady, where I will question you further,' he continued, turning to Lady Molynieux. 'And when you are brought to trial and the evidence of your complicity is revealed, I have no doubt that the jury will find you guilty of high treason. For that, you will be sentenced to a traitor's death.' There was a pause and Topcliffe smiled slyly. 'Think of yourself and your children,' he continued. 'If you give me the names of the other Jesuits you have sheltered and disclose the places where they have stayed, it is in my power to help you. You need not die.'

Lady Molynieux straightened up. 'Then I would rather die!'

At this, Jane burst into tears and sank to her knees. 'Please, God! Have you no pity?' she begged, clutching Topcliffe's cloak.

'What's this?' Topcliffe smiled. He reached down and lifted her head. 'Sweet, innocent Mistress Rufford, where is your precious faith now?'

Thomas took his sister by the hand and raised her to her feet. 'Come,' he said, 'do not waste your tears appealing to his conscience. He has none! There is not an ounce of goodness in him; there are many who have borne witness to that!'

'Faith!' interrupted Lady Molynieux. 'You, Master Topcliffe, are wholly ignorant of faith. We endure for our faith and we do so with gladness in our hearts. Faith gives us courage and takes away our fear. In the end, it will save us.'

'You should be most fearful, my Lady. Your God will not save you now!' Topcliffe replied. 'Take these traitors away!'

Once more, his burly accomplice sprang into action. 'Get out! Get out!' he screamed and dragged the priest by the scruff of the neck over to the main door and threw him down the entrance steps. Two soldiers in the courtyard outside came running to help.

Topcliffe seized Lady Molyneiux by the arm and led her to the door.

'I will do as you bid,' said Lady Molynieux, pulling

herself free from his grip. 'But you will not lay your hands on me! You do not frighten me!' She went to offer assistance to the priest.

Jane's whole body began to shake with sobs. Topcliffe gazed at her with hungry, greedy eyes. 'I hope to have the pleasure of your company again soon, Mistress Rufford,' he said.

'You exist on the misery and suffering you cause to others,' Thomas said, his lips quivering with emotion. 'You are a most detestable creature.'

Topcliffe turned to face him, his face impassive. 'Nor will your God save your brother – another Jesuit traitor!'

'What? What do you know about John?'

'That he is taken, a couple of nights ago at a house in Holborn.'

The words crashed around Thomas's ears. He staggered forward, winded, as if he had been thumped in the stomach.

'There was no secret hide beneath the fireplace in that house!' laughed Topcliffe's accomplice. Thomas stared after him; his eyes wide with terror and disbelief.

'No! It cannot be; it's impossible!' Thomas tried to swallow but couldn't. Blood pounded loudly in his ears and everything went dark around him. He tried to focus on Topcliffe. Perhaps it was another ploy, another trap. But seeing the smile on Topcliffe's face, the glee in his eyes, Thomas knew that it was true: his brother was taken.

# CHAPTER 24

THE PURSUIVANTS ARRIVED shortly before dawn at Lady Molynieux's house in Holborn, where John Rufford had taken lodging in the apartment on the upper floor. Armed with swords and staves, they rushed upstairs and hammered on his door. John woke and looked about frantically but there was no other exit, no hiding place in that small, cramped room. Then the door gave, there was a wild scrabble of feet on the landing and the parlour was invaded by the light of lanterns. This time there was no escape; John Rufford's good fortune had deserted him.

John was led down the narrow stairs and out into the street. It was a cold, damp morning. Though it was still early, the news of an impending arrest had spread quickly and a threatening mob had gathered around the house. They pressed from all sides, eager to catch a glimpse of the Jesuit traitor and give vent to their hatred. The soldiers forced a way through and John was unceremoniously bundled away.

He glanced back over his shoulder and thought he glimpsed the steward from Broad Oaks in the crowd. The man had a broad, sardonic smile on his face as he counted out coins and then returned them to a small leather pouch he was holding.

John was taken to a large private house in the Strand. While the rest of the soldiers stood outside, the captain of the guard escorted him into a dimly-lit room where several commissioners had already gathered and were sitting in silence at a long table. Presiding over them was the chief commissioner, a clean-shaven, man of about forty years of age, with well-defined cheek bones and a long straight nose. He had bright, intelligent eyes and a penetrating stare. He sat without stirring, calmly deliberating his opening move. John braced himself for the inevitable interrogation.

'Sir, let us not waste each other's time. We know who you are and indeed what you are,' the chief commissioner said.

John looked silently at him, drawn by that resolute gaze.

'Although you travel under many false aliases, we know that your true name is John Rufford,' the commissioner continued, 'and that you are a Jesuit priest. Do not try to deny it!'

Jesus! How can they know that? John felt a sharp stab of fear. He deliberated for several seconds. The face of the steward outside the house in Holborn flashed before him. He had been betrayed. 'As always, you have been well informed,' he answered. 'I do not deny it.'

'Good,' exclaimed the commissioner, rubbing his hands together. 'We have a few questions to put to you. Let us hope you continue to show common sense in the rest of your answers.'

'I will answer all your questions as far as my conscience will allow.'

'Who sent you over to England?' barked a voice from the far end of the table.

'The Superiors of the Society.'

'Why?'

'To return lost souls to God.'

'No, sir! Your mission is to seduce people away from the Queen's allegiance and compel them to the Pope's. You are a traitor!'

John turned his head in the direction of the outburst. A young nobleman, with an angry complexion had risen to his feet and was glaring at him, while a grey-haired, elderly gentleman sitting adjacent to him was silently nodding his approval.

'There is no conflict between the allegiance due to the Queen and that due to the Pope,' John replied. 'The history of England and of all other Christian states shows this.'

'In spite of the fact that Her Majesty has been excommunicated by the Pope,' returned the chief commissioner.

'I recognise her as the true Queen of England, though I am also aware that there has been an excommunication.'

'Give us a plain and straight answer!' bellowed the young nobleman angrily, and moved rapidly around the table towards John.

'I have told you what I think and will not give you any other answer!' said John resolutely.

The nobleman approached. He examined John closely and began to remove his velvet doublet. 'What's this?' he demanded, gripping the coarse gown that John was wearing underneath.

'A vest.'

## CHAPTER 24

'No! It's a Jesuit hair shirt!' the nobleman roared and started ripping it off with his enormous hands. 'Why don't you wear these clothes in the open? Instead, you prefer disguises and assume false names. No decent person behaves in such a manner.'

'My Lord, I must protest at such rough treatment,' John pleaded, fending off the assault as best he could.

The chief commissioner nodded, slightly embarrassed by his colleague's behaviour. 'Master Young!' he exclaimed reproachfully, waving the young man aside. 'This is neither the time nor the place. We must conduct ourselves with a little more restraint, if you please.'

The young man grunted his disapproval and, with great reluctance, dragged himself back to his seat.

'Thank you,' said John, adjusting his torn gown and re-fastening his doublet. He breathed a sigh of relief but there was to be no respite.

'How long have you been acting as a priest in this country?' pursued the commissioner, determined to continue with the interrogation.

'Nearly two years.'

'How did you land? And where? Whom have you lived with since then?'

'If I name any person who has harboured me, or mention any house where I have found shelter,' John replied, 'innocent people will suffer for the kindness they have done me. Such is your law. For my part I would be acting against charity and justice, so I pray you will excuse me for not answering.'

The commissioner shifted in his chair. The stubborn intelligence of his prisoner clearly irritated him.

'If you refuse to disclose the places where you have

stayed and the persons with whom you have been in contact, then we must presume you have conspired to do mischief to the State.'

'Not so.'

'I told you so,' the young nobleman shouted, rising again to his feet and overturning his chair. 'I knew he would not reveal any names. We're wasting our time here!' He swayed as if drunk, gesturing vigorously and cast a threatening look at the commissioner. 'Traitors must not be allowed to dictate to the Queen's commissioners,' he snarled.

For a few seconds the commissioner scrutinised John without speaking.

'If you will not answer,' he said at last, leaning forward and spreading his hands on the table before him, 'then you leave us no choice. We will have to force you to answer.'

# CHAPTER 25

THE SQUALID, COBBLED streets of Southwark seemed busier than usual as the late afternoon sun dipped below the tenements. The taverns, gambling dens and stews were crowded with the usual drunks, gamblers and pleasure seekers who haunted this lawless district south of the river. The all-pervading stench from the rotting filth was enough to make any man throw up his gorge.

Thomas looked neither left nor right as he staggered by a group of ragged, grubby men spilling out from The Antelope. 'There goes an eager one! I bet he's out for a taste of some pretty young drab!' cried one of them.

'No! By the look of 'im, 'ee's out for a fight, I'll wager,' shouted another.

'No! He's a stranger to these parts. Make no mistake, there goes a lost soul if ever I saw one,' cried a third, less drunk than his companions.

But Thomas was oblivious to their drunken heckling. His muddled thoughts were far away, stirred up by the hopelessness of the situation. Earlier that same morning, he had left Sir Francis Walsingham's office in Cheapside in a state of despair and had gone into the city. There he had crawled from one tavern to another, becoming more inebriated as he went, hoping to drown his fears and his guilt. Later, he had crossed London Bridge and passed under the Great Stone Gate where the severed heads of traitors were displayed on spikes; a gruesome warning that the same fate awaited anyone who challenged the authority of those in power.

The stench of decay filled his nostrils and made him nauseous. With his heart thumping against his ribs, he hurried from the bridge, turning right past the church of St Mary Overies and Winchester House, and on past the Clink prison. Here he paused and looked down at the dirty, bony hands of the debtors reaching out through the bars from their underground cells. The prisoners relied on their families or kindly well-wishers for their food. Regretting that he did not possess so much as an apple or a scrap of bread, Thomas lowered his head and stumbled past. Now, without quite knowing how or why, he found himself wandering bleary-eyed down yet more foul and hazardous alleys towards Bankside, going over his visit to Cheapside again and again.

'Your brother, Father John Rufford, is under close confinement in the Tower, where he is being interrogated further. He is not permitted any visits,' Walsingham's clerk had told him. 'And as for his scheming accomplice, Lady Molynieux, she has been transferred to the Gatehouse in Westminster where she awaits trial.'

When Thomas pursued the matter, demanding an audience with Walsingham, the clerk's expression became apprehensive. With downcast eyes, he said that Sir Francis was gravely ill and unable to see anyone. 'Even the Queen fears for her Old Moor's state of health. You can take the matter up with Sir Robert Cecil if you think it will do any good.'

'That crooked man!' The words rang out again in Thomas's mind. He knew that Lord Burghley's son had been Walsingham's protégé for some time; he would never entertain a petition on behalf of one of the Jesuit Order – that 'generation of vipers' as he regarded them. To Thomas, it seemed his brother's situation was no better than those of the debtors in the Clink.

Thomas turned down a shadowy alleyway. Presently he reached the river and stood at its edge, staring vacantly down into its dark, turbulent waters. He was afraid. He wanted to let himself fall. He had always believed that John was protected by divine providence, that he would never be captured; had God suddenly deserted him? And of course, his own guilt was ever-present. He had imagined that he would be there to help his brother in his time of need, to fight their enemies – but that's not how it had happened. There was no glorious struggle, only the betrayal by a trusted servant who Thomas himself had inadvertently shown the way, as if he had been one of Walsingham's most reliable intelligencers.

And of course, he could not forget kind-hearted Lady Molyneux. What harm had she ever done? Was there to be no end to their sufferings? What was he to do now? The situation seemed hopeless; the more isolated Thomas felt, the more he despaired. Perhaps, this time the game was up.

Suddenly the sound of oars splashing on the water intruded upon his anguish. Excited voices grew louder and drifted across to where he was standing. A wherry was arriving at the water steps a short distance up river filled with revellers in search of solace in the shadowy world of Bankside. The boat lurched dangerously as, one by one, its passengers scrambled ashore. Their laughter grew even louder as one of them fell on the slippery steps.

'Stupid, blind fools! What have they got to laugh about?' Thomas thought indignantly. 'How can they carry on in such a manner, without heed for the misery that surrounds them? They care only for one thing – as much pleasure as they can find!' He turned away in disgust but curiosity overcame him and he glanced back as the last passenger disembarked onto the steps. The short, corpulent figure lumbered ashore, carelessly throwing the boatman his fare. The boatman doffed his hat begrudgingly at the pitiful recompense for such back-breaking work.

The rotund dignitary reached the top of the steps. He adjusted his violet-coloured doublet and breeches and placed a large feathered hat over his thinning hair then set off briskly, keen to catch up with his fellow passengers who were already heading towards the nearby bear garden. He had gone no more than half a dozen paces when he stopped abruptly, suddenly aware that he was being stared at. He turned slowly and looked across at the solitary figure standing at the water's edge; at the moment of recognition, a sickly smile crept over his face.

Thomas sobered up in an instant. This man was no stranger, no dignitary. 'You!' he exclaimed, recognising the steward from Broad Oaks. 'You have the temerity to come here ... to laugh and be merry after what you've done! You are the cause of all our troubles.'

Consumed with hatred, shaking with fury, Thomas strode menacingly towards the steward. Swaggering, the steward confronted him, positioning himself with his back to the river. 'Think! Do not act unwisely, Thomas Rufford, for I am protected more than you realise.'

Thomas halted just a few feet away. He thought he detected slight nervousness beneath the steward's blustering. 'You make me sick, with your fine, new clothes,' he cried. 'How could you betray your friends? Your mistress? At Broad Oaks, you were treated not as a servant but as a member of the family. Lady Molynieux showed you nothing but kindness and generosity.'

'I am now in the service of Sir Robert Cecil, the future Secretary of State,' the steward said, with a slight tremor of his lower jaw. 'And Lady Molynieux should have known better than to continue in the way she did.'

'Have you no care for what happens to her?'

'I care only for myself!' the steward snapped. For the first time, there was an irritable note in his voice. 'She thought only of her precious traitor priests. It was they who benefitted from her substantial wealth; I received nothing from her. She brings this terrible weight to bear upon herself by her own actions.' He paused, gathering himself. 'And I've heard rumour that she showed personal favour to many of them, including your lecherous brother!'

The words had scarcely been uttered when Thomas drew his sword and made a furious lunge at him, stabbing him in the chest. The steward collapsed in a heap but it was more from shock, for the wound was superficial.

Thomas hovered above him, pinning him to the earth with the point of his sword. 'I swear I could kill you right here and now,' he growled.

The steward closed his eyes and swallowed. 'Do that and your whole family will perish. Your brother's life already hangs from Topcliffe's manacles in the Tower, and as we speak the safe haven that was Broad Oaks is being plundered once more. Robbed and ransacked. Desecrated by the Queen's own command. Not so impenetrable after all!'

'Jane!' A look of horror flashed across Thomas's face. Although she had pleaded with him to let her come to London he had stubbornly refused, insisting that she must stay behind at Broad Oaks. What menace had he exposed her to?

'You would add to your crime should you neglect your virtuous sister,' scoffed the steward, observing Thomas's fearful expression with sadistic amusement. 'You should return to Broad Oaks with all speed and rescue her.'

'I should strike you a blow that would rid all England of the dark, evil shadow you faithless heretics cast upon her,' said Thomas.

'But that would only hasten your own self-destruction,' replied the steward, gaining confidence.

Thomas was about to speak when he was distracted by the sound of bawdy songs intermingled with raucous laughter. He glanced over his shoulder and saw the same three drunks he had passed outside The Antelope staggering towards him.

As they grew nearer, their discordant singing faltered.

'Hey! What are you about?' cried one of them.

'It's 'im again! I said 'ee was looking for trouble!' slurred another.

'Help me! This man's a papist traitor!' the steward shouted.

Thomas shot a hateful glance at his smiling face. 'You stinking coward!' He plunged his sword into the traitor's stomach. 'My brother is revenged!'

The steward desperately sucked in a mouthful of cold air, his lips quivering. Struggling to muster his draining strength, he strained to lift his head but it fell back helplessly. The glint in his eyes faded.

For a few moments, Thomas straddled his victim like a conquering warrior. He stared down at the lifeless body beneath him. Then he staggered backwards, his face ashen. Hot and nauseous, he stared at the glistening blood on his sword. With trembling hands, he wiped the blade against his breeches. He looked up at the three dumbfounded spectators. Slowly and deliberately, with his eyes still fixed on them, he retreated past the water steps and turned into the narrow alleyway which led away from the river.

Thomas hurried along the alley. Occasionally he glanced back but no-one was following him. After only a short way, the passage opened out onto a muddy field; the bear pit, an eight-sided, roofless, wooden amphitheatre loomed up before him, a temple of death where half-starved dogs were unleashed against chained bears. A crowd of excited men and women were gathered outside, barring his way and he had to elbow his way through. The roars of the spectators combined with the baying of the frenzied dogs made him shudder. He had to get away from this terrible place as quickly as possible.

He rubbed his sweating forehead. He shut his eyes but immediately saw the mocking smile of the steward and the insolent, cruel eyes of Richard Topcliffe staring back at him. He imagined his brother in the Tower and then his sister at Broad Oaks, and suddenly he felt ashamed. His reckless desires had been too powerful to resist. He must return to Broad Oaks at once.

He ran from the crowds of Bear Alley, keeping to the southern fringes of Southwark. After a short while, he reached the main road from Sussex to London where he turned north again. Finally, working his way up Long Southwark towards the bridge, he stopped at a horse trough and washed his face and hands. His distorted countenance reflected in the dirty water. His throat was parched. The beer had suddenly turned bitter, leaving an unpleasant taste, and his head ached. He must cross to the other side of the river.

He hurried under the Great Stone Gate and back across the narrow roadway of London Bridge and into the city then followed the side streets before turning right into Fenchurch Street. His horse was stabled at the Boar's Head Inn just beyond Aldgate; if he rode all through the night, he could be at Broad Oaks by late morning.

# CHAPTER 26

JANE ENTERED THE chapel at Broad Oaks. She was alone and though it was not cold, she was shivering, her hair dishevelled and untidy, her clothes disorderly. She clutched a small, broken statue of the Virgin which she placed on the altar table in front of her. The Virgin's face had been mutilated and the arms of the statue were missing, smashed during the previous day's violence. As she knelt before the altar she crossed herself with a shaking, unsteady hand. But Jane did not see the desecration. She was looking inwards, searching deep within herself for an answer.

Several maids glanced in at her as they passed the open door but none entered. Each of the maids' faces displayed the same subdued expression. Despondency permeated the house; though everyone knew what had happened, no-one mentioned it. Every now and then one of the younger maids burst into tears, before being ushered away gently by an older servant to some quiet corner.

Outside, though it was nearing the end of March, winter seemed reluctant to release its grip, unleashing a final assault of howling winds and squalls of snow. In the Great Hall, the principal usher was in hushed conversation with an elderly servant who had just come downstairs carrying a tray still laden with food. Bread, meats, cakes and a glass of wine, all of it untouched.

'But she would not take it!' the distraught servant said.

Suddenly, the main door was thrown open by a strong gust of wind which swirled around the Hall, making the heavy velvet curtain across the main window billow wildly. Plates toppled off the sideboard and the tallow candles on the newel posts of the great staircase guttered and were snuffed out. The servant fumbled his grip on the pewter tray, sending it crashing to the floor. The principal usher shuddered and went over to the door which had been fastened only by the latch; the oak crossbar which would normally have been in place lay splintered to one side.

'There's someone approaching!' he said, holding the door but not closing it. 'I think – yes, it is! It's Master Thomas!'

Jane, still kneeling before the broken statue, had begun to read from a small leather-bound prayer book. Her lips moved feverishly but the unspoken words failed to bring her any comfort. Pausing, she lifted her head, listening to the disturbance downstairs.

Then, above the din, she heard a loud, urgent voice. 'Jane! Where is she? Where's my sister?'

Jane instantly recognised the familiar voice. She felt a rush of relief and anxiety. She had barely risen to her feet as her brother appeared in the doorway.

After more than twelve hours in the saddle, Thomas was exhausted. His face was grimy, his breeches and boots caked with mud. For what seemed like an age, they stared at each other, neither of them speaking.

Thomas removed his cloak and stepped a little closer. 'My dear, sweet sister, what has happened to you?' he said.

The memory of Jane's ordeal was written on her sad face. 'Help me!' her eyes seemed to say.

'They say God is merciful and good ... but I fear my faith is weak,' she said in a voice that was barely above a whisper and sapped of emotion. She glanced past Thomas at two chambermaids who had crept warily into the room, pausing just inside the door.

'In their eyes, and mine own, I am disgraced,' she went on coldly. 'My life is shamed and I pray that I may never see the light of day again.'

'No! Please, no!' Thomas longed to take away her pain and suffering, but some unknown fear held him back.

Jane sensed her brother's hesitation. 'Poor Thomas!' she whispered. 'How can you possibly understand?' Her voice started to quiver and her eyes glistened with tears. 'Topcliffe ... he was too strong and I was too weak.' She broke off.

'Topcliffe!' Thomas screamed, hurling his cloak across the room. 'He is the devil incarnate! Why, he even carries a warrant for his shameful lust!' He began to pace up and down the room. 'Where is he now?'

'Returned to London, Master Thomas,' interceded one of the maids, stepping forward timidly. 'They stayed but a few hours.'

Thomas sighed heavily and glanced at his sister. 'He is like a gorged hawk which has satisfied his appetite and then flies away to his nest, back to his mistress.' He spat out the words. 'I'll kill him! I will pursue him without rest and avenge the wrong he has done you.'

Jane's tears began rolling down her cheeks. 'Thomas, I beg of you. Do not seek revenge for my sake. That will not erase his loathsome crime only serve you greater ill.'

'But he has violated your honour! He is guilty of the most hideous of crimes! Let him die! And all those like him!'

Not realising his strength, Thomas grabbed his sister's arm. Jane grimaced and tried to pull away. Thomas held tight and drew her closer. He pulled up her crimson sleeve and saw the lacerations on her forearm and wrist.

His eyes met Jane's and filled with tears. 'I am so sorry, Jane,' he sighed. 'Please forgive me. I am the one who should be punished. It is I who should be ashamed.'

'The scars I bear will remain with me forever' Jane said, quickly covering her arm again and lowering her eyes. There was a quiet despair in her voice that disturbed Thomas and he was overwhelmed with pity, tenderness and love for his sister.

'Jane, I cannot begin to understand the torment you are suffering. Is there any relief I can bring?'

'Let us weep together. Perhaps that will help to wash away the stain,' Jane said, and fell helplessly into her brother's arms.

† 

In the days and weeks that followed, melancholy pervaded Broad Oaks. Jane wandered listlessly from room to room; at night she cried herself to sleep.

Though Thomas tried to comfort her, share her pain, his pity seemed only to aggravate her misery.

Thomas spent hours alone in the Great Hall, meditating. He was irritable and impatient, often losing his temper with the servants if they disturbed him. He thought about his sister and Lady Molynieux and agonised over John. Guilt weighed heavily on his conscience. His killing of the steward sickened him. The feelings of excitement and inspiration he had experienced at Long Melford, Rowington and St Winefred's had passed. The day he had set out from Broad Oaks with his brother, with such eager readiness to discover some divine truth, had become a distant memory.

# CHAPTER 27

FOLLOWING HIS INITIAL interrogation at the house in the Strand, John Rufford was led away to the Tower of London. There the soldiers handed him over to the governor, a tall, distinguished man, bearing the title of Queen's Lieutenant. After a brief introduction, John was taken to the Salt Tower at the south-east corner of the inner ward, handed over to a warder and assigned a small, cramped room on the first floor.

Entering his cell, John was immediately hit by the pungent smell of urine. He blinked his eyes several times and, as they grew more accustomed to the gloomy interior, observed that the room was completely bare.

'Am I to be denied a bed? Where am I to sleep?' he inquired.

The warder rolled his eyes. 'Bless you, sir, there are no beds for prisoners in the Tower.'

John stared despairingly at the cold stone floor. The warder, seeing the injured expression on his prisoner's face, disappeared through the low doorway and returned moments later clutching a bundle of straw.

'It's not much, I'm afraid, but at least it will ward off the cold,' he said cheerfully, spreading it carefully on the floor. 'I will fetch you a bed if any of your friends are willing to provide one,' he offered, straightening up and brushing some loose straw from his breeches. 'Or some more clothes, perhaps?'

John was aware of the powerful odour of sweat emanating from the warder as he moved nearer and studied him more closely. Though the offer to help could easily have been a trap to entice John to reveal the names and whereabouts of his friends, the warder had a sympathetic look in his eyes. There was no hint of malice. 'May I know your name, gaoler?'

'Bennet, Sir!'

'Then God bless you, Master Bennet. I am most grateful for the straw but a bed is a luxury I cannot afford!' John said.

Reaching into his pocket, he gave the warder a groat for his troubles. The warder smiled his thanks. 'As you please, sir!' he said and turned and left, securing the door with bolts and a great iron bar.

The cell was cold and dark, the only available light seeping in from a tiny window which overlooked the moat. John crossed to what had previously been another window but which was now blocked up. The names of all the orders of the angels, from the Seraphim and Cherubim, through to the Archangels and Angels, were scribbled in chalk on its stone surrounds. He crossed himself and wondered who had been the previous occupant: another martyr to the faith perhaps.

Removing his leather belt and using the sharp, pointed edge of the buckle, John began painstakingly chiselling the initials 'IHS' into the stonework. Above these, he added 'Ad Majorem Dei Gloriam'.

He bowed his head, commended his soul to God,

prayed to the Blessed Virgin and lay down to sleep on the bed of straw.

† 

John had expected to be brought for interrogation immediately after being imprisoned in the Tower but to his surprise he was left undisturbed for more than a week. Grateful for these few days of solitude, he drew consolation from his meditations and spiritual exercises. With bribes and a little coaxing, he persuaded the warder to provide him with a few books and some candles by which to read them.

One morning during the second week of his confinement, he heard the almost welcome sound of the warder's footsteps climbing the stairs up to his cell. Presently, a light appeared under his door. The heavy iron bar was removed, the bolts drawn and the door was pushed open.

'I am ordered to bring you at once to the Lieutenant's lodgings, to sit before the Lords Commissioners,' announced the warder gravely. He wiped his forehead, smearing dirt across his perspiring brow.

'What time is it?' asked John, rising to his feet and straightening the Jesuit cassock which he had reverted to wearing.

'Nearly eight o'clock, Sir.'

'So I am sent for at last!' John adjusted the rope cincture around his waist and stepped forward. 'And who are my inquisitors?'

'The Lieutenant of the Tower, the Queen's Attorney-General and the secretary of the Privy Council.'

CHAPTER 27

'Then I should consider myself honoured!'

†

The warder knocked loudly at the door and, without waiting for a reply, showed John into a spacious, brightly-lit room. Three gentlemen, dressed in court robes, were sitting at a table. In the middle sat the Lieutenant of the Tower, whom John had already met. On his right sat the Queen's Attorney-General, his long face framed by his high, starched white ruff and a sheet of rolled up parchment in his small, leather-gloved hands. On the other side, sat the secretary of the Privy Council, a man in his fifties, with a wizened face and dark, distrustful eyes.

It was he who spoke first. 'We have brought you here in order that you may clarify certain matters for us.' He leaned forward, scratching his coarse whiskers, peering at John. 'We have a friend of yours in the next room. Perhaps you would care to renew acquaintances?' A playful smile crossed his lips. He beckoned the warder standing at the door. 'Show our guest in.'

The door opened and a figure appeared on the threshold. 'Come, come,' said the secretary, perceiving the visitor's hesitation.

John turned around, not certain if it was another trick. Immediately his eyes widened. Lady Molynieux, advanced slowly into the room. Everyone was silent as they watched her laboured movements. Her eyes were dark from lack of sleep. With incredible self-control, she stifled any hint of recognition that would betray them both.

'I think there is no need for introductions,' said the secretary. He paused deliberately, waiting for the laughter of his fellow inquisitors.

Lady Molynieux began to speak, cautiously at first then growing bolder. 'Is this the man you told me about? But I do not know him, Master Secretary. I'm afraid you have been misinformed and have wasted everybody's time.' Her eyes narrowed a little as she peered at John. 'Though undoubtedly, he does have the look of a priest.'

She genuflected. John bowed to her in acknowledgement but remained silent.

'What pretence!' cried the secretary. He stirred uneasily in his chair. 'Come, priest, confess to knowing this woman. Admit that Lady Molynieux has offered you the security of her home at Broad Oaks on several occasions.'

'But I do not recognise her,' John replied. 'And you should understand how I always answer questions like this. I never mention by name any place or person whom, unlike this Lady, I may happen to know.'

'You try our patience!'

'And you try mine!' retorted John. 'You should not insult me with your contemptible tricks.'

'Such impudence!' The secretary's face turned a violent red. 'Take her away! Let us not waste any more time with this creature.' He jerked his head in Lady Molynieux's direction then leaned back in his chair to ponder his next move.

John glanced at Lady Molynieux. To him, her face appeared more beautiful and serene, the eyes more defiant. 'May our Lord, Jesus Christ and His most holy

Mother watch over you,' he said softly, making the sign of the cross.

As the warder escorted her from the room, Lady Molynieux held herself upright.

'Now, let us get down to the serious business. You have recently received a packet of letters from your fellow priests in the Low Countries, have you not?'

John turned to face his new inquisitor, the Attorney General. He was looking not at John, but at the parchment he was holding in his hands. 'I deduce from your silence that you have,' he went on. 'And what did these letters contain?'

Again, John made no answer.

The Attorney General persisted. 'We understand that they have come out of Spain and contain correspondence between several in your society relating to matters of state.'

'I read but one or two of them and they were concerned solely with the financial assistance of Catholics abroad. We have nothing to do with politics,' John protested.

The Attorney General raised his eyes. 'And what has become of the letters now?' he asked.

'Burnt them, I think,' replied John.

'Burnt them,' repeated the Attorney General meditatively.

'Oh, come now,' roared the secretary of the Privy Council, thumping his fist on the table. 'Did you not forward them to your Superior, Father Henry Garnet?'

John flushed guiltily. 'I forget,' he stammered. Behind his back, he clenched his hands. He must not allow himself to falter. 'The burden of proof lies with you and you have no evidence with which to condemn me.'

The secretary threw his hands in the air.

'You say you have no wish to obstruct Her Majesty's Government,' interrupted the Attorney General leaning forward over the table. 'Tell us, then, where Father Garnet is. He is an enemy of the state and you are obliged to report on all such men.' He fixed John with a penetrating stare.

'He is not an enemy of the state,' John replied indignantly. 'On the contrary, I am certain that if he were given the opportunity to lay down his life for his Queen and country, he would gladly do so. I do not know where he lives, and if I did, I would not tell you.'

'Then we'll see to it that you tell us before we leave this place,' cried the secretary. He snatched the parchment from the Attorney General's grasp and thrust it at John.

John tentatively began to read:

*'If you shall find him obstinate, undutiful or unwilling to declare and reveal the truth, you shall cause him to be put to the manacles and other such torture.'*

A chill ran down his back; it was a warrant for his torture. He looked up at the faces of the men sitting before him. The Lieutenant of the Tower had remained silent the whole time; his expression betrayed dismay and conflict. Under John's searching look, he quickly averted his gaze. The Attorney General and the secretary of the Privy Council, however, stared resolutely back at him.

John summoned all his courage. 'With God's help I shall never do anything that is unjust or act against my conscience or the Catholic faith. You have me in your power. You can do with me what God allows you to do – more you cannot do.'

# CHAPTER 28

John was conducted from the Lieutenant's lodgings, via a cold, dank underground passage to the vaults beneath the White Tower. The warder, carrying a lighted candle, seemed restless and uneasy, and tried to hurry along the solemn procession as though he wanted to be done with a necessary but unpleasant task. Presently, they entered a vast, dark chamber. It was warm and there was a strong odour of sweat and urine. As John's eyes adjusted to the darkness, he glimpsed a figure in the shadows hunched over a desk at the far end of the room. The man was sorting through various devices and instruments of torture, almost as if he were caressing them.

The warder approached the solitary figure, shuffling his feet across the stone floor as he went. The two guards, one tall and thin, the other a dark, dishevelled, muscular fellow with a flat nose, nudged John towards the middle of the room.

'By order of the Queen and Privy Council, I hand this man over to you!' the warder announced in a trembling voice, handing over the piece of parchment. He looked as if he wanted no part in what was to follow. He turned round, shot a pitying glance at John and departed.

Without looking at it, the tall, ominous figure placed the parchment on the desk. Raising himself to his full height, he turned around to face his prisoner. 'Father John Rufford. We meet at last! My name is Richard Topcliffe...' He spoke slowly, articulating every syllable.

'I know who you are,' John interrupted. 'You are a veteran in evil. The devil himself has devoured you!'

Topcliffe's face was impassive. 'Come, Father Rufford. Why not admit the truth and answer our questions? It will save you so much trouble.'

'I cannot,' replied John, and fell to his knees, his hands clasped together in prayer.

At Topcliffe's command, the two guards dragged John across the floor to a pillar, one of several wooden posts which supported the roof. His wrists were forced into a pair of iron gauntlets and he was ordered to climb some wicker steps. His arms were lifted up and an iron bar passed through the rings of one gauntlet, through an iron staple which had been driven into the top of the wooden post and then through the rings of the second gauntlet.

With a sadistic smile on his face, Topcliffe kicked away the steps and John was left hanging by his hands and arms. 'Now will you confess?'

'I cannot and I will not.' John could barely utter the words such was the excruciating, unbearable pain he felt. Blood rushed into his arms and hands and he could already feel his flesh swelling above the irons.

'Then I will take my leave of you,' Topcliffe said coldly. 'I will return only when your body has become so weak and your hands so swollen that you will beg to be let down.'

The two guards kept close watch over him. Every now and then, to alleviate their boredom, they tormented him. 'You know if you keep this up, you will be a cripple all your life,' said the tall, thin one.

'That is, if you live,' sneered the other.

'Topcliffe is the master of torture and he has not finished with you yet. You will be hanged from these manacles every day until you confess.'

Their voices droned on and on as they persisted with their taunts throughout the morning but John remained steadfast, refusing to take the bait. Then sometime after one o'clock, with his whole body drenched in perspiration, he succumbed to the pain and fell unconscious.

The two guards leapt into action, as though carrying out a drill they had practised many times before. While one supported the weight of John's body, the other quickly slid the wicker steps under his feet. After a few minutes John came round but, as soon as did so, the two guards immediately let him hang again. This routine was repeated again and again, every time John fainted, which was some eight or nine times during the course of the day.

Finally, just before the Tower bell rang at five o'clock, Topcliffe returned and consulted with the two guards. After a few moments he went over to John, a wide smile playing on his lips. Prowling around the limp body hanging before him, he launched straight into another attack.

'Are you ready now to obey the Queen and her Council?'

John's eyelids flickered open. 'I have nothing to say,'

he replied hoarsely.

Topcliffe reflected for a moment. 'I am returned directly from the Queen and her Secretary. They say they know for certain that Garnet meddles in politics and is a danger to the state. And this the Queen asserts on the word of a Sovereign, and the Master Secretary on his honour. So unless you choose to contradict them both, you must agree to hand him over.'

John closed his eyes again. 'Clearly, they do not know the man.'

'Come,' retorted Topcliffe, his face only inches away from John's. 'Why not admit the truth and answer our questions?'

'I cannot and will not,' John whispered.

Topcliffe flew into a rage. 'Then hang there until you rot off the pillar!' he screamed. Reaching the doorway, he stopped and glanced back. 'I will see that you get your martyrdom, priest! Then he slammed the door shut behind him.

# CHAPTER 29

IT HAD BEEN six months since Thomas's return to Broad Oaks. Somehow, amidst all the turmoil and uncertainty, all the pain and suffering, the necessities of everyday life continued, as they inevitably must. Each new day came with its hustle and bustle, as servants and maids busied themselves with their routine chores.

Nevertheless, it was a strange normality; life had changed in many ways for both Thomas and Jane. Recently they had taken to sitting together in the same room, often without saying a word, Jane reading from the scriptures while Thomas reflected on what had happened. Neither spoke of the future or what it might hold.

The sun was particularly strong this morning and its bright light filled the small study. Jane looked up from her book and glanced at her brother. 'I do not wish to be a burden or a hindrance to anyone anymore,' she announced. 'So, I've come to a decision. I will go abroad, to the convent at Louvain.'

'To the convent at Louvain!' Thomas repeated, surprised.

'Yes. I will devote the rest of my life to God. Only He can take away my pain and heal my wounds.'

Thomas knelt before his sister and held her hands. His eyes searched hers as if trying to discover the secrets of her soul. His face was calm and his voice gentle. 'When God calls, it must be a wondrous, marvellous thing. You are indeed most blessed. I wish nothing but good for you but you are still young, you have your whole life before you. Think what you are doing. Sister, I love you dearly; be careful you do not do this for the wrong reasons. You are unhappy and there are painful memories for you here at Broad Oaks. Perhaps it would be better if you return home to Mythe Hall and discuss the matter with Mother and Father.'

'You don't understand!' exclaimed Jane with a flash of temper. 'My life is over. I cannot love or be loved again, so it is better I go.' Her voice cracked with emotion and her body began to tremble. Thomas looked tenderly at her.

At that moment, there was an abrupt knock on the door and a maid came in. She paused when she saw Thomas kneeling before his sister and Jane's face streaked with tears.

'Beg your pardon,' she said.

Thomas sighed heavily and rose to his feet. 'What is it?'

'If you please, Master Rufford,' the maid whispered hesitantly. 'A man told me to give you this.' She handed Thomas a letter. 'The gentleman is in the Great Hall and awaits your response.'

But Thomas scarcely heard her because as he broke the seal of the letter, something fell to the floor. He stooped to pick it up. Orange peel, crudely cut into small crosses and stitched together in pairs had been strung onto a thin silk thread to make a rosary. He looked at the opened letter.

'Sweet Jesu!' he cried. 'It's from John.' Holding the delicate rosary in one hand, he started to read aloud.

*'My dear brother and sister in Christ, it is through the goodness of Almighty God and the benevolence of my trusted friend the warder that I am able to write you a few short lines. It would bring me great consolation to receive your correspondence by return. Be reassured that I am well. My room is comfortable and the food is plentiful and good, though I would be indebted to you if you would send something for the warder's troubles, for he has shown me great consideration. He is particularly fond of oranges. I confess that I find it hard to accept my confinement but we each of us have our cross to bear. No-one is free from suffering, from sorrow, not the Pope nor the Queen, so I pray each day and I beg for your prayers too. We cannot hope to understand the glorious mysteries of God, but we must not despair. And we must not let our hearts be filled with hate for those who hurt us, for hate never yet dispelled hate; only love can dispel hate. Remember, love is a holy, holy, holy thing and in the end, love will redeem us.'*

At the foot of the page, under the closing lines, *'Now, I must bid you farewell till we meet again. God's most humble and obedient servant,'* John had scribbled his signature.

Jane wiped away her tears. Her face was transformed. Jumping up, she instructed the maid to invite the bearer of the letter into the study.

'We must write to John at once,' she said to Thomas.

'Yes ... yes, we must,' murmured Thomas. He stared after the maid. 'Yes, and bring some wine too!' he called, as she hurried from the room.

As they waited to meet the guest who had brought them such unexpected news, Thomas's attention returned to the letter and the rosary. Handling the precious object with great reverence and glancing repeatedly at the letter, he grew more pensive, more curious. The handwriting, he thought, was more like that of a young child who was still mastering the skill, with untidy, oversized letters and large gaps between the lines. His brother's hand was normally so neat and precise.

The maid returned a few minutes later, flushed and smiling flirtatiously at the handsome young man standing beside her. She curtsied and hastily disappeared again, this time to fetch the wine.

'Sir, you are indeed most welcome. Please, you will take a drink with us,' said Thomas. 'I am Thomas Rufford and this is my sister, Jane. Pray tell me, my friend, whom do we thank for delivering such welcome news?'

The stranger was tall, elegant, about twenty-five years of age; he wore fashionable clothes and at his side he wore both dagger and sword. 'My name is Henry Giffard,' he said, bowing courteously and removing the gold-laced cape from his shoulders, revealing a red silk doublet. 'I am a soldier and a gentleman, the son of Sir Richard Giffard, Lieutenant of the Tower.'

'The Lieutenant of the Tower!' exclaimed Thomas.

His mood changed instantly. 'Is this some kind of cruel jest? He is responsible for our brother's continuing imprisonment.'

'My father is a devoted and loyal subject who regards the high position he holds as an honour; he is proud to serve both the Queen and the country he loves,' Giffard retorted. He looked from Thomas to Jane and saw the hurt and sadness in their eyes. 'But his loyalty does not blind him to the sins perpetrated in the State's name. And I should have said the *former* Lieutenant, for as soon as he settles his affairs at the Tower, he will resign his office.' He lowered his head. 'He no longer wishes to be used as an instrument in the torture of innocent men.'

Thomas stared at him. 'Torture?' he repeated. 'Are you saying our brother has been tortured? But there is no mention of it in his letter.'

'Sir,' replied Giffard, without raising his eyes. 'I regret that the order was given to put your brother to the manacles.'

Thomas looked again at the childlike handwriting. Of course, he thought, such brutal treatment would have affected John's ability to use his hands, let alone to hold a pen and write. He closed his eyes and sighed. Bringing the letter up to his lips, he kissed it gently. As he did, he thought he detected the faint smell of oranges. He placed both the letter and the rosary on the table.

'Afterwards, when my father went to visit your brother in his cell,' Giffard continued, 'he was so moved with pity and compassion that he immediately instructed the warder to do whatever he could to ease his suffering.'

'Your father was not present at my brother's torture?' Jane inquired.

'No.'

'He may not have been present in the torture chamber,' Thomas said abruptly, 'but in standing aside in silence, I consider him equally guilty.' His face distorted with fury, he seized Giffard by the collar and began shaking him from side to side.

Giffard rocked back on his heels but he offered no resistance to Thomas's violent assault. Jane pulled her brother away.

'Master Giffard,' she began breathlessly. 'I believe your father to be a good, honourable man, for it takes great bravery to act upon one's conscience in the face of such pressure. And in your actions, you too have shown great courage.'

Giffard read the pain in her sad eyes and was deeply moved. 'You are very kind Mistress Rufford,' he said, 'but it is your brother who should be commended for his bravery. For in spite of his suffering, they have not been able to wrench a single word out of him that would incriminate his friends. I confess I am in awe at the self-sacrifice and courage of men and women who persevere with their beliefs against all the odds.'

'You have sympathies for the old faith, then?' Thomas asked, rubbing his face with his hands to try and disguise the embarrassment he felt at his vehement outburst.

'On the contrary, Master Rufford. I stand by the new teachings,' replied Giffard. He faced Thomas and they stared at one another for several moments. When Giffard spoke again, his voice was low and his tone reflective. 'Master Rufford, I am recently returned from three years in the Low Countries. I am saddened to find such a chasm in our great country. I was a witness to much cruelty and death in Flanders – on both sides. And to what end? It only bred more hatred, more suffering. It is my sincere hope that every man should be able to choose his religion, without fear of violence. I pray for greater tolerance. Only then will we be reconciled with one other. Only then will our country be at peace and its subjects free to laugh and sing together.'

'If only it were so!' said Thomas. 'But I fear there are many who do not share your hopes and perhaps never will.'

'I agree but that should not prevent us from doing what our conscience tells us is right. It matters not that you are of the old and I of the new; it is what you feel in your heart and soul that truly matters.'

'You speak of tolerance, sir, but how can we stomach the depravity of men such as Richard Topcliffe and that abuse which forces innocents to flee abroad for sanctuary.' He went to his sister and kissed her gently on the forehead.

Jane lowered her eyes. She sat down and picked up John's letter from the table.

'... *hate never yet dispelled hate, only love can dispel hate.*' She gazed at her brother, her eyes glistening with tears.

Thomas fell forward, burying his face in his sister's hair. The close friendship that had always existed between them, which had been absent for the past weeks, had returned.

'If you will grant me leave, Mistress Rufford, so that

I may speak my mind,' Giffard said, his voice shaking. 'I have heard Topcliffe's vile boasting and I am truly sorry for what has happened. His abominable offence is now made public and he will have to answer for it. But you, Mistress Rufford, are a most remarkable woman. Do not run away; do not hide yourself away from the world.' As he spoke, he took Jane's hand and squeezed it gently. 'I beg of you, look upon me as your friend. If you will allow, I will visit again. If I can help in any way, if you feel the need to talk to someone – please, let it be me. If you did, it would surely bring happiness into the heart of this unworthy nobleman.' He brought her hand to his lips and kissed it.

Jane was startled by this unexpected demonstration of feeling and she flushed with pleasure. She tried to mask her emotions but she was aware of a joyful feeling within, of life and love returning to her heart.

The maid re-appeared, bringing the wine and some cups, but no-one noticed her. Thomas took Giffard by the elbow. 'You have spoken sincerely, Master Giffard, and I am pleased. My sister is indeed a rare treasure and we are most grateful for your kindness. We insist that you rest here before returning to London with our reply.' He poured a little wine into the three cups. 'Please forgive my misunderstanding,' he went on, clearing his throat. 'I have grown so accustomed to the lies and greed of those stewed in corruption that I had forgotten that some people still retain their honesty and integrity.'

The letter from his brother, his sister's courage, Giffard's capacity to understand and his talk of tolerance and reconciliation; these had brought renewed hope to Thomas. Without realising it, his faith had been rekindled.

†

The rest of day passed quickly and Thomas was conscious of the growing friendship between Henry Giffard and his sister. It was not until two o'clock in the morning that they retired to their beds.

On the way to his room, Thomas paused at the chapel. He entered and closed the door softly behind him. He placed a lit candle on the table in front of him, next to the broken statue of the Virgin, then dropped to his knees.

'Teach me what to do; show me how to live my life…' he prayed, lifting his eyes towards heaven. 'I humbly submit myself to thy will, O Lord.' He prayed for those he loved: his father and mother, his brother and his sister. He prayed for Lady Molynieux and all those friends he had met during the struggle of the past few years, and he prayed for the souls of those who had died. And, with a calmness and sincerity which was a revelation to him, he prayed for his enemies and those people who hated him. He prayed for those in high office who drafted the many cruel laws against Catholics and for those who carried out such orders. He prayed for the pursuivants and the spies and the gaolers. He even prayed for Richard Topcliffe. With tears of remorse, he recalled killing the steward and asked God to forgive him and have mercy on his soul. Thomas prayed with all his soul that he would be strengthened by faith and hope and love.

## CHAPTER 29

He spent more than an hour in the chapel, praying and meditating, before eventually returning to his room. He sat on the edge of the bed and removed John's letter from his pocket, tilting it over the flickering candle on the bedside table. As he began re-reading it, his jaw dropped and his tired, bloodshot eyes widened in disbelief.

# CHAPTER 30

Unwittingly, Thomas had stumbled upon the device used by Jesuit priests and Catholics interned in the many London prisons to send secret or coded messages to their friends on the outside using 'invisible' orange juice. Their writings would only appear on the paper when it was held over direct heat.

Astounded, Thomas held the parchment closer to the flame. He held his breath, scarcely able to believe his eyes as the heat from the candle began to expose a clandestine correspondence; in the white spaces between the lines of charcoal was another, far more secret communication from his brother.

Thomas read silently for several minutes. John wrote that it was three weeks before he was able to use his hands. He had coaxed the warder to bring him some large oranges, so he could exercise his fingers by cutting up the peel. *'All the time I secretly stored the juice for later!'*

Thomas fingered the rosary in his pocket and smiled, shaking his head at his brother's guile. Suddenly he grimaced as the flames from the candle began licking his fingers. He cursed himself for being so clumsy and edged back slightly, wary of setting the letter alight but fearful also that the words might vanish forever once it was taken away from the heat. He need not have worried; the words remained.

As Thomas continued to read, the true reason behind the secrecy was revealed. *'I have been informed that I am to be tried and condemned within a matter of weeks and to prepare myself for execution.'*

'Execution!' Images of Anthony Babington and the priest, John Ballard, flashed through Thomas's mind.

*'While I am glad to lay down my life for our Saviour,'* John went on; *'He has provided me with a means and an opportunity of escape.'*

Thomas leapt to his feet, overturning the table and sending the candle and an empty wine mug rolling noisily across the bare oak boards. For a moment he remained perfectly still, waiting for the sound of footsteps on the stairs or in the corridor outside his room. But all was silent. Swearing to himself, he fumbled across the floor, retrieving first the mug and then the candle. Crossing to the fireplace where a few smouldering embers still remained in the grate, he relit the candle and set it down on the oak mantel.

Escape ... from the Tower? Surely that was impossible. How was John planning to do it? Was the warder involved and if so, could he really be trusted? *'There is a fellow brother who is imprisoned in a squat tower opposite me,'* he read, *'in the south-eastern corner of the battlements. This tower is close to the moat. It would be possible to lower a man by a rope from the roof of this tower to the wall beyond the moat. I ask that you come, at midnight on 3rd October, to the far side of the moat, opposite the squat tower.'*

Thomas swallowed hard. From his brother's description, he recognised the squat tower as being the Cradle Tower, the very same tower where their own father had been imprisoned following the Babington affair. He began pacing up and down his room, his mind racing; 3rd October was only one week away.

*'Once in position, you will meet with some other 'friends' to whom I have sent the same letter. You will bring a rope and tie it to a stake. From our high position we will throw an iron ball attached to a stout thread. You must find the cord and tie it to the free end of the rope. We will then draw up the rope by pulling the other end of the cord which we will be holding in our hands and finally, make our descent to freedom. By the Grace of God, we will succeed.'*

Thomas could feel beads of sweat trickling down his forehead and he went to the window. As soon as he threw open the heavy shutters, the bright moonlight flooded in. He opened the casement and gulped in the cool night air. From beneath his window, the sweet perfume of flowers drifted up.

Thomas leaned his elbows on the window ledge and gazed at the moonlight and the shadows. He didn't know what to think. The plan appeared well devised and every detail had been accounted for. But to attempt such an audacious escape from under the very noses of the gaolers was fraught with danger; if they were discovered, all their fates would be sealed.

And who were the other 'friends' John had referred to; could they be trusted? Did the warder suspect anything? Should he confide in Jane? Thomas sighed and looked up at the heavens. Despite all his doubts and fears, he was certain of one thing: nothing on earth would prevent him from being there to help his brother.

He closed the casement and returned to his bed but it was not until after four in the morning that he eventually fell asleep.

# CHAPTER 31

Next morning, Thomas was awakened by a young chamber-boy bringing a wooden bathtub to set before the newly-lit fire, and placing a clean shirt and ruff to warm.

Thomas prised open his eyelids, blinking at the sunlight streaming in through the casement. Outside, he could hear birds and cattle lowing in the distance. He stared up at the ornate plaster ceiling, at the pairs of boxing hares, painted in shades of red, brown and green, and outlined in gold. Then he remembered the letter from John.

He sat up and drew a long, shaky breath as he recalled its hidden secrets. He was still seized by an overwhelming need and desire to act. Whatever reservations he might have about such a dangerous venture, there was no doubt in his heart. He would go to London without delay.

He threw off the coverlet and shuffled to the bathtub; bathing in hot water with clean linen towels had become a rare luxury.

Afterwards, Thomas felt restored and better able to think straight. Quickly, he dressed in the clean clothes, ate a slice of warm manchet and drank some weak morning ale. Then, carrying his boots, he hurried from his room and along the corridor. Reaching the top of the oak staircase, he paused; Broad Oaks seemed particularly quiet and empty.

He pulled on his boots and ran down the stairs into the stillness of the Great Hall. Approaching the heavy oak entrance door, he saw that the new wooden crossbar had been lifted from its sockets and was leaning upright against the wall and the two iron door bolts had been pulled back. Lifting the latch, he stepped outside.

The air was clear and sharp. The grass was saturated with dew while further away, the woods were turning from lush green to pale yellow and russet. Closer to the house in the orchard, maturing trees had sagging branches laden with swelling, ripening fruit. And above everything, there was a bright blue sky.

Thomas crossed the courtyard and entered the stables. Inside, the smell of horses and straw filled his nostrils. Saddles, bridles and harnesses hung on the stone wall behind a row of five horses. Nathaniel, the diminutive stable boy, was softly whistling a tune while effortlessly grooming a chestnut gelding. Every now and then he leaned forward and whispered in the horse's ear, 'There's a good boy! There's a good boy!' The horses seemed to respond to his gentle voice and kind touch. At night, Nathaniel often slept in the stables on some straw, curled up close to his companions.

A few moments passed before the boy glanced up and saw Thomas. He doffed his cap. 'Good day to you, Master Rufford. What can I do for you on this fine morning? Shall I saddle a horse?'

Thomas smiled and nodded his acknowledgement.

He stepped further into the stables. 'I am pleased to see you treating your animals with the care and respect they warrant, Nathaniel.'

'Why, but of course! There's no sense in any other way!' the boy said, surprised at such a curious remark. 'How else am I to gain their trust and friendship and their loyalty?' He began stroking the gelding's smooth, glistening mane with his child-sized hands. 'We must inspire respect and affection ... not terror!'

'There is a wise old head on those young shoulders,' said Thomas, smiling. 'Your father is the principal usher here, is he not?'

'Yes, sir. Been in service at Broad Oaks for nearly twenty years, he has. Did you know that when he first arrived, he worked in the stables too! Always treated right and proper, he was. Lord Molynieux – God rest his soul – saw to that. But now...' Nathaniel hesitated, resting his head on the gelding's heaving flank. 'Poor Lady Molynieux! My father says the world has gone mad ... turned upside down.'

Thomas looked at him sympathetically. The confident, assured manner which the young stable boy had so easily displayed a few moments earlier had vanished, and his expression was now one of doubt and confusion.

'I have heard rumours in the village that Lady Molynieux will never return to Broad Oaks,' Nathaniel continued. 'That the estate will be confiscated by the government.' His eyes filled with tears. 'Tell me that won't happen, Master Rufford ... tell me it won't.'

'Only God knows what will happen, Nathaniel. We must put all our faith in Him. We must be strong and not lose heart. Lady Molynieux is a good, honest woman and they are bound to set her free soon.'

'But some of my friends in the village poke fun and tease me. They say that we will be evicted from Broad Oaks and we will have nowhere to live.'

'Then they are not your true friends and what they say does not matter.'

'But I'm afraid they may be right. And if we are thrown out, who will take care of my horses?'

'My brother once told me there is nothing to fear but fear itself. Broad Oaks belongs to Lady Molynieux and her family; they cannot simply take it away from her.'

Nathaniel frowned. 'But Lady Molynieux is imprisoned! She is helpless!'

Thomas slung an arm across the boy's shoulders. 'Then we shall have to see what we can do about it, won't we? Why, I will even go and see Queen Elizabeth herself, if that's what it takes.'

'You mean ... you'll see...'

Thomas started walking along the row of horses, patting each one in turn. 'Nathaniel, how quickly can you prepare and saddle a horse for me?'

'They are all fed and watered, Master Rufford. Look, you can see how strong and healthy they are.' There was pride in the stable boy's voice. 'I can have one saddled in no time at all.'

'Good! Excellent! Then I leave for London within the hour,' said Thomas. Giving the young stable boy one last look, he hastened away.

Hope flickered again in Nathaniel's large eyes and a broad smile returned to his face.

Thomas emerged from the gloomy stables and filled

his lungs with the rejuvenating, cold morning air. Then, he strode purposefully across the courtyard towards the house.

†

In the Great Hall, Jane and Henry Giffard had returned from a stroll around the garden and were sitting talking in front of the large bay window. They reminisced over happier times in childhood when summer days that seemed to last forever were spent playing games with much-loved brothers and sisters. They talked of friendship, and confided their hopes and aspirations for the future. Jane gazed intently into Henry's handsome face the whole time. It was as if they understood each other better than anyone in the whole world.

During a brief lull in their conversation, Jane caught sight of her brother trying to steal unnoticed glances across the room. 'Ah! There you are!' she said cheerfully. 'We wondered where you had got to.'

'What? I – I've just come from the stables,' Thomas muttered vaguely.

Jane looked at him inquisitively. 'What is it, Thomas? What's troubling you?'

'I have decided to leave for London,' Thomas said slowly. 'Yes, London. At once! I cannot stand idly by while our brother and Lady Molynieux remain in such peril. I cannot wait around Broad Oaks any longer; at least if I'm in London there may be something I can do.' He paused, glancing from Jane to Henry Giffard and back again. For the present, he dare not tell them about the secrets in John's letter; that he was to be an accomplice in his brother's planned escape. It would be safer if they did not know.

'But what can you do? What can any of us do?' Jane asked. 'It is true Lady Molynieux is not closely confined and is therefore permitted visitors but they will never allow you to see John, never! You will only torment yourself further.'

Henry Giffard went to Jane's side, making a clear show of his support for her. 'Master Rufford, I fear that Jane is right about your brother,' he said. 'It will be impossible to see him. You will not even be able to bribe your way inside, such is the government's fear of Jesuit priests. And if you are seen loitering anywhere near the Tower, you will put both yourself and your brother at even greater risk.'

'I care nothing for my own safety,' Thomas said. 'I know you speak in earnest, Master Giffard, but I must go, my mind is decided.' He looked at Jane. 'In the end, all our lives belong to God … you have shown me that.'

'Then allow me to accompany you, Master Rufford,' Giffard offered. 'I fear you will not succeed alone.'

Jane was about to speak but her voice was drowned out. 'No!' cried Thomas, shaking his head. 'I am much obliged to you for your kind offer, Master Giffard. Thank you, but no. I am responsible and I alone must go to my brother's aid. I must give of myself if I am to receive that which I seek.' A sudden rush of self-belief swept through him; a firmness and sense of purpose. Nothing would prevent him from doing what he knew to be right.

Giffard and Jane listened to him in silence.

'But there is something you can do,' Thomas went

on, addressing Giffard. 'Will you safeguard Broad Oaks while I'm away, see to it that the everyday matters of the household are properly attended to. It must be ready to welcome home Lady Molyneux.'

'Yes, of course, but...'

'And ... will you take care of my sister.'

Henry Giffard looked from Thomas to Jane. 'I am humbled that you should consider asking me,' he said. 'That you are prepared to entrust the safe-keeping of your sister to someone you barely know, to someone who many of the old faith would say should not be trusted.'

Thomas smiled. 'I trust you,' he said quietly.

'Then the answer is yes. I will be honoured to do so.'

'Good. That's settled then.' Thomas spoke with relief and satisfaction. 'Now, if you will excuse me, I must pack a few things into a saddlebag for the journey.' As he reached the foot of the stairs he glanced back, a mischievous glint in his eyes. 'And besides, it will give you the chance of being together – I know how fond of each other you have already become!'

'Why, Thomas!' exclaimed Jane, flushing hotly. 'What nonsense you talk! It is you who should not be trusted.'

# CHAPTER 32

IN THE STUDY of his Westminster house, Richard Topcliffe was pacing up and down the room. It was evident from the twisted expression on his face that he was in an especially foul temper. The room itself was small and simply furnished; against one wall there was a sideboard with several lighted candles upon it; against another was a large chest with an embroidered scarlet cloak draped over it while in the centre of the room, there was a rectangular table with a half-empty flagon of wine and a number of wine cups. Three of Topcliffe's followers were seated at the table, nervously listening to their master's tirade.

'Why? Why?' Topcliffe demanded furiously. 'Why am I prevented from carrying out my duty? It is intolerable. I tell you, there is much that lies hid in this Rufford, this Jesuit. I must be allowed to deal with him. Let me rack him and the truth will burst forth.'

One of his companions leaned back in his chair. He was a large man and his peascod-bellied doublet only just covered his round bulging stomach. He appeared less frightened than the others. This was Anthony Munday, the longest serving of Topcliffe's unsavoury accomplices. 'But you have full authority…' he began, his voice tired and lethargic.

'I have the authority of the Queen herself,' Topcliffe screamed. 'Well, 'tis more of an understanding really. But the warrant for my work in this particular case was issued by the Privy Council and now, owing to that feeble-minded governor at the Tower, it has been revoked. We should not feel sympathy for these traitors! They are behind every plot and conspiracy that ever sought to remove our glorious Queen from her rightful throne. Their allegiance is to the Pope not Queen Elizabeth!'

Topcliffe paused, as if considering whether he had said everything he wanted to say. He lowered his head and fixed his gaze on Munday. 'It is a glory to kill Catholics. Why, I have helped more traitors to Tyburn than all the noblemen and gentlemen of the court. My objective is to extinguish the Catholic religion in this country once and for all.'

There was a brief silence as everyone weighed Topcliffe's words.

'Aye, that is the objective of us all!' shouted a thin man with a red, perspiring face. He had removed his cloak and doublet and his white linen shirt was open to the waist. He was staring with glazed blood-shot eyes into his empty cup and dumbly nodding his head in agreement though it was clear that he had spoken without any real conviction.

'Well, in the case of the Jesuit John Rufford, you can set your mind at rest,' Munday said. 'His guilt is a foregone conclusion. He is finished!'

'Fools! Imbeciles!' retorted Topcliffe. 'What is the life of one stinking Jesuit! But if they had granted me just a little more time, I would have succeeded in loosening his tongue and acquired the names and houses of all his fellow traitors. I would have ravaged their entire network within a matter of weeks.'

'But there are so many of them,' moaned the third companion. 'They are everywhere! They roam the streets of London, they move freely about the country…'

'Ah! Stop your bellyaching!' interrupted Munday, making a rude gesture with his plump white hand. Embarrassed by Topcliffe's earlier rebuff, he was not slow to point out his companion's shortcomings. 'So, we must double our efforts,' he added, casting a sideways glance in Topcliffe's direction in a thinly-veiled attempt to court his master's favour once more.

Topcliffe took several turns about the room in silence. He stopped and glared coldly at the dissenting aide.

'Then we shall raid every suspected safe house in London and beyond until we are satisfied,' said Topcliffe. He rummaged in his pocket, pulled out a crumpled piece of cloth and threw it onto the table. He nodded slightly as a sign that Munday might open it. The cloth was unravelled to reveal a map of London, drawn street by street. 'We shall systematically search every square mile of the city, beginning with those places we know to be Catholic.' Topcliffe's bony fingers pointed out several places on the map, moving from one location to another in rapid succession. 'Here, in Hern's Rent, and here in Montague Close. And in the inns and taverns. We shall hunt them down wherever they may hide and we shall employ whatever means are necessary. They will have no relief from their sufferings and pain.'

'Of course, you know we will do everything you ask of us,' said Munday, still trying to ingratiate himself with his master. 'But first, come and sit down. Here, have a drink!' He poured Topcliffe a large cup of wine.

Topcliffe made no answer and remained standing.

'Our sources indicate some reliable leads which we will pursue with vigour,' Munday continued. 'Anyone suspected will be brought in for interrogation. Be assured, it will not be long before we enjoy success. Let us drink to that!' Raising his cup, he took a large mouthful of wine.

'Do not take our task too lightly, Munday, for these are no ordinary traitors,' Topcliffe warned sternly. 'We will need all our guile and cunning if we are to accomplish our objective.' He reflected for a moment and then, leaning forward, added in a barely audible voice: 'You will, of course, bring those we need to question directly to me, here in this house?'

'But of course!'

Topcliffe's scrutinised the others around the table, silently demanding their absolute obedience; without hesitation, each man in turn dutifully swore his compliance.

Topcliffe gave a small grunt of satisfaction and nodded. He took the cup of wine and straightened up. 'Rufford … Rufford…' he repeated slowly several times. He drained the cup and wiped his mouth with his handkerchief. 'Mark me, my business with that family is not yet ended.'

# CHAPTER 33

THE DAY AFTER his departure from Broad Oaks, Thomas arrived in London and took lodgings in Bishopsgate, in The Black Bull, one of the many courtyard inns in the city. His chamber was on the first floor and, though cramped, was clean and warm with a fire in the grate and a fine wool coverlet on the bed. The room opened out onto a wooden gallery above a cobbled courtyard, and was accessed by an external staircase which Thomas particularly liked; he could come and go without being observed. To the rear of the courtyard were the stables.

That night, despite being exhausted after his journey, Thomas was restless and unable to sleep. He tried to read for a while in an attempt to distract himself but it was no use. A passing watchman called out that it was 'one of the morning' but all was not well. Thomas's head was a confusion of tangled, troubled thoughts. He imagined all manner of reasons why the escape would or would not succeed, who the other accomplices were. Should he have told his sister about the scheme? Should he have burned his brother's letter, rather than hiding it in a secret drawer in his bedchamber where it might be discovered?

He sighed, angry with himself. He extinguished the

candle and stretched out on the bed but the stillness of the room only served to amplify the rhythmic, contented snoring coming from the adjacent room. As Thomas listened, the infuriating noise seemed to grow louder, as though his inconsiderate neighbour were being deliberately spiteful.

Exasperated, he sat up again. His mind quickly reverted to his brother's scheme; though he went over it again and again, something still bothered him. It was then that he came to a decision. In the morning, he would go to the Tower. He knew it was risky but he needed to reconnoitre the land, to gauge for himself the height of the tower and the width of the moat, the distance his brother had to traverse. He needed to familiarise himself with the smallest details of the planned escape.

Somewhat reassured by his plan Thomas lay back, closed his eyes and eventually fell asleep.

A little after dawn the next morning, still feeling rather groggy, Thomas slipped quietly from his bedchamber. He crept down the outside stairs of his lodging, across the courtyard, through the vaulted archway and out into the street. It had rained during the night and the chill morning air refreshed him. It was the first day of October.

Thomas looked up and down the street, to see if there were any suspicious characters loitering about. Even at such an early hour Bishopsgate was beginning to stir. Shopkeepers were already busy at their counters, apprentices rushed to and fro carrying out their masters' barked commands and women with baskets went about their chores. Though everything looked safe enough, Thomas was nervous that his face would betray his true purpose so he pulled his woollen hat lower and, quickening his pace, hurried off down the street.

As he neared the city the noise and the chaos and the throb of activity increased. A young apprentice, slouching against a lean-to, called out to passers-by: 'What do ye lack? What do ye lack?'

'Buy some fine pippins!' cried a woman with a basket over her arm. 'Or pears!'

'Hot pies, still warm from the oven!' called another.

Thomas, deep in thought, raised his head. His stomach groaned for some food. He handed over a ha'penny to the pie-woman and went to stand in the doorway of a drapers shop. Savouring the warm minced beef flavoured with sliced prunes, raisins and chopped dates, he stared absently about him. One thought consumed him; that he would see his brother safely to freedom, or die in the attempt. Everything else receded into shadows. The noises and smells of the city, the men and women scurrying like ants between the tall claustrophobic buildings, all seemed like a dream to him. For now, he was disconnected from their world of turmoil and confusion.

A man suddenly lurched into him, knocking him off his balance. The stranger's face was red and distorted; even at this early hour, he was obviously drunk. Seeing the startled look on Thomas's face, the man stared back at him, his eyes squinting as they tried to focus.

'Idiot! Out of my way!' he cursed, pushing Thomas aside and, staggering on his thick legs, he moved towards Threadneedle Street. As he reached the corner, he paused and glanced back over his shoulder. Thomas looked back at him, and caught his breath. 'Dear God!' he muttered, stepping back into the shop doorway.

The swaying figure in the peascod-bellied doublet was no stranger at all. Thomas tried to remember his name; he recognised him as Topcliffe's accomplice the day they arrested Lady Molynieux at Broad Oaks. Anthony Munday, that was it.

Thomas hesitated. What should he do? Should he confront Munday or ignore him? Perhaps Munday, in his drunken stupor, had not recognised him. But then, as abruptly as he had appeared, the man disappeared round the corner.

Thomas knew that if he were recognised by Topcliffe or any of his gang, if they had the merest hint of what he was about, it would result in immediate death not only for his brother but for himself. He tried to convince himself that Munday was so inebriated that when he did eventually sober up, he would have no recollection of running into Thomas. No, he must simply put this encounter from his mind; nothing could be done about it.

He must go directly to the Tower. He must see for himself what needed to be done and concentrate on saving his brother.

† 

By ten o'clock in the morning Thomas had reached Tower wharf. He walked towards the south eastern corner of the Tower, surveying the moat and the outer fortifications as he went. The weather was calm. The city of London was behind him with its houses and shops, taverns and churches all crammed together and the mass of people swarming about its narrow cobbled streets.

Thomas turned to look at the Thames. A gentle breeze played on his face and the sunlight glinted on the crests of the grey-green ripples. He could feel his spirits rise. The encounter with Munday had completely slipped his mind.

He turned back; directly facing him on the far side of the moat was the squat tower accurately described in his brother's letter. Thomas was right: it was the Cradle Tower where he had visited their imprisoned father three years before. And it was from the roof of this very same tower that his brother was going to slide down a rope to freedom.

The distance from the battlements on top of the tower, across the moat and over the ten-foot-high wall at its edge to where he was standing was greater than he had envisaged. Thomas began to fret that the rope he had brought from Broad Oaks was not going to be long and strong enough. If only he knew who the other accomplices were. They needed to confer and go over the plan, to ensure that nothing was left to chance.

Thomas noticed an elderly man with grey hair limping slowly along the wharf towards him. At his side, bearing his considerable weight, was a young woman with fair hair, wearing a black cloak. In her free hand she carried a wicker basket full of autumn fruit: apples, pears, plums and cherries.

Suddenly, Thomas felt conspicuous and he quickly removed his hat and smiled awkwardly as they approached. 'Come, I see your basket is heavy. Let me help you,' he said boldly.

The woman stared curiously at him, wary of this unexpected offer of help but, seeing only the benign expression on his face, her manner relaxed. 'You are most kind, sir!' she replied. 'But we do not have far to go, my father and I. Just to the cottages there. We shall cope.'

Thomas glanced to his right and noticed a row of dilapidated cottages at the far end of the wharf. With rotting timbers, smashed glass between the leaded panes and much of the thatch missing, they were nothing more than hovels.

'Then it will be no trouble for me to help.'

'Thank you,' said the woman as Thomas took the basket from her grasp. 'I am a trifle tired, it is true. I confess life is a struggle these days. But I shouldn't complain; it is nothing compared with the burden of the poor wretches in there.' She inclined her head towards the Tower. 'I do pity them so.'

The old man beckoned Thomas closer. 'Her husband, God rest his soul, perished in the Clink ... dysentery. Died in one of the underground cells, he did.'

Thomas faltered, remembering the outstretched, scavenging hands of the prisoners that day he had passed the Clink prison months earlier.

'Aye, lad!' continued the old man. 'And this only a year after he had served with Drake aboard the Revenge at Gravelines and returned a hero.' He paused, drawing deep, laboured breaths. 'He may have been a hero for scattering the Spaniards to the four winds, but what happened to him and his shipmates afterwards was a scandal! Cast adrift with nothing, without any pay, without any food, nothing! Ending their days in filthy, disease-ridden debtors cells! There's the Queen's gratitude for you!'

'Oh, Father! You must be mindful of what you say,' his daughter scolded. 'You must forgive him,' she added to Thomas. 'My father is easily excited. He doesn't mean to insult our Queen. In his heart, he does not believe Her Majesty intends any suffering or harm to her loyal subjects, especially those who defend this country against her enemies. But then, are there not innocent victims on both sides?'

Thomas was uncertain where their sympathies lay and contented himself with listening and smiling without replying.

'Here it is. This is where we live,' said the woman, pointing to the ramshackle house on the end. No sooner had the words left her lips, than its rotten wooden door swung open and two little girls came running out to greet them.

The children, no older than nine or ten years of age, kissed and hugged their mother and grandfather. They were eager to discover the contents of the basket but as soon as they saw Thomas holding it, they became self-conscious, clutching their mother's dress and staring up at the stranger with frightened faces.

Thomas looked down at their grubby bare feet. 'Here!' he said balancing two apples in the palm of his hand. 'There's one each!'

The eldest girl shook her head.

'But they're good and juicy!'

There was a moment's deliberation, a testing of each

other's will, before the youngest girl stepped out from beneath her mother's cloak, quickly snatched both apples from his grasp then turned on her heels and scurried back to the house, her older sister close behind.

As the mother smiled at her daughters, the lines around her eyes deepened.

'Forgive their lack of manners,' the old man grunted. 'My daughter is not strict with them. She is far too lenient when she should punish them. That's the only way they will learn. Mark my words; they will grow up spoilt brats!' He vanished into the house, muttering to himself.

'Perhaps my father is right,' the woman began softly. 'But I cannot bring myself to be hard on them. They have already endured so much. I only wish to spare them any further pain and sorrow.'

Thomas handed over the basket. 'Perhaps, it is because you possess that which is most precious of all – the love of a mother,' he said. Quickly bidding her farewell, he turned and walked back along the wharf.

'Sir!' the woman cried out after him. 'May we know your name?'

'Rufford. Thomas Rufford.'

'Then may God bless you, Thomas Rufford.'

†

Drawing level with the Cradle Tower once more, Thomas looked again at its sombre appearance. His attention was drawn to a tall, round, three-storey tower set further back and to the right: the Salt Tower. As he scanned its grey walls, he saw a figure staring straight back at him from a first-floor window. He inhaled sharply.

'God have mercy!' he exclaimed joyfully. Though the window was some distance away and its opening was narrow, there was no mistaking the familiar features of his brother's bearded face or the characteristic way John had of tilting his head to one side when scrutinizing someone.

Thomas's face lit up. His first impulse was to remove his hat and signal his brother. He took two or three paces forward but then stopped and glanced around nervously. The wharf was deserted, he was alone again, but dozens of wherries scurried to and fro plying their trade on the river. He must not arouse suspicion.

He began to pace up and down and at each turn he stopped in exactly the same place and raised his head. He repeated this several times until John finally recognised him. His brother greeted him with signs and blessed him. For a few precious moments, the brothers gazed at one another intently.

All too soon, John gave a sign that he must go and stepped back into the shadows. For a while, Thomas stared up at the dark opening of the window, the smile still fixed on his face. As he replaced his hat, he was conscious once more of the gentle breeze on his face and the sound of the river behind him as the tide turned. Dogs barked in the near distance, the cries of boatmen wafted across the water, music, laughter – but all of these things seemed empty and insignificant. Nothing could distract him from the task which lay before him.

As he retraced his steps, Thomas felt uplifted,

renewed in some way. He headed back into the city and The Black Bull in Bishopsgate.

# CHAPTER 34

All the next day Thomas remained in his room, preferring quiet solitude to the noise of the city. The thought of his brother's escape obsessed him and the vision of them being reunited constantly played in his mind. The day seemed endless.

That night, Thomas sat on his bed with his back against the wall and rested his chin on his raised knees. Occasionally he got up and stretched his legs, taking a few restless steps around the tiny room before returning to the bed and assuming the same position. Sleep was impossible. He prayed to God for the strength and courage he was going to need.

Next day, the 3$^{rd}$ of October, Thomas again remained idle. Occasionally, he glanced out of his tiny window, his attention attracted by the noisy arrival of a dray in the courtyard below and the servants unloading heavy barrels and casks, or by a groom carrying buckets of oats for the two huge horses and scraping a dung fork noisily across the cobbles as he disappeared into the stable.

Later, after an early supper of stew, some bread and a pot of ale, which the landlord's young daughter brought to his room, Thomas gathered his belongings and set out on his mission. He was prepared for sacrifice or to endure suffering; his conscience and the cause demanded it. He knew the risks to which he would be exposed but he was resolved not to spare himself. There was no turning back.

Emerging into the early evening sunlight, Thomas rubbed his eyes; two almost sleepless nights had left him weary and exhausted. He tried to straighten his dirty clothes. Over one shoulder he carried his leather saddlebag concealing the length of rope, together with a clean pair of breeches and a workaday doublet for John. At his side, he wore both his sword and rapier. He would use the sword as the stake. He pulled his hat low and set off along Bishopsgate.

His route took him into Gracechurch Street and from there along New Fish Street until he came to London Bridge and the river. He gazed at the dark water flowing between the narrow arches under the bridge. Still and peaceful now, but he had heard tales of boatmen who, for a wager, would try running these falls at high tide. When the tide turned, the water could rise ten feet or more, roaring and crashing between the arches, funnelled by the boat-shaped starlings on which they were supported. Any small boat attempting such a foolhardy deed would certainly have its hull split in two and its boatmen would be spewed out into the Pool of London. There was a saying that wise men go over the bridge, fools under it. He shook his head incredulously, then turned eastwards and proceeded towards Billingsgate.

He looked at the wharves piled high with bales and casks, the loading tackle which seemed to resemble the gallows and the boats and barges moored against the jetties. Lanterns twinkled and his nostrils twitched at the burning pitch of torches on the walls. A few merchants and their clerks were hurrying in and out of the shadows between now-deserted warehouses, eager to go home after a day's profitable business.

A wicket gate creaked on its hinges as Thomas pushed it open. He passed through and walked on, away from the industry of Billingsgate, downriver past Custom House towards the Tower.

He reached the row of cottages at the edge of Tower Wharf and stopped. The night was dark, clouds obscured the moon and the autumn chill made him shiver. He cupped his hands and blew, then wrapped his cloak tighter. He was gripped with a raw feeling of anticipation. His stomach grumbled and he felt nauseous. It can't be long now, he thought.

When a distant watch cried twelve o'clock, Thomas heard the sound of oars splashing in the water, followed by the thud of a boat against the water steps a short distance along the wharf. He pressed himself flat against the wall and listened … nothing. He waited a while longer … still nothing. His hunched shoulders relaxed. His first glimpse of the figure cautiously crossing the wharf towards the moat took him by surprise. The man glanced nervously about him, then pulled from a sack what looked like a stake or iron bar some three or four feet long and pushed it into the ground. Thomas squinted, but in the darkness it was difficult to see who it was. He licked his dry, cracked lips. Summoning all his courage, he stepped out from his hiding place and walked slowly towards the crouched figure.

Alert, the man leapt to his feet and turned to face him. 'Thomas! You gave me such a fright!' he muttered softly, removing his hat and wiping his brow. 'I knew you would come!'

Thomas breathed a sigh of relief and smiled. 'I am pleased to see you my friend,' he said, and he clasped the man's shoulders embracing him warmly. It was Nicholas Owen.

Thomas stood back and peered across the moat at the squat tower outlined against the night sky. 'I pray God is with us this night.'

'Amen,' came Owen's whispered reply.

Thomas turned round. 'I heard a boat ...' he said, looking past his friend towards the river.

'Yes! And two of our brothers are at the oars,' Nicholas said. 'Two more trustworthy souls you couldn't hope to meet. John Lillie was released from the Clink some six months ago. He has vowed to fast one day every week for the rest of his life should your brother get away safe! Then, there's Richard Fullwood. He managed to escape from the Bridewell.'

Thomas shuddered. The Bridewell was notorious for its barbarity; though mainly reserved for whores and vagabonds, Catholics were often sent there to have confessions forced out of them.

'We aim to take your brother as far as possible by river,' Nicholas went on. 'There is a relay of horses for us at a house in Richmond. From there we will go across country to Uxendon, where we will meet up with the Jesuit Superior.'

'I have brought some rope,' said Thomas, groping in his saddlebag, 'but I fear it may not be strong enough.'

## CHAPTER 34

'It looks good to me. Go ahead, tie it to the stake!'

Thomas fumbled with the rope, but his fingers were clumsy and would not respond. He struggled with the knot until one end of the rope was securely fastened to the stake whilst the other was left free.

Then they waited ... and listened. And as they waited, they fell silent, each occupied with his own thoughts. Thirty minutes turned into one hour, and one hour turned into two, and all the time Thomas clenched his teeth so hard that he felt the muscles of his throat grow taut.

He looked despairingly at Nicholas. 'Why does it take them so long? What could have happened?' he asked.

Nicholas was silent.

Thomas stared into the darkness. 'Something must have gone wrong,' he said, his voice barely audible. He lifted his face to the night sky and began in a soft whisper: 'Almighty Father in heaven, from the depths of my heart, I beseech You. In Your divine and loving mercy, deliver to us our brothers; safe from all...'

A stifled cry came from the river, cutting short his prayer. Thomas and Nicholas spun round as they heard the pounding of heavy feet approaching.

The figure of a man suddenly appeared out of the darkness and came running towards them, stopping only a couple of feet away from where they stood.

'What is it John? What's the matter?' asked Nicholas.

'The tide is turning,' replied John Lillie, breathing heavily. 'We dare not risk waiting any longer or it will be too bad!' There was alarm in his voice and his eyes flashed urgently from Nicholas to Thomas and back again.

Nicholas sighed and put a consoling arm around Thomas's shoulder. 'Perhaps it was not God's design that we should succeed tonight ... but do not despair; He has only postponed the day. We will return again tomorrow night.'

'No, wait!' Thomas exclaimed, pulling himself away. 'Please, I beg you. Give them a while longer. I know they'll come.'

'The river is rising fast,' John Lillie said impatiently. 'The current is growing ever stronger. If we are to go by river at all, we must leave now.'

At that moment, there was a dull thud on the soft earth behind them. All three men turned. An iron ball, two inches in diameter, lay on the ground no more than three or four feet away from where Thomas stood. A thin cord was fastened to it and stretched out into the darkness beyond. A lifeline. It was exactly as described in John's letter.

Thomas threw himself down on the ground, seized the loose end of the rope and hurriedly secured it to the cord. He gave three sharp tugs on the cord and knelt waiting beside it.

He thought he could hear the tread of a sentry in the distance away to his left. He held his breath but the footsteps came no nearer and then disappeared altogether. A soft breeze cooled the sweat running down his face. He tried to gather his thoughts, to reassure himself that all would be well, but his imagination conjured up guards running onto the wharf at the very moment his brother slid down the rope to freedom.

Suddenly the cord, with the rope safely attached to it, jerked violently. It slithered across the ground like a snake and, as it was pulled taut, cleared the wall at the edge of the moat and rose up towards the tower.

Thomas gazed after the rope as it disappeared into the shadows. Slowly and cautiously, he edged forward, his eyes straining to pierce the darkness.

A startled cry came from behind. He was about to turn back to his companions when he caught sight of two figures on the battlements of the small tower directly opposite.

# CHAPTER 35

ON THE FLAT roof of Cradle Tower, John Rufford and his accomplice John Arden were desperately hauling the rope towards them. Its passage was sluggish and alarmingly noisy but at last they held the end of the thick rope in their hands and at once wrapped it twice around the nozzle of a cannon before securing it with a double knot.

'Look!' cried Arden despairingly, pointing at the rope.

John's gaze followed his companion's outstretched arm. He gave out a muted groan. The distance between the roof of the tower at one end and the stake at the other was so great that the rope, instead of sloping down, stretched almost horizontally between the two points.

John glanced across at the strained expression on Arden's pallid face. More than seven years of imprisonment had left him weak in both mind and body and he looked much older than his forty years. Arden had always said to him that it would be the simplest thing in the world to slide down the rope to freedom; now John realised the truth of the matter. To make their escape, they would have to heave and pull themselves every inch of the way along the rope's length. John was not sure they would be able to make it.

Arden wavered. 'I don't think we'll make it across,' he whispered.

'There is no going back, not without the risk of betraying both ourselves and our friends down there,' said John, trying to conceal his own doubts. 'Do not be afraid, God is with us.'

Arden smiled. 'You're right, of course. It is better we take this chance of escape than stay locked up here. I shall certainly be hanged if I remain.'

Minutes later, after a short prayer, Arden clambered over the battlements and steadily, inch by inch, worked his way along the rope. He pulled himself doggedly along and, after ten minutes of strenuous exertion, he fell exhausted onto the wharf.

The instant his feet touched the ground, Thomas took the rope and gave it a wrench before exchanging a glance with Arden, whose weary, perspiring face lit up with a triumphant smile. Nicholas threw a cloak over Arden's shoulders and then turned round again to face the Tower. All three men were silent.

On the roof of the tower, John felt the tug on the rope - Arden had made it across. Now it was his turn. He paused for a moment, commending himself to God and the Blessed Virgin. He felt another tug on the rope, this time more impatient. Gripping it with his right hand and pulling himself along with his left, he began to move off face downwards, at the same time, twisting his legs around the rope to prevent himself from falling.

He had gone no more than three or four yards when his body swung round under its own weight and he found himself hanging precariously beneath the rope.

As he slipped, his head and arms quivered violently with the strain. By some miracle, his hands clung on to the slackened, drooping rope.

His body was rigid. He adjusted his grip a little and inched slowly along, but the pain in his wrists and forearms was excruciating, and he made little progress before he was forced to stop again. Beneath his doublet, the shirt clung to his back, drenched in sweat. He was close to fainting. Close to defeat.

On the wharf below Thomas, who could distinguish his brother's motionless silhouette suspended perilously from the rope, looked on in terror. He moved forward, clutching at Arden's sleeve. 'He's not going to make it! He's going to fall!' he said.

The noise of the river behind seemed deafening.

John's strength was failing fast. He struggled to move his hands or his feet. He must move on or fall. In the darkness, he heard a soft, whimpering moan; it was some time before he realised the sound was coming from himself. From the depths of his soul, he prayed to God. Moments later, as though his prayer had been answered, he was overcome with a sense of peace; though his body was still racked with intense, throbbing pain, he seemed not to feel it. With renewed strength, he began to drag himself along the rope once more.

Every moment Thomas expected his brother to plummet into the depths of the moat below, or for a guard to appear on the battlements and start hacking at the rope with a sword. Now and again, John's agonising progress ground to a halt as the pain threatened to overwhelm him once again. Each time, Thomas raised his hands to his eyes, hardly able to watch. It seemed as though more than half an hour had elapsed when in fact it was only a matter of minutes before his brother, with a last desperate effort, finally reached the far side of the wall.

But there, with his feet just scraping the top of the wall and the rest of his body hanging behind, John's strength finally gave out.

Thomas scaled the wall, seized hold of his brother's legs and pulled him over and down onto the wharf. They both collapsed in a huddle on the damp earth, coughing and wheezing.

Nicholas Owen crouched beside them and produced a small, brown bottle from a leather pouch he was carrying. Carefully removing its stopper he leant forward. 'A little restorative – some cordial water,' he whispered, and tilted the bottle against John's parched cracked lips.

After another fit of coughing, John wiped his eyes and looked about him, not quite sure where he was. Thomas leaned forward and cradled his brother's body in his arms. He looked at John's sallow face and a feeling of compassion such as he had never known before flooded his heart. Tears streamed down his cheeks as he gently rocked his brother to and fro.

'We thought ... I thought you were never going to make it. But now you are safe. It is a joyous moment for us all!' A deep bond had always existed between them but now it seemed even more profound.

A faint smile crept over John's lips and his eyes fixed on Thomas. 'It is true. There is no joy like the joy of freedom.'

'Forgive me Master Rufford, but we are none of us safe yet,' interrupted Nicholas. 'We must get away from here as quickly as possible.'

'I have some friends with a house in Spitalfields,' Arden announced. 'By your leave, I will go there directly. I will be safe there … I know I will!'

Nicholas considered for a moment. Perhaps it would be better if they travelled by different routes. He looked around nervously. There was no time to debate the matter; every minute they delayed risked discovery. He agreed. 'Yes, go! And God's speed!'

Arden thanked them for their help and bade his farewells. He reserved an especially tender embrace for John. Vowing that they would meet again soon, he turned and set off briskly towards the row of cottages at the far end of the wharf, glancing back only once before disappearing into the darkness.

Nicholas turned to John, whose colour was slowly returning to his face. 'Father, we must go now! If we help you, do you think you can make it to the boat?'

John was half carried, half dragged to the waiting boat. Beneath the arched sailcloth canopy, he slumped onto a thickly cushioned bench. Lillie and Fullwood sat facing him and were already lowering the oars into the water.

'Thomas?' enquired Nicholas, steadying himself as he too descended into the boat.

John glanced over and leaned across. 'Come with us Thomas!' he said, beckoning his brother.

Thomas hesitated. He stared across the surging river towards Horsleydown on the southern side, at the dark jumble of buildings along its bank and the flickering lanterns at the foot of the water stairs. He gazed up at the heavens, at the stars, radiant and sparkling in the vast expanse of darkness. He was captivated by the magnificent beauty of it all. He thanked God for the life of his brother and for all those who risked their own lives to help him. He thanked Him for Nicholas Owen, Anne Ferrers and her sister, Eleanor at Rowington, his own sister, Jane, and of course Lady Molynieux … yes, he must not forget Lady Molynieux. Now, Thomas had an overwhelming desire to return God's favours.

'Master Rufford! What are you doing? What are you waiting for?' Nicholas cried.

But Thomas was deep in thought and it was several moments before he looked into the boat and gazed steadily into his brother's face. 'You go. You must go on without me. You will be in Richmond by dawn and in Uxendon by sunset. You are safe now. Go!' He paused. 'I will return to my lodgings. I must attend to some unfinished business in London.' A faint smile appeared on his face. 'Goodbye and God's speed!' He stepped away from the boat.

The oars splashed and skipped on the water as the boat turned into the strong current and headed upriver towards London Bridge. For a long while, John looked back at the shore with a slightly quizzical but joyous smile.

†

With a final glance at the boat, Thomas slipped away, retracing his route along the path beyond Custom House, and then on through the narrow alleyways and silent warehouses of Billingsgate. Every now and then, he glimpsed the river between the tall buildings. His mind wandered, contemplating the night's events but even now, so shortly afterwards, he could not remember details or the order in which things had happened. Only that his brother was now safe.

Despite the cold night, he threw open his doublet and inhaled the air. His spirit soared and his heart was full of hope. He thanked God but reminded himself there was now another life to save.

Striding past sacks of spices and tuns of wine, he failed to hear them at first but then, through the darkness, away to his left, he detected the sounds of shouting and cries for help. He lifted his head. There they were again, louder ... desperate. And this time he thought he recognised the voices.

Two men appeared, still clumsily pulling on their clothes and carrying lanterns. They brushed past him and ran towards the river in their bare feet.

The river! All manner of thoughts flashed through Thomas's mind as he ran. Two minutes later he reached the riverbank, but already the water was alive with boats and there, wedged against the piles beneath the bridge, was his brother's boat. With the water level still rising, each new wave crashing into its hull threatened to capsize it and throw its occupants into the river.

'They need to get alongside if they are to assist!' Thomas shouted impatiently, gesturing wildly at several of the smaller boats which had formed a semicircle around the trapped vessel.

'What? And risk being pulled in themselves!' snapped a man standing at the water's edge a few feet away.

Thomas looked around him at the crowd which was already lining the bank. 'But there must be something we can do,' he muttered angrily. Instinctively, he stepped forward. Water lapped over the edge of his boots. He could clearly see the helpless figures in the boat being thrown around like dolls, desperately hanging on. 'Please God, don't let them perish!' he said aloud.

'Look yonder!' shouted someone and everyone's attention was drawn to the top of the bridge.

Lights danced. Thomas could see a basket swinging from the end of a length of rope being lowered down to the stricken boat. If only John and the others could get into it, they could be pulled to safety.

By now, however, a large sea-going merchant ship had braved the tide and crept alongside. On board, the sailors were shouting and repeatedly waving their arms at the shadowy figures on the bridge. Then, displaying tremendous daring, they began hauling the poor men to safety. One … two … three men in rapid succession were pulled onto the deck of their ship. Only one man now remained: John. As he struggled to his feet, an immense wave struck, overturning the small boat and sweeping him into the rapids.

'Oh no! God have mercy!' exclaimed Thomas, scarcely able to watch. He turned to the man nearest him and seized him by the arm. 'What are you standing there gaping at? We must help him!' he screamed and he rushed into the water dragging the man along with him.

'You mad fool!' the man protested, struggling against Thomas's grip. 'We'll both drown!' He wrestled himself away and staggered back to the water's edge, shivering.

'Look! See how far the idiot is going!' remarked someone, seeing Thomas wade up to his waist through the icy water. From various sides, several other onlookers urged Thomas to come back. Two large, broad-shouldered men, standing at the water's edge without coat or shoes, threw themselves into the river and swam out to him.

Thomas thrashed about, trying to resist them but they were stronger than he was and, after a few moments, he relented; he knew it was hopeless.

'Look over there!' shouted an excited voice.

Thomas looked up and stared in disbelief. By a small miracle, his brother had managed to grasp the rope let down from the bridge and was now being hauled to safety. Moments later, cheers rang out from all sides as John, soaked and exhausted, was finally dragged onto the bridge. The smile on Thomas's face broadened into a wide grin.

The two men who had rushed into the water to rescue Thomas gradually released their grip. 'Come along then,' said the older one. 'Come along … It's all over.' He started wading back to the side.

'Yes … yes, of course,' Thomas stammered. Strands of wet hair hung across his face, dripping. As he struggled through the water, he realised how tired and cold he was.

Within a matter of minutes, the swarm of small boats, wherries and skiffs had vanished and the sea-going merchant ship was already heading down river, towards the Custom House wharf, from where it would put ashore the three men it had rescued. The crowd along the bank, still buzzing with excitement, began to disperse, drifting slowly back to their homes.

Thomas stood shivering on the bank. He felt odd, as if what he had witnessed were unreal. The roaring of the water filled his ears, adding to this strange sensation he felt. At the bridge, the lanterns which had illuminated the rescue had now disappeared and the bridge was dark once more. He could no longer see his brother.

'Where would they take him?' he thought. He pushed his way past a couple of stragglers and started to run, as fast as his cold, numb legs would carry him. After a short sprint, he arrived at the bridge. The chain that would normally bar the entrance for the nightly curfew was resting loosely on the road; the sentry who should have been on duty was nowhere in sight. Above the noise of the river, he could hear voices and the sound of boots on the roadway.

Moments later, John appeared beneath the archway. Blood trickled down his face. His hair hung in wet clumps and his clothes dripped water onto the stone flags.

'John! John!' Thomas ran towards him, then stopped abruptly.

A Constable of the Watch stepped out of the shadows and stooped to pick up the chain; at the same time two other gentlemen appeared on either side of John. One was a tall, prosperous-looking man with broad shoulders, the other a squat, older man of about forty. They were talking excitedly and congratulating themselves. John stood between them, dazed, swaying to and fro like a drunken man.

'There, look at that!' said the younger man, nodding

his head in Thomas's direction. 'Another fool who fancied a soaking!' He laughed and at the same time gave Thomas a friendly wink. 'Mind, Master Ripley and I were nearly too late with this fellow,' he continued. 'We only just pulled him out in the nick of time.'

Thomas moved closer and embraced his brother. 'John ... John,' was all he could say.

For a second or two the young man scrutinised them, his handsome face assuming an inquisitive expression. 'You know this man? Who is he?' he asked.

Thomas pulled himself away. 'Thank you,' he said, his voice faltering. 'Thank you for saving my brother's life.'

'This man's your brother!' exclaimed the young man. 'Well, I never!' and he gave a loud burst of laughter.

Thomas remained silent, incapable of saying another word.

'Eh, lad, don't fret now,' interrupted the older man in a voice which reminded Thomas of Lord Molynieux. 'Don't fret, my friend. Your brother is out of trouble now, thank God.'

The expression on Ripley's face was so good-natured that Thomas responded with a smile. 'Master Ripley, I shall not forget what you and your companion have done,' He glanced at the young man. 'I am bound in eternal gratitude to you both.'

'Master Stephen Harwood, at your service,' the young man said, extending his hand to Thomas.

'And how was it, sir, that your brother and his companions happened to be on the river at this hour? Up to no good that's certain.' The cold, stern voice jarred and Thomas was suddenly aware of the constable staring at him intently.

Thomas's mind raced to invent a plausible excuse for his brother's river trip.

'Now, now…' interrupted Ripley, observing Thomas's hesitation. 'Is it not enough that a man's life has been saved? Let us not ask such questions. We are all tired and want to be away to our beds.'

The constable scowled but said nothing. Ripley turned to Thomas, his face beaming. 'Never have I met such a brave and courageous man as your brother,' he said. 'As we pulled him away from death, we could see how weak he had become. He somehow managed to hang on. I know not where he found the strength.'

'From Almighty God!' came John's faint whisper. 'It is His will I am saved!'

'Perhaps it is as you say,' said the constable coldly. 'Perhaps it is simply because you had the good fortune that these two men were around.' He reflected for a moment and shrugged his shoulders. 'What do I care what you were doing on the river!' he said. He turned away and went to replace the chain across the bridge.

'So, my good friend,' Ripley said cheerfully, linking his arm in Thomas's and moving away from the constable. 'Your brother has suffered much. My friend and I were intending to return with him to our lodgings in Cheapside where he could recover. Of course, you would also be most welcome… But forgive me, perhaps you reside close by and would like to care for him yourself?' he added hastily, as if reading Thomas's thoughts.

Thomas nodded. 'Yes … I will look after him now,' he said simply. His radiant smile convinced them.

'Ah! Then we are your assured friends and wish you both a safe journey,' said Harwood. He clasped Thomas by the shoulder and shook him gently.

Thomas's eyes filled with gratitude.

†

Arriving back at The Black Bull, Thomas helped John climb the stairs to his lodgings, and gently laid his exhausted brother on the bed. Within minutes, John was sound asleep. Thomas crossed to the window and gazed out at the night sky. Dawn was only a few hours away.

# CHAPTER 36

THE NEXT MORNING, a small knot of people were gathered on Tower Wharf opposite the Cradle Tower: several merchants and their young clerks; a plump, well-nourished shopkeeper in his apron; a group of local women, and a Tower guard, who had a scared expression on his face. They were muttering to one another and shaking their heads. Now and then, their conversation died away and they stared at the battlements and the rope which was hanging down against the wall of the tower.

Attracted by the bustle of activity on the wharf, a rabble of children raced to the scene and quickly surrounded the guard.

'What's happened?'

'Look yonder! A rope!'

'I reckon someone must 'ave escaped from the Tower!'

'That'll do! Be off with you!' bleated the guard, biting his lip and making threatening gestures with his pikestaff.

Shouting noisily, the children scattered and ran off into the distance in search of some other sport. As the guard watched them disappear, the frightened expression on his face turned to panic. Solid shapes had appeared out of the shadows and were moving along the wharf towards him.

At the same instant, the crowd's mood changed. Some men stared with wide eyes and their mouths half open, while others shifted uncomfortably and looked away.

'That's the Lieutenant of the Tower,' said one.

''Ere, isn't that Richard Topcliffe?' whispered another. 'There's bound to be trouble now.'

Topcliffe was shaking his fists. His head jerked violently from side to side and, though still several feet away, he could be heard venting his fury at a thin, little man behind him. The man was unable to walk and was being dragged along by two guards.

'You incompetent imbecile,' Topcliffe raged. 'How is it possible that you could allow such a thing to happen?' He stopped abruptly, turned so that he was only an inch away from the man's terrified face. 'Well?' he added.

'Please, Master Topcliffe, I beg you. Don't blame me!' The distressed voice belonged to John Rufford's warder. His face was grey and his lips trembled as he spoke. 'I knew nothing of the escape, nothing at all … as this letter left by the priest shows.' Unclenching his fist, he began unfolding a piece of parchment.

Skimming through the first part of the letter, where John stated that he was exercising his right to escape – he had committed no crime and was therefore being wrongfully held in prison – the warder quickly reached the sentence he was searching for. 'My warder should not be held liable,' he read aloud. 'I protest before God that he was not privy to my escape, and would never have allowed it if he had known.' The warder looked up hopefully.

'The letter proves nothing, damn you!' Topcliffe retorted. 'These Jesuits are all liars and traitors and are not to be trusted, none of them! Aye, and Rufford is by far the worst I have ever met! If you did not suspect, then you must have been in collusion and I will see to it that you pay for your mistake with your life.'

The warder continued to protest his innocence but his pleas were to no avail and his words drifted away on the morning breeze.

Topcliffe pushed forward, working his way impatiently through the crowd with his elbows until he was at the front. He stared across the moat at the Cradle Tower and at the rope hanging down the wall. Lowering his head, he glanced at the iron stake still in its position next to his right foot. He swore and kicked out at it with his right boot but missed. He cursed again. Turning to the Lieutenant of the Tower, he said, 'I hold you equally responsible for this shambles! I see it as a gross dereliction of duty and you should seek the Queen's pardon. I think you should give serious consideration to your position.'

'Master Topcliffe, I declare I am the Queen's true and devoted subject,' replied the lieutenant warily. It was clear from his demeanour and the deliberation of his step that he regarded Topcliffe's presence on the wharf as wearisome and exasperating. 'I regard it as an honour and privilege to serve my sovereign and England and I have expended all my energies in the faithful execution of my duties. I have, at all times, acted carefully and diligently.'

He lowered his eyes, as if something were weighing on his conscience. 'But it is with deep regret that I look upon this whole sorry affair of the Jesuit John Rufford. I have this very morning tendered my resignation.'

Topcliffe nodded his approval. 'Then you have made a sensible decision, sir.'

'Master Topcliffe, you misunderstand me. I have resigned not because of the escape!' the Lieutenant snapped. 'I have witnessed the terrible consequences of your work and am left disgusted ... ashamed. What you do is heinous and wrong. You offend God and the Queen and I am morally bound to heed my conscience.'

Topcliffe leaned forward. 'Then you disappoint me. This conscience you speak of would make cowards of us all! I do whatever is necessary in such matters, and with the Queen's consent too. These Jesuit vipers are guilty of treason and I will not be satisfied until John Rufford is found.'

One of Topcliffe's henchmen stepped forward, a lumbering giant of a man. He could smell opportunity and was keen to exploit the situation by rendering any sort of service that would win his master's favour. 'By your leave, Master Topcliffe,' he said, 'I will send hue and cry to Gravesend and to the Mayor of London for a search to be made in London and all the liberties. There will be nowhere safe for these traitors to hide.'

Topcliffe turned and smiled derisively at the lieutenant. 'There, you see, Sir Richard. They are all doomed!'

'You can't hope to find them,' said Sir Richard disparagingly. 'If they have friends who are prepared to go to such lengths to do all this, you can rely on them having horses and hiding places to keep them well out of your reach.'

'No-one is out of my reach!' retorted Topcliffe angrily.

A look of exasperation came over the lieutenant's weary face. 'You will excuse me, Master Topcliffe, but I have important business to attend elsewhere.' He turned his back and walked quickly away.

Topcliffe glared after him. 'No-one is out of my reach,' he repeated. 'Do you hear what I say, damn you?'

There was an empty silence as the words chased in vain after the departing lieutenant. The crowd and the guards drew a collective breath. They glanced furtively back towards Topcliffe awaiting his response, but none came.

With everyone's attention distracted, and sensing that this was his chance, the warder suddenly sprang into action. He shoved his two guards aside, thrust his way through the startled crowd and ran across the wharf.

'Hey! Come back!' shouted Topcliffe's henchman, and then: 'After him, after him!'

The guards made haste to follow, but being well-acquainted with the warder, they were somewhat sluggish in their pursuit. The warder, consumed by panic and in fear of his life, was far too quick, and soon disappeared between the dilapidated buildings at the end of the wharf.

'We'll catch up with him. Don't you worry,' the henchman reassured Topcliffe. 'I will see to it myself.'

'It is of no matter. He has nowhere to run,' Topcliffe sneered. 'Call your men back.' He tugged uncomfortably at the sleeve on his doublet and frowned. 'I have seen enough here! Let us go and see what tongues we can loosen.' He turned and set off back along the wharf with long strides, his long black cloak flapping in the breeze.

The guards hurried in his wake. The crowd, subdued yet at the same time excited by all that had happened, talked in muted whispers as they dispersed. Amongst them, the young mother Thomas had met two days earlier, along with her elderly father, headed back to their cottage, their faces displaying contented, slightly wry smiles.

# Chapter 37

Before dawn that same morning John Rufford, weak and exhausted after only a few hours rest, left the Black Bull on his brother's horse and headed west to Father Garnet's house at Uxendon. Before taking his leave, he gave Thomas his blessing for what still lay ahead.

Thomas remained in the upstairs room, sitting on the edge of the bed, silently contemplating. His hair was dishevelled and there were dark pouches under his eyes telling of nervous strain and the previous night's excitement.

He finally crawled off the bed and crossed the room to a small table in the corner, where there was a wooden bowl filled with cold stale water. After washing his face, he rubbed his teeth with a cloth dipped in honey and vinegar and combed his hair. He glanced down at his sage-coloured doublet and shrugged his shoulders; it would have to suffice. Thomas was determined to seek an audience with the Queen to petition for the immediate release of Lady Molynieux.

He passed under the archway into Bishopsgate and strode out in the direction of the river. Within twenty minutes he was on a barge destined for the palace at Richmond where the Queen and her court had recently moved so that she could enjoy hunting and hawking in the Royal Park.

There were several other passengers on the barge, crowded together on cushioned benches beneath a wooden canopy. As the barge swayed in the strong current, the ladies present fought to stay upright on the velvet cushions, trying in vain to retain their dignity.

Thomas gazed absently at the bank as the river began to curve southwards. To the right was the jumble of buildings that made up the palace of Whitehall; beyond that the bulk of Westminster Hall and the imposing, majestic Westminster Abbey. Lambeth Palace appeared to the left, with its twin towers pointing reverently towards heaven. London is much better observed from the river, Thomas mused. The early morning sunlight and a fresh breeze as the barge sped along were a merciful relief from the suffocating stench of the City streets.

Thomas's thoughts returned to the task that lay before him. He knew it was improbable that he would be granted an audience with the Queen, but he had to try. He had to explain the injustice of Lady Molynieux's imprisonment, to tell her that the arrest was a fraud perpetrated by Richard Topcliffe and that Lady Molyneiux remained the Queen's faithful servant.

Thomas was relying on the fact that Lord Molyneiux was still held in high regard by some of the leading luminaries at Court, many of whom still secretly harboured Catholic sympathies, to get him access. Maybe the fact that he was a Rufford would arouse curiosity. By the time the trees of Richmond Park came into view, Thomas had dispelled any lingering misgivings. He would go to any lengths and make any sacrifice for what he believed.

After the other passengers had all disembarked and gone their varied ways, Thomas climbed the water stairs and gazed at the sprawling palace before him. The Privy Lodgings faced the river, three storeys high, with white stone walls and an expanse of glittering windows. Above its many octagonal and round turrets, all capped with pepper-pot domes or cupolas, the sun appeared through dreary, leaden clouds. Behind the main palace building, Thomas could see the Great Hall and the Chapel. To the west were the domestic buildings, dominated by the louvred roof of the Great Kitchen, while between these buildings and the river was the orchard, surrounded by high brick walls. The palace gardens, which were encircled by two-storey galleries, lay to the east of the main palace.

At the main gate to the palace, a Yeoman of the Guard ordered Thomas to halt. He did not obey at once but advanced slowly along the gravel path.

The guard, scowling, blocked Thomas's way with his pikestaff. 'Are you deaf?' he shouted. Three other guards standing close by stared curiously at the unfashionably dressed stranger.

'My name is Thomas Rufford. I am here for an audience with Her Majesty on a matter of utmost importance.'

'My friend, do you not know that Her Majesty attends to no public business while she is at Richmond?' the guard replied. 'Now, away with you!' He turned his back.

'I am the son of a true knight of the realm,' Thomas

protested, 'and a close friend of Lord Molynieux, a personal favourite of the Queen. You must grant me entrance.'

The guard was unyielding. 'My orders are explicit: Her Majesty is not to be disturbed. And I always obey my orders. Now, do as you are bid and leave, if you know what's good for you.'

'Then I refuse to go!' Thomas said. 'I care not for my own safety while the life of my friend, Lady Molynieux is in peril!'

The guard stared, plainly deriving satisfaction from Thomas's agitation. 'Take him away,' he said to the other guards.

But before they could carry out their orders, they were distracted by the sound of noisy laughter and loud voices away to their left. Thomas saw three men striding along the path in front of the privy lodgings and heading directly towards them. They were led by a tall, imposing figure in a fur-lined cloak. As he drew nearer, Thomas saw he was also wearing the gold livery collar of the Order of the Garter.

'God's death! It's the Lord Chancellor!' whispered one of the guards nervously.

Seeing the uninvited stranger, the Chancellor stopped and looked inquiringly at the young guard on the gate.

'Who is this man and what business brings him here?' he asked.

'My Lord, he states he has come for an audience with the Queen,' the guard replied respectfully. 'He refuses to leave, even though I informed him that such a meeting is impossible.'

'Be assured I mean no harm, my Lord,' Thomas began.

'But I will not leave without telling Her Majesty the truth about the arrest of Lady Molynieux. I know that when Her Majesty hears the facts, my dear friend will be acquitted of all these false charges. Lady Molynieux is a frail old woman...'

The Chancellor interrupted him. 'What is your name?' he asked.

'Thomas Rufford, my Lord.'

The Lord Chancellor studied him intently. For some moments they looked at one another in silence, and it was in that look Thomas was reprieved. The Lord Chancellor sighed. 'Well, Master Rufford, I think you are somewhat naïve if you presume that you can stroll in to a royal palace and demand an audience with the Queen, however legitimate the reason.' He paused, reflecting for a moment. 'But I also judge you to be an honest man, so if you will follow me, it is possible I may be able to gain you get a few minutes with Her Majesty.'

As he was led in through the gate, Thomas saw that the guards were whispering and grumbling amongst themselves.

Entering the Palace, he was amazed at its splendour. Staterooms, rich with Flemish tapestries and turkey carpets; fine portraits; ornate ceilings of chequered timber and plaster decorated with roses and portcullis badges. Everywhere there was a riot of jewelled colours – and a heaving mass of courtiers hoping for the Queen's patronage.

The Lord Chancellor led him into a lavish Presence Chamber, where still more nobles and ladies-in-waiting were gathered. The room buzzed with conversation. All those present bowed politely and greeted the

Lord Chancellor with the reverence his high office commanded, whilst moving aside to let him pass. They looked at Thomas, a lowly stranger, with suspicion.

Thomas was told to wait. He rested his hand on the Lord Chancellor's sleeve. 'Thank you,' he murmured.

'I am not doing this on your account,' the Chancellor retorted. 'I do it out of my respect for Lord Molynieux. He was a good and trusted friend throughout the many years he served at this Court.' He broke off and a smile played on his lips. 'Although this is not the first time the Rufford family have received my benevolence,' he added. 'Was not your father imprisoned in the Tower for his involvement in the Babington Plot?'

'My father was innocent of any crime,' Thomas snapped angrily.

'That may be so, Master Rufford,' he said. 'And Lord Molynieux clearly believed your father to be so. So much that he implored me to intervene on his behalf. Contrary to my better judgement, I agreed.' He sighed, breathing heavily.

The Lord Chancellor was pale and shaking as if he had an attack of the fever. 'My Lord, you are not well,' Thomas said, steadying him.

'It is nothing,' the Chancellor replied irritably, wiping his sweating forehead with a white lace handkerchief. 'And so,' he went on, pulling himself together, 'I declared to Her Majesty that, although your father was a known recusant and had proven associations with Anthony Babington, he was most certainly ignorant of any plot and that the real conspirators had already been dealt with. She deliberated for some considerable time. Walsingham and Burghley had convinced her of the guilt of Babington and the others, but she detested the cruel manner of their executions and regretted the fate of the Queen of Scots. Her Majesty stated that she wished to bring the whole sorry affair to a close and subsequently ordered your father's release.'

Thomas was astounded; he had been unaware of the political diplomacy employed to secure his father's release. Before he could say anything, the Lord Chancellor had crossed the room and was standing before a great doorway, guarded on either side by a Yeoman of the Guard brandishing gilt battle-axes. After a brief pause, he entered the Queen's Privy Chamber.

Thomas glanced around the room at the lords and ladies, handsomely dressed in their velvets and jewels. He could sense their power and ambition. But Thomas no longer desired such things. Such sweet perfume had a bitter taste. The waiting seemed endless. Thomas glanced nervously at the closed door at the far end of the room. Perhaps the Chancellor had been unable to persuade the Queen.

Thomas got to his feet. He was so close. He edged forward; he would not accept defeat. Suddenly, the door to the Privy Chamber burst open and the Lord Chancellor re-emerged.

'Well?' Thomas demanded impatiently.

The Chancellor smiled. 'Her Majesty is in good humour, having just returned from a successful hunt. She will see you at once. Now, if you would follow me.' He turned round and re-entered the Queens Privy Chamber, bowing politely as he did so.

Thomas stepped inside and instinctively made a low and deferential bow.

Elizabeth was sitting at the head of the Privy Chamber and was quite alone. She was strangely attired in a dress of silver cloth with slashed sleeves lined with red taffeta. The front of her dress was open, displaying her wrinkled bosom. The collar of her robe was very high, and adorned with rubies and pearls. She wore a garland on her head and, beneath it, a great red wig. Her long, thin face, which was beginning to betray the signs of age, wore an expression of benevolent welcome.

She nodded in response to Thomas's greeting, rose from her seat and moved five or six paces to where he stood. 'Good day, Master Rufford!' she began. 'Sir Christopher tells me you wish to see me over the matter of Lady Molynieux. Very well. I am glad to receive you and will listen to what you have to say.' She scrutinised Thomas's face with her intelligent eyes and then glanced across at the Lord Chancellor.

'Thank you, Your Grace,' Thomas said, conscious of the violent beating of his heart. 'If I may be so bold to trouble Your Grace … I … I,' but his words tailed off. The Queen's gaze disconcerted him and drove all his carefully prepared speeches from his mind.

'You are nervous – calm yourself!' Elizabeth said. 'You may speak freely.'

Thomas steadied himself. Images flashed through his mind: Lady Molynieux; his brother; his sister; his parents; his friend Anthony Babington; the stable boy; the priests in the hide. He knew he must not fail them but there was something else, too. A presence within him was dictating how he should act; a greater, higher will than his own.

He continued with renewed confidence. 'Most mighty

and merciful Majesty, for the sake of Lady Molynieux, I humbly beg of your clemency. She is a most true and faithful servant, and has never given your Majesty any cause for displeasure.'

'Yes ... and her husband was a respected and trusted nobleman of this court,' interjected Elizabeth. 'I was much grieved to hear of his death. He is sadly mourned by us all.'

'He was indeed a good man,' agreed Thomas. 'Bound by his faith and his conscience. As is his lady wife – and yet she is being persecuted for it!'

Elizabeth gestured with her hand, every finger of which was adorned with large glittering rings. 'The fire burns so! It hurts my eyes,' she complained, shielding her brow even though there was a great screen before it and the Queen was six or seven feet away. She returned swiftly to her chair.

'On the contrary, Master Rufford,' intervened the Lord Chancellor, feeling the need to defend the Queen's position. 'There is no persecution against religion.'

'Nor do I have any desire to make windows into men's souls,' Elizabeth declared wearily.

'But is not the very law itself a most heavy oppression when it is a felony to receive a priest purely for one's spiritual needs?'

'I do not punish my people for their beliefs,' Elizabeth reiterated. 'But neither am I ignorant of the dangers to myself or my crown posed by these dissolute rebels and traitors. If my people break the law, then they shall be punished.'

'And the punishment for Lady Molynieux, this most honourable gentlewoman, is to be thrown into the darkest of dungeons to rot!'

'Master Rufford! Remember who you address!' The Lord Chancellor rebuked. He cast an anxious glance towards the queen.

Elizabeth's white face cracked into a sardonic smile. She began speaking in a low, deliberate tone. 'Your candour and honesty are admirable qualities, Master Rufford, but I did not expect to receive a lecture.'

'Forgive me, Your Majesty, if I caused offence,' Thomas said, bowing his head. 'But I must speak the truth. I would be a poor man indeed, without courage and void of all honour, if I did not.'

'You are certainly audacious, Master Rufford; a trait I believe you share with Lady Molynieux.'

'She is a woman of many virtues, Your Grace.'

'Yes, Lady Molynieux is a most remarkable woman,' agreed Elizabeth. 'For example, are you aware that she spoke out vehemently against the Oath of Supremacy?'

'But you know she is your Majesty's obedient servant.'

'And there are those who swear she conceals priests in her household, where the Catholic Mass is celebrated openly and with ceremony.'

'Lady Molynieux has concealed nothing save honesty and honour,' answered Thomas. 'She is the innocent victim of the trickery and deception used to trap her.' He explained the truth behind Topcliffe's devious scheme. 'She is as good and honest as the day and does not deserve this punishment,' he concluded.

Elizabeth rose from her chair, clearly irritated by Thomas's tone. 'I have never given my permission for such duplicity,' she retorted. 'Those who have exceeded their authority will be answerable to me!'

## Chapter 37

'Your Majesty, all we ask is for greater tolerance,' said Thomas. It was imperative that he added a plea for the plight of all Catholics. He wanted to say more; but something held him back.

'That's impossible!' the Lord Chancellor said loudly. 'Take heed, Master Rufford, there are some who have been imprisoned for petitioning such nonsense!'

Elizabeth sighed heavily. 'If I grant this liberty to Catholics I lay myself, my honour, my crown and my life at their feet.'

'But your Majesty ... you are our only hope!'

'Enough!' shouted the Queen. 'I have heard enough!' She went up to Thomas, staring directly into his face for several moments before turning abruptly and returning to her chair.

Thomas did not regret what he had said but he feared he might have gone too far.

Elizabeth was silent for several moments, twisting the rings on her fingers as she contemplated. 'Returning to the matter of Lady Molynieux,' she announced suddenly. 'I am satisfied you have told the truth, Master Rufford. I have much affection and respect for Her Ladyship and deeply regret what has happened.' She turned to the Lord Chancellor. 'It is my command that no sentence should proceed against her; in regard she is a noblewoman, and her loyalty to me has never been called into question. It pleaseth the Queen's majesty that she be set free.'

Thomas stared at her. 'I thank your Majesty for her most gracious pardon.' As he spoke, he heard the chime of bells from the clock tower. It was mid-day and the world outside was intruding once more.

Elizabeth slumped back into her chair. 'Now, leave me, I am tired.'

The Lord Chancellor ushered Thomas away. As he left, Thomas looked one last time at the lone figure slumped in the chair. He saw not Elizabeth, the Queen, Gloriana, but Elizabeth the woman, frail and tired. How quickly the glories of the world pass away, he thought.

'Please inform My Lord Chancellor that I have taken lodgings at the Black Bull in Bishopsgate,' shouted Thomas, descending the landing steps to a waiting barge. 'I will return there and await Lady Molynieux's release.'

The guard who had challenged Thomas earlier looked on suspiciously and then pulled a subordinate aside and said something to him in a low voice. The other guard glanced at Thomas and hurried away.

As the barge pulled away, Thomas was infused with a warm glow. He held his head higher and his eyes glowed with a lustre that illuminated his whole face.

# CHAPTER 38

The Black Bull was peaceful when Thomas returned that evening. A few of the other lodgers were sitting around the tables, eating and drinking, engaged in quiet conversation. Some of them nodded to him as he entered. After eating his supper and drinking several jars of strong ale Thomas retired to his room, exhausted and slightly drunk but content.

He slept late, worn out by the momentous events of the previous day. With his head still buried in the pillow, he barely registered the creaking floorboards on the landing outside his upstairs room. Nor did he hear the impatient shuffling of footsteps and the murmur of men gathering.

There was a rap at the door. Thomas groaned and turned over. The knocking was repeated, and then again, more urgently. 'Alright … alright, give me a minute,' Thomas said groggily, rubbing his eyes. He threw back the coverlet, and crossed the small room in his stocking feet. He lifted the latch and opened the door.

'You!' he gasped, instantly awake.

It was not the landlord or his daughter who stood before him, as he had expected, but the sinister form of

Richard Topcliffe and two of his hired thugs.

'Good day to you, Master Rufford!' Topcliffe sneered. Snapping his fingers, he signalled the two ruffians who immediately forced Thomas back into the room. Topcliffe followed them and the door was closed and locked behind him.

Caught unawares by the speed and strength of his assailants, Thomas stumbled and fell awkwardly, cracking his elbow. Slumped on the floor, he tried to raise himself but couldn't move. He looked up at the two giants hovering over him and then at Topcliffe.

'Where is your brother ... that Jesuit traitor?' Topcliffe asked quietly.

Thomas's mind raced. He must play for time. 'I ... I ... I, don't understand...' he stuttered, finally managing to prop himself against the bed. But no sooner had he spoken than the thug nearest to him lunged forward and dragged him to his feet. Thomas let out a high-pitched scream as his injured arm was almost wrenched clean out of its sockets.

'Let us not play games, Master Rufford.' Topcliffe leaned forward, close enough for Thomas to smell his stale sweat and foul breath. 'You are not as accomplished at lying as your brother. It is no coincidence that I find you in London, though I think you should have fled while you still had the chance. Your brother escaped from the Tower the night before last, as you well know. The bridge watchman tells me that there was a commotion on the river during the night: an overturned boat and several men pulled to safety. One man was hauled on to the bridge and taken away by a younger man; a friend or brother, the watchman thought.' There was a triumphant tone in his voice as he spoke. 'So I want to know who, besides yourself, helped him and where he is hiding now.'

'If my brother has escaped as you say, then it is God's doing,' said Thomas. 'And I rejoice at the news.'

There was a dull thud and Thomas crumpled as the other thug caught him with a well-aimed blow in the stomach. Thomas couldn't breathe. The next instant, a heavy boot kicked him in the stomach again, breaking two of his ribs. Thomas retched. For several minutes, he lay on the floorboards, writhing in pain. Coughing and spluttering, he was hauled to his feet again.

'Tell Master Topcliffe where your brother is?' the thug screamed, twisting Thomas's arm behind his back.

Thomas winced as intense, searing pain saturated his whole body.

'Or perhaps you would rather I ask your sweet, delicious sister,' said Topcliffe quietly. 'I am certain I would be able to persuade her to tell me.'

The relish in Topcliffe's voice made Thomas's skin crawl. 'I know what you are Topcliffe,' he gasped 'and I see in you the greatest corruption in human nature.'

A heavy fist struck Thomas viciously across his face; the blow reverberated around the room and blood trickled from the corner of his mouth. Topcliffe drew the rapier from his belt and held it against Thomas's throat.

'Then you know I will stop at nothing to get what I want!' he snarled, baring his yellowing, rotting teeth. 'I will ask you again! Where is that stinking, Jesuit traitor, brother of yours? Where?' He pressed the blade firmly into Thomas's throat and drops of blood began to appear.

'I do not know,' replied Thomas, swallowing hard.

'You are lying!' Topcliffe's face twitched with anger. 'Tell me the truth, tell me where he is!'

The thug tugged Thomas's hair, ripping out a tuft and jerking his head backwards. Thomas remained defiantly silent.

'I have greater power than anyone in the kingdom on these matters, so it is futile to resist,' Topcliffe continued. 'I am closer to the Queen than anyone! I am above the law!'

'But you are not above the law of God!' said Thomas. Immediately, he felt the thug tighten his grip.

Topcliffe snorted. 'I am a reasonable man, Master Rufford. Tell me what I want to know and I may spare you. Yes, even reward you, if you choose to co-operate.'

'Whatever you could offer would not be enough to make me betray my brother or my friends.'

'Ah! You're all the same!' Topcliffe turned his back and spat into the empty grate. 'Don't you understand? These priests rely on your silence, your foolish bravery while they hide away like the cowards they are. There is a new order in England and it is my duty and my honour to protect my sovereign and keep her safe from traitors such as you.' Topcliffe crossed the room. 'Bring him!' he barked, unlocking the door. 'Let us return to Westminster. His tongue will loosen once he has experienced the delights which await him there.'

'Look!' cried the thug, still keeping a firm grip on Thomas. 'Look at what he's wearing!'

Topcliffe spun round. Dangling on a chain outside Thomas's torn shirt was the Agnus Dei given to him by his sister. Topcliffe's lips curled into a cold smile and with slow, deliberate steps, he closed in on his helpless prey.

'How stubbornly you cling to your old superstitions,' he said. He ripped the small oval disc from around Thomas's neck. 'This popish trish-trash is enough to imprison you!'

'You cannot imprison our faith!' Thomas's voice was weak yet defiant.

'Faith!' Topcliffe laughed mockingly. 'You think this will save you?' He held the Agnus Dei in front of Thomas.

'Yes ... I believe God's love will save us all.'

Topcliffe turned away. 'Come! Let us make haste!' he shouted impatiently, and stepped out on to the landing.

Thomas was allowed just enough time to gather up his boots before he was bundled along the landing to the top of the stairs. They were in a hurry it seemed, as if they wished to remove their quarry unobserved, to carry him away to their secret place where they could finish their grisly work away from inquisitive eyes.

Thomas went down the timber staircase one step at a time. Waves of pain washed over him and he started to shiver. His eyes half-closed, he thought he was going to faint. He stumbled on the stone cobbles, jarring his elbow again, and moaned softly.

'Get up, damn you!' Topcliffe screamed.

Thomas lay still. He could hear the heavy footsteps of the thugs charging down the stairs and braced himself. The footsteps stopped and now he could make out the sound of other voices approaching from across the yard.

'The air bites this morning! It chills through to the

bone!' remarked an imposing voice.

Thomas listened; the voice sounded familiar.

'You are still unwell, my Lord; you should have stayed at home.'

'You will catch your death on a morning like this,' said another.

Thomas lifted his head and there, passing beneath the archway and entering the courtyard was the Lord Chancellor, escorted by two of his aides and a rather flustered landlord.

The Lord Chancellor was waving his aides' protests aside. 'We are the Queen's to command...' He stopped short. 'Master Topcliffe! What are you doing? Where are you taking this man?' he asked indignantly.

'Ah! Good day, my Lord Chancellor!' Topcliffe replied, unruffled. 'I am delighted to inform you of the arrest of Thomas Rufford for his complicity in the escape from the Tower of his brother, the Jesuit traitor, John Rufford.' He reached the foot of the stairs, beaming with satisfaction.

'You have proof, Master Topcliffe?'

Topcliffe looked surprised. 'What need do we have of proof where traitors are concerned!' Seeing the Lord Chancellor's impassive expression, he went on. 'He refuses to say anything at present, so we are removing him to my house for further interrogation. Never fear, he will divulge the truth before long!'

'The truth!' snapped the Lord Chancellor, stepping up to Topcliffe. 'I was with this man at Richmond yesterday, hardly the place where you would expect to find a fugitive from justice. Leave him be!'

'Richmond!' repeated Topcliffe, the smile vanishing

from his face.

'Yes. He was there to petition the Queen concerning the matter of Lady Molynieux's wrongful arrest…'

'Lady Molynieux! But I don't understand, my Lord. I made the arrest myself!' interrupted Topcliffe. 'She was caught harbouring a Jesuit priest! What more evidence do you need?'

'Yours was the worst evidence I have ever known,' retaliated the Lord Chancellor. 'The Queen is most displeased. Her Majesty retains the utmost affection and respect for Lady Molynieux and at her command, I am here to right the injustice you have brought upon that poor woman.'

Topcliffe was incredulous.

Thomas struggled to his feet. 'Lady Molynieux, how is she?' he asked. 'Is she released?'

The Lord Chancellor looked at him and smiled. 'Her Ladyship is blessed with a wondrous constitution, Master Rufford,' he said cheerfully. 'In spite of her period of confinement, she retains her good health and high spirits. My coach will take you both to Broad Oaks.' He gestured through the archway to the street beyond.

'I am forever in your debt, my Lord!' Thomas said. Clutching his boots in his hand, he lurched towards the archway.

'My Lord! I must protest!' Topcliffe said. 'This man is guilty! All the Ruffords are traitors!' He urged his accomplices to stop Thomas from leaving but they remained where they were, glancing nervously at each other. They feared Topcliffe's violent temper but they also knew that the Lord Chancellor's authority was not to be challenged. Topcliffe started to move.

'Master Topcliffe!' barked the Lord Chancellor. 'You will accompany me, if you please!'

Topcliffe hesitated. He, too, did not underestimate the Lord Chancellor's power.

'There are ugly rumours being spread around court at the moment,' continued the Lord Chancellor, his voice threatening. 'About a repugnant crime committed by one of Her Majesty's most trusted servants. Such a scandal could ruin a man's reputation and destroy what favour he currently holds with the Queen. Perhaps we can discuss it on our way to Richmond – you may be able to shed some light on the matter.'

Topcliffe nodded dumbly. 'As my Lord wishes,' he said.

†

Grimacing with pain, Thomas climbed into the coach which was waiting on the other side of the archway and sank into the cushioned seat facing Lady Molynieux.

'I am pleased to see you safe and in good health, Lady Molynieux,' he said gasping for breath.

'Thank God we arrived when we did!' Lady Molynieux's expression was pale but full of compassion. Taking his hands in hers, she kissed them gently, wetting them with her tears.

Thomas smiled as he glimpsed the crucifix she was still wearing defiantly around her neck. 'Yes, thank God,' he whispered. He let out a long, contented sigh and closed his eyes.

# CHAPTER 39

It was a long, uncomfortable journey to Broad Oaks. The coach pitched from side to side as the wheels repeatedly encountered deep ruts and potholes in the dirt-track roads. At every jolt, Thomas felt a piercing, stabbing pain in his chest from his cracked ribs; an excruciating ache throbbed through his whole arm and there was a burning sensation in his neck. Yet in spite of this, he felt restful and strangely happy. His world now seemed quiet. He would have been glad to lay down his life for his brother, for his friends, for his belief. Our souls, our very existence, depends upon truth and love, he thought. And in this old, honest faith, all was well within him.

As the wheels rolled noisily across the gravel path on the approach to Broad Oaks Lady Molynieux turned to Thomas, about to speak. Discovering that he was asleep, she roused him gently.

The coach slowed to a halt and the imposing figure of Master Samuel, the principal receiver, appeared at the door. Samuel looked up as first Lady Molynieux and then Thomas stepped from the coach. His tired expression was suddenly transformed into one of delighted amazement.

'My Lady!' he cried. For several moments he stood motionless, beaming, unable to speak. Two women servants appeared in the doorway behind him and rushed forward. They fell sobbing into the arms of their mistress.

'It is good to see you, my dears,' smiled Lady Molynieux drawing away. 'But let us first take care of our good friend, Master Rufford.' She led Thomas inside, out of the drizzling mist which had now begun to descend.

In the Great Hall, everything was the same: the enormous oak-beamed roof and the Flemish tapestries hung on the walls. The fire crackled merrily in the hearth. Before Thomas reached the dining room, someone swooped out of a side door and began hugging and kissing him.

'Thomas! My dear Thomas ... we have all been beside ourselves with worry!' said Jane, tears of joy running down her cheeks.

Another door swung open and Nathaniel, the young stable boy, came hurtling in, throwing himself into his mistress's protective embrace. He looked at Thomas, not thanking him with words, but with the jubilant expression on his face. Then he raced back to his beloved horses to tell them the wonderful news.

Manservants and maids flocked into the room. Henry Giffard took his place by Jane's side; loving eyes glistened with tears of joy. After a while, Thomas was taken to the adjoining ante room where Lady Moynieux and Jane, together with Henry Giffard, attended him.

Two maids hurried in, bringing bottles of ointment and wash-basins brimming with hot water. Lady

Molyneux, assisted by Jane who could not take her eyes off her brother, carefully bathed and dressed Thomas's wounds.

Later, after they had all taken some refreshment and were feeling somewhat rejuvenated, Thomas recounted his adventures in London and Lady Molyneux told of her confinement in prison.

Jane and Henry Giffard hung on their every word, marvelling at John's incredible escape from the Tower and his near drowning in the river, at Thomas's extraordinary meeting with the Queen and at the timely arrival of the Lord Chancellor at the Black Bull to deny Topcliffe his sport.

'But did you really see and speak to Queen Elizabeth?' asked Jane.

Thomas laughed. 'Of course! After all, I had given my promise!'

There were a hundred and one questions Jane wanted to ask but all she could say was, 'It's a miracle ... it's a miracle!'

'Yes, God be praised!' Holding Thomas's hand, Lady Molyneux kissed it gently. 'I love you as though you were my own son. We are all saved thanks to your courage and faith.'

Thomas smiled. 'There are many who possess far greater bravery and have a much stronger conviction than I.'

'Yes, that is true indeed!' agreed Henry Giffard, glancing at Jane and making her blush. 'And I am glad to hear of your brother's safety. He has suffered so much for his Faith ... you have all suffered so much.'

Jane gazed lovingly at Henry. Her heart, though still

scarred by the painful memories of the past, was being healed by the love she had found with this fine man.

'And if you were to ask John, or indeed, to ask any of us,' Thomas remarked, not letting go of Lady Molyneux's hand, 'whether we would give in and submit or go through the same suffering again, then our answer would be the same. And it is because of this Faith, this belief in God, this love we share and which binds us together, that we shall all be free.'

Giffard nodded silently and looked at Jane. She smiled radiantly back at him.

Thomas leaned forward. 'It gladdens my heart to see that warm smile return to my sister's face and that bright light shine again in her eyes,' he said to Giffard. 'I will be glad to call you brother and I know you will be most welcome in my father's house.' He turned to Jane. 'It seems to me that life without love is incomplete.'

Suddenly Jane burst into tears. 'What is it?' asked Giffard.

Jane shook her head. 'I would never have believed I could be so happy,' she whispered. Through her tears, she smiled at Henry and Thomas.

The two maids reappeared, bringing fresh candles. It was late and Lady Molyneux was suddenly conscious once again of the privations she had suffered as a prisoner. Thomas, clutching his broken ribs, was beginning to feel the full effects of his injuries.

'I think it is time we said good-night,' said Lady Molyneux. 'Let us rest and see what new joy waits for us tomorrow.' And she got up and glided out of the room.

†

The next day a coded letter arrived from John, telling them of his safe arrival in Uxendon. There was great rejoicing and celebration at the news, though the mood became quieter and subdued when they discovered that John intended to continue with his mission in England. Following his escape, he would be hunted with even greater determination and ferocity, together with anyone who gave him shelter. There would be no respite from danger. And yet in spite of their misgivings, everyone at Broad Oaks felt strengthened by John's unwavering dedication and commitment.

†

The weeks passed as Thomas continued to convalesce. Christmas came and went. The dark winter nights gave way to the lengthening days of spring as his health was restored.

'I have learned so much from those I have met these past years,' Thomas said, as he and Jane wandered along the path between the flowerbeds.

Spring buds burst open under the warm sun and a pleasant perfume pervaded the air. There was an explosion of white, yellow and lilac coloured blossom and the new green of feathery leaves on the trees. As Thomas looked around, he thought it would be difficult to be more contented.

'Such honest folk and good friends all … and bound together by unity of purpose, by simplicity and purity. I have been asleep when I should have been active. I have done nothing so far but now I want to make amends. I know it will require the greatest effort, for it is still easy for me to be tempted or led astray, but I know my Faith will guide me and the love of my friends will sustain me.'

Jane stopped walking and held her brother by the arm. 'You are a good man, Thomas,' she said, her lips curving into a smile. 'You have grown so much since we were last at Mythe Hall. I am happy that you have found peace.'

'And I am delighted for you, sister, that you too have found what your heart desires.' Thomas paused, staring into the distance wistfully. 'My dear sister, let us return home; it has been so long I wonder if we shall recognise the place.'

'Yes, I think it is time,' Jane replied.

They walked on in silence for a while, before Thomas added: 'I mean to look after Mother and Father, you know. And of course, there will be so much work to do at Mythe Hall. I am keen to get started.'

'That is good.'

'And Nicholas has agreed to assist me with some building alterations I have in mind.' Thomas broke off suddenly and turned to Jane observing her downward gaze. 'But of course!' he continued, smiling broadly at his sister. 'It is right and proper that Master Giffard will join us … otherwise, how will he ask Father for your hand?'

†

One week later, Thomas, Jane and Henry Giffard reached the ancient stone bridge near the hamlet of

## CHAPTER 39

Mythe. Crossing over the bubbling stream, they swept left, urging their wearied horses uphill along a winding track, then downhill through a copse of birch and alder shimmering in the early morning sunlight, then up again, until they came over the crest of the final steep hill and stared down into the valley before them. Nestling there was the familiar sight of Mythe Hall.

Thomas pulled up his horse, sat back in the saddle and closed his eyes. He felt a gentle breeze playing on his face, as though it were the very breath of life itself. He opened his eyes and looked up. The sky was cloudless, the pale blue vast and limitless. He felt the warmth of the rising sun gently caressing his aching limbs. A joyous feeling of freedom filled his entire being.

'It's going to be a fine day,' he said aloud.